MURDER
AT THE
LOCH

BOOKS BY DEE MACDONALD

DEE MACDONALD

MURDER AT THE LOCH

bookouture

Published by Bookouture in 2025

An imprint of Storyfire Ltd.
Carmelite House
50 Victoria Embankment
London EC4Y 0DZ

www.bookouture.com

Storyfire Ltd's authorised representative in the EEA is Hachette Ireland
8 Castlecourt Centre
Castleknock Road
Castleknock
Dublin 15 D15 YF6A
Ireland

ISBN: 978-1-83525-508-7
eBook ISBN: 978-1-83525-507-0

ONE

It was a glorious October afternoon, with not a cloud in the sky, and Ally McKinley was sitting gazing at Loch Soular, which was still and calm, without even a ripple to disturb the reflection of the surrounding mountains and heather-clad foothills. Autumn light was shining through the trees onto the carpet of golden leaves all around, a picture postcard view of one of the most beautiful spots in the Western Highlands of Scotland.

It was views such as this that had brought Ally up here from Edinburgh in the first place, at the grand old age of sixty-eight. That and the old malthouse, which had been sitting forlornly on the hillside in Locharran. No longer used to store the malt for the famous local whisky, the building had been unused and unloved, and was now transformed into The Auld Malthouse B&B, Ally's pride and joy. Apart from the grey, stone castle on the hilltop, it was the oldest building in Locharran. Ally could see the castle now, in all of its turreted glory, reflected in the water, almost like a clip from a Disney movie. And a short distance in front of her was the rustic, old wooden boathouse, where the rowing boat lived during the winter months. It had already been put inside this year, although today would have been perfect for a row round the loch, she thought.

As she looked out across the water, she spotted something yellow floating a little way away. It was quite large, possibly a sack or something, and she wondered what kind of person would find their way to this beautiful spot to dump their rubbish. If only the boat hadn't been put away for the winter, she'd have rowed over there and attempted to retrieve whatever it was from the water.

The only sound was that of Flora, her young Labrador, who was busy digging in the sandy mud, and Ally sighed as she heard a vehicle approach, knowing the blissful silence was about to be broken. She'd had a busy morning and was just beginning to really relax. Turning round to see who it might be, she recognised – even at a distance – the earl's Land Rover. It was, after all, the earl's land, the earl's loch and the earl's castle, so she could hardly resent his presence.

The muddy Land Rover drew to a halt a hundred yards from the track leading down to the loch, and out jumped Hamish Sinclair, Earl of Locharran, and owner of everything in sight. He was in his seventies now and still had an eye for the ladies, including Ally when she first arrived in Locharran. Age might have withered him (Ally had declined to find out), but it certainly hadn't dulled the roguish twinkle in his eye. Septuagenarian or not, he was still a handsome man, with a close resemblance to Sean Connery, and with the added attraction of being an aristocrat with thousands of acres, a village, a loch and a castle to boot. What was there not to like? Even so, Ally had made it abundantly clear that she was only interested in friendship; lotharios had never been her type.

Ally watched him approach, jaunty in his kilt, thick sweater and gilet, his feet encased in sturdy boots.

'Isn't it a glorious day, Alison!' he shouted by way of greeting. 'I hoped I might find you here at the loch.' He plonked himself on a nearby large boulder.

What did he want? Ally wondered. They'd become friends after she'd told him, in no uncertain terms, that there was to be no 'hanky-panky' and, so far, he'd respected that.

'I need to have a wee chat with you,' he said, beaming. He cleared his throat. 'Alison, I think I told you that I was married once?'

Ally nodded, recalling the conversation when he'd told her of his short-lived marriage, which had ended in the tragic demise of his young wife.

'I'm so glad I found you,' he continued, 'because I wanted you to be one of the first to share my wonderful news! I'm going to get married again!'

Ally stared at him in amazement. 'Who are you going to marry?' was all she could manage to say.

'A wonderful woman, Alison! Her name is Elena Alexandrescu. She's a Londoner, but her parents originated from Eastern Europe.'

'However did you meet her?' Ally asked.

'Well, I was in London, in a taxi heading towards my club, when a lady suddenly stepped out into the road. The poor driver only just missed her. I got out to make sure she wasn't harmed, and she wasn't hurt, but she was greatly distressed. I insisted she got into the taxi, and we took her back to her hotel. She was very grateful and asked me if I would join her for a drink in the bar. Well, Alison.' Hamish smiled almost shyly. 'Believe it or not, after we'd been chatting for only a few minutes, I felt as if I'd known her all my life!'

Ally smiled back. She'd never seen this side of her friend. 'Does she still live in London then?'

Hamish nodded. 'Yes, but she works in tourism and so travels all over the world. She'd just returned home from a conference in Singapore and was terribly jet-lagged, poor thing.

We had dinner that night, and then every night of my stay. She is *very* beautiful. She has lovely green eyes just like yourself, and I'm very partial to green eyes, as you know!'

Hardly able to believe what she was hearing, Ally said, 'So when will you be seeing her again?'

Hamish beamed. 'I'll be seeing her soon because she arrives tomorrow!'

'*Tomorrow*? Are you sure you know what you're doing, Hamish?'

Hamish frowned. 'I thought you might be pleased for me,' he said a little petulantly. 'I thought you'd approve of my settling down with one woman. And we want to get married as soon as possible because Elena wants several children you know.'

'Have you told anyone else about this?' Ally asked.

'I've told a couple of close friends – and Desdemona, of course.' Desdemona was the sister of his late wife. 'And I couldn't resist telling my awful cousin. He's so obsessed with the idea of being the next Earl of Locharran that I couldn't resist the urge to get him worried!'

'So how old is Elena?' Ally asked hesitantly.

'Oh, she's thirty-two! I couldn't be happier at the thought of having my very own son to carry on the line!'

Ally smiled. 'Hamish, has it not struck you that there's a fifty-fifty chance she might have a daughter?'

'In which case,' he said happily, 'we'll just have to keep at it until she has a son. Daughters can't inherit, you know, unless there's been some major change in the Locharran entail that I don't know about.'

They both sat silently for a minute, gazing out at the loch.

'So is she travelling up on her own?' Ally asked.

'Not exactly,' Hamish replied. 'She's coming with her sister.'

'Her sister?'

Hamish nodded. 'Elena said she couldn't possibly leave her

sister behind, and she insisted her sister had to be the brides-maid. They're very close and don't have any other living family.'

'Well, take time to get to know Elena properly before you go setting a wedding date,' Ally said.

'Yes, yes,' he said impatiently. 'Now, why I wanted to see you was because I'm planning a little dinner up at the castle on Saturday evening, a sort of welcome, you know? And I'd very much like you to come to meet Elena because I respect your judgement, Alison.'

'Saturday evening?'

'Unless you have a prior engagement? I mean that you're to come as a couple, as I know you're friendly with our retired vet!'

Ally had met Ross Patterson, the supposedly retired vet, when he'd stood in for his son at the surgery when Ally had brought Flora in for her initial examination and booster vaccination. They'd hit it off straight away, had become great friends and, more recently, lovers. He was a gentle and considerate lover, but mostly they enjoyed just being together, the warmth of each other's bodies, a feeling neither of them ever expected to experience again. He was still a good-looking man, tall, with crinkly blue eyes, silver hair and upright posture, and Ally had fancied him at first sight.

She couldn't wait to tell Ross this piece of incredible news, and neither could she wait to meet this Elena!

'Informal, of course,' the earl continued. 'No dressing up, just smart casual. I've asked the minister and his wife along too, but I'm not sure if I'll invite anyone else or not. Simon, who will be my best man, is abroad at the moment, and dear Desdemona's away in London.' He sighed. 'I've asked Mrs Jamieson, to make us a special meal. Do you think Elena might like venison?'

'I've no idea,' Ally replied, 'so why don't you ask her?'

'Or beef Wellington?' Hamish went on happily. 'Mrs J cooks a wonderful beef Wellington. Isn't this *exciting*?'

It was mind-blowing, Ally thought. An old earl in his mid-seventies, planning to marry a lady less than half his age, in a village which was a hotbed of gossip and which regarded even herself as a 'Sassenach', although she was from Edinburgh, not England. How they'd deal with the surprise addition of a new Countess of Locharran was anyone's guess!

'Well, I must be off.' Hamish got to his feet. 'We'll expect you both for drinks at seven, then dinner at eight, what-ho!'

'Hang on a minute, Hamish,' Ally said. She'd noticed that the yellow shape she'd spotted earlier had drifted closer to where they were. 'Can you see that thing in the water?'

'Could be a sheep, or even a young deer,' Hamish said dismissively. 'Happens all the time.'

Whatever it was, it was still floating in their direction, half-submerged. But as it got closer, it began to look a little less like the bag of rubbish Ally had originally thought it was.

'Hamish,' Ally said, her heart thumping, 'that does not look like an animal, unless animals have taken to wearing yellow coats.'

The earl pulled some binoculars out of his gilet pocket and looked steadily for a couple of minutes before he said, 'Alison, would you be kind enough to call the police? I fear we are indeed looking at a body.'

'Oh, Hamish!' said Ally, feeling suddenly sick.

Hamish continued to squint through his binoculars. 'It could well be a woman's body.'

'A woman's body? Are you certain?'

'No, but I suppose it could be a man with long blonde hair,' Hamish said.

That did it. 'I'll call the police,' said Ally, digging out her mobile phone.

TWO

Detective Inspector Bob Rigby hailed from Birmingham originally. His Scottish wife had persuaded him to take this post, covering the Western Highlands, 'because nothing ever happens up there except for the occasional brawl at closing time'. He'd hoped, he told Ally, for a few quiet years before retirement. Things were not turning out exactly as he'd expected.

Rigby arrived. The earl's wooden rowing boat was brought out of the shed before being moored alongside and, having asked permission to use it, Rigby rowed out with a young police constable to bring the body back to the shore. A little later, while he questioned Hamish, Ally sat in the police car with a friendly woman officer until it was her turn.

Ally knew she was never going to feel quite the same about this little loch again.

'It was so peaceful and quiet,' she told Rigby. 'Then, when the earl arrived, we chatted for a bit, and that was when I drew his attention to the something I'd seen earlier floating at the far end of the loch, drifting in our direction. That was when Hamish got out his binoculars and realised it was a person.'

'Hmm,' said Rigby. 'And do you know who this woman is?'

'No, I've never seen her before.' *And I don't ever want to see her again*, Ally thought, shuddering at the sight of the pale, lifeless woman, with her staring eyes and her white-blonde hair.

'We can only suppose she was a tourist,' Rigby said.

'Perhaps she just tripped and fell in? Maybe she couldn't swim?' Ally suggested.

Rigby shook his head. 'And just *happened* to get bashed on the head first?'

'Probably not then,' Ally said sadly.

'Definitely not,' said Rigby.

Ally was glad to get home, and as she made her way up the lane, she realised it was the anniversary of the date when she'd first seen the malthouse. It had been 17 October, two years before, when she'd initially seen the old stone building on the heather-clad hillside, the castle towering above and the village beneath. Her family had thought she'd gone raving mad when she announced her intention to sell her warm, comfortable Edinburgh flat to head north and west to this remote spot, 'where it rains all the time,' they said. Furthermore, her son pointed out, she was – then – *sixty-six years old*! Surely this was the time to take up knitting, evening classes and go on cruises? Isn't that what old people did? Ally didn't want to do any of that. Even her daughter, Carol, down in Wiltshire, had tried to dissuade her from making such a move. 'I don't suppose we can blame the menopause at your age,' she'd said sadly, probably convinced then that it could be the early signs of dementia.

Sometime in the not too distant past, health and safety regulations had decreed that the malt must be stored elsewhere, and the distillery appeared to have forgotten about the old malthouse for several years before someone decided it should be sold. Ally had thought she might have a battle on her hands to be allowed to add many more windows, but the building wasn't listed and the local council had been surprisingly amenable. Now her three en-suite guest bedrooms had stunning views down to the village, the river and the larger Loch Arran, which was a sea loch, in the distance.

These rooms had been full all summer, her first summer here, but now there was only the occasional late tourist looking for accommodation. In another couple of weeks, at the end of October, the clocks would be turned back an hour, the days would shorten, and Ally would probably close The Auld Malthouse B&B for the winter, only opening up again for Christmas and the New Year.

Locharran itself was a sturdy little village alongside the Altbeag River and nestling in the glen at the foot of the mountains. It boasted a church, an elementary school, a post office and general store, a fish and chip shop, and even a little bistro, run by an English widow called Linda, who had become one of Ally's closest friends. They were both incomers and so viewed with a certain amount of wariness. Linda, too, would most likely close her bistro, except perhaps at weekends and Christmas, and the village would doze quietly throughout the winter.

Ally sat down beside the log burner in the spacious kitchen, which was her favourite room. There was an oil-fired Aga opposite, which provided the central heating, off-white painted wooden kitchen units, and a large pine table. The architect had done a fine job, and the builder has managed to retain the beamed ceilings throughout the ground floor, making the kitchen, the dining room and the sitting room feel cosy and characterful.

She realised that she was still shaking and felt the need for something stronger than tea. Ally wasn't normally a whisky drinker but, on this occasion, she poured herself a small measure and tried to digest the afternoon's events: Hamish Sinclair, Earl of Locharran, Lothario of Locharran, now planning marriage to a woman less than half his age! And another woman's body has been found floating in the loch! She could hardly wait to tell Ross. It was a good half-hour walk to his house, but Ally felt that this incredible news was best delivered in person.

Ross lived outside the village in a converted barn, with outbuildings that he'd transformed into holiday lets. Like Ally and Linda, he, too, was less likely to be doing much business in the winter, except at Christmas and particularly New Year, when everyone headed north to experience a Highland Hogmanay. The area then came alive again, for about ten days, then dozed off until Easter.

Ross was a kind, patient man and was well respected in the village. Ally had never expected to find love again at her late age, and Ross had admitted to feeling exactly the same.

As she walked, Ally thought fondly of Ken, her late husband, who'd also been a patient, kindly man, if not exactly adventurous. She recalled long evenings when, as a headmaster, Ken had marked dozens of exercise books, while she dreamed of escaping to France or Italy to lead a simple life in a rustic village growing olives and grapes. Goodness only knows what he'd have thought of Locharran! Perhaps she had left it a bit late for France or Italy, but at least she'd made some sort of escape.

Flora had been happy with the extra walk, although she lay down exhausted when Ally finally arrived at the barn.

'Have I got news for you!' she greeted Ross, who was in the garden stripping down an old Windsor chair which he planned to re-varnish.

'And what's that?' he asked, laying down a wad of sand-paper and standing up to give her a kiss.

'First of all, there's been what appears to be a *murder*! I saw the body first, while I was sitting by the loch chatting to the earl.'

Ross raised an eyebrow. 'What were you doing with the earl?' he asked with a wicked smile.

'I wasn't doing anything. I was just sitting there, minding my own business and enjoying the serenity, when he appeared and we got chatting. I'll tell you about that in a minute, but it was then that I saw again what turned out to be a body floating in our direction.'

Ross looked shocked. '*What*? Are you *serious*?'

'Yes. It was a woman, a young woman, wearing a yellow coat. I had to call the police.'

'Did you recognise her?'

Ally shook her head. 'I'd never seen her before. But it appears she might not have drowned accidentally because there was a nasty cut on the top of her head.'

'My God, Ally, you must need a drink!'

Ally nodded, realising in that moment just how shaken up she still felt. 'I went home and had a wee whisky before I felt steady enough to walk down here!'

Ross took her in his arms. 'Why didn't you call me? I'd have come straight up.'

'I know you would, but I wanted the walk. And that's not all! We've been invited to dine at the castle on Saturday evening.'

'The castle? What's that all about?'

'We've been invited to meet the lady that Hamish intends to marry!'

'*What*?' Ross stared at Ally in disbelief.

'You heard! He's planning to get married again!'

'Who the hell's going to marry that silly old goat?' Ross

asked. Though he and the earl had actually become quite good friends in recent months, Ross had always privately maintained that if Hamish hadn't been landed gentry and had been obliged to earn a living for himself in the real world, he'd be penniless.

'A young woman by the name of Elena,' Ally replied.

Ross raised an eyebrow. 'How young?'

'I believe she's thirty-two.'

Ross shook his head slowly from side to side. 'Where did you hear this gem from, for goodness' sake?'

Ally laughed. 'Straight from the horse's mouth! From the bridegroom himself! That's what we were chatting about.'

'My God!' Ross exclaimed, looking at his watch. 'I'd better not offer you another drink, I suppose, but let's have some coffee while you tell me all.' He led the way into his huge open-plan kitchen-cum-diner-cum-living-room and began to prepare coffee in the state-of-the-art machine which, after some hissing, delivered two hot, frothy cappuccinos. 'I'm still trying to get my head around what you've just told me!'

'Hamish met her in London – nearly knocked her off her feet. Literally, I mean! She stepped out in front of his taxi.'

'He's planning to marry a woman he nearly ran over? This is becoming more and more ridiculous, Ally! *Why*, for God's sake?'

'No, he's fallen in love with her! Feels like he's known her all his life. Apparently, she's very smitten too. He's also hoping they might produce an heir so that his horrible cousin can't inherit,' Ally replied.

'This all beggars belief! A woman supposedly murdered in the loch, and Hamish Sinclair is planning to marry a lady half his age!'

'Well, the fact that Hamish and I found that poor woman in the loch has nothing to do with Hamish's plans to get married. And, after all, we've found love in later years, haven't we?' Ally said.

'Yes, but we're the same age, and we're not exactly planning to have a family!'

'That's true,' Ally agreed. 'Should be an interesting dinner though.'

THREE

One thing was clear: the lady in the loch was certainly not from Locharran. Nobody had been reported missing, and Detective Inspector Rigby had been having a major headache until Ivan, the barman from the Craigmonie Hotel Bar, informed Rigby that he'd been expecting his fiancée on the bus from Inverness the previous day, and she hadn't arrived. He'd met her on his last trip home to Lithuania. Ivan had then been persuaded to look at the woman's body and had been horrified to discover that it was indeed his fiancée, Kristina.

Ally and Ross heard all of this in the Craigmonie Bar when they popped in for a drink that evening. 'I was to meet her at the bus stop in Locharran,' Ivan had wept. 'I couldn't go to the airport because Callum was away and I was running the hotel. But then she called me. She told me her flight was late and she missed the bus, but a nice lady was giving her a lift.'

According to Murdo McConnachie, the village postman and a font of knowledge when it came to village gossip, the distraught Ivan, a heavy drinker anyway, then commenced a two-day drinking binge to assuage his grief and was later found unconscious in his room by Callum Dalrymple, the hotel manager.

Ally was beginning to wonder just how many brides-to-be were heading to Locharran, but knew that Hamish's Elena would not have arrived by bus because Hamish had told her that he would be driving to Inverness to meet her and her sister at the airport. Presumably, by now, they were both safely ensconced up at the castle.

So far as Ally could ascertain, no one in the village had any knowledge whatsoever of the earl's proposed nuptials except herself, Ross and possibly Donald Scott, the minister, who had also been invited to the Saturday night dinner. In any case, Elena's arrival would scarcely have been noticed amidst the furore over Ivan's fiancée. If Mrs Fraser, the earl's housekeeper, and Mrs Jamieson, the cook, were at all aware of the reason for the sisters' arrival at the castle, they hadn't spread the news, so Ally could only assume that Hamish had spun them some tale to put them off the scent. And since the village shop was such a hotbed of gossip, they would definitely have plenty to say on the subject if they knew. In the meantime, they'd doubtless still find plenty to talk about, and Ally steeled herself as she went to buy some eggs the following morning.

Locharran Stores was run by two spinster sisters, Queenie and Bessie McDougall, who were well into their seventies. Queenie, the elder, was the boss, and spent most of the day stretched across the counter to see and hear anything and everything of interest, while Bessie did as she was told.

'Well, Mrs McKinley, I canna believe what I'm hearin'! It was yersel', wasn't it, that saw that poor woman's body in the loch!' Queenie paused for a brief moment. 'In the company of the earl, I'm told?'

Ally sighed. *Here we go again*, she thought. Queenie considered her to be the local femme fatale, convinced she'd been having an affair with the earl *and* the vet! It was hardly surprising, she supposed, because Hamish had a bit of a reputation as a ladies' man, and it was beyond Queenie's comprehension to imagine that they could just be friends.

'The earl came along while I was sitting quietly by the loch,' she said, 'and he happened to have some binoculars and could see the body before it actually got to us.'

'Och, poor, poor Ivan! So, are ye still pally with the vet, *as well as* the earl?'

'I'm friends with both,' Ally said shortly. 'Could I have some eggs please?'

'Bessie!' Queenie hollered into the dark storeroom at the back of the counter. 'Eggs for Mrs McKinley please!'

Some scraping and rustling sounds emanated from the storeroom before Bessie, in her usual scruffy jumper and droopy skirt, emerged and deposited a box of a dozen eggs on the counter. 'New laid,' she informed Ally, who doubted it.

Queenie wasn't finished yet. 'Mrs Fraser told me this morning that the earl's been acting sort of funny and has gone off to Inverness to meet two ladies who're now staying at the castle.'

Mrs Fraser and Mrs Jamieson, both of whom had been with the earl for at least forty years, generally knew everything that was going on up at the castle.

'I just wondered if ye might know what they're doin' here?' Queenie asked hopefully.

'I haven't the first idea,' Ally said, digging out a five-pound note. 'Let me pay you for the eggs.'

Before Queenie could do any more interrogating, Ally picked up her eggs and her change and headed quickly out of the shop.

. . .

The next day was Saturday, and Ally was trying to decide what to wear to the earl's dinner party. She'd bought a dress in Inverness back in the springtime but as yet had had no occasion to wear it. It was a dark green, wool midi-dress, but it had been such a long time since she bought it, she wasn't sure if it would still fit. Ally took the dress off its hanger and offered up a quick prayer. The prayer was answered: it fitted. Just. As a long-legged five feet, ten inches, she often had trouble finding outfits that were long enough.

She studied herself in the full-length mirror in her bedroom and reckoned she didn't look too bad, her rapidly greying hair still highlighted and lowlighted by that miracle-maker hairdresser in Fort William. Thank goodness she'd had it cut a couple of weeks ago.

'You look lovely,' Ross said, putting an arm around her when he arrived.

He was looking pretty good himself, Ally thought. Originally from Glasgow, Ross had lived in Locharran for around forty years, so he pretty much had the measure of the place. He'd worked hard to set up his veterinary practice, now passed on to his son, also a vet, who had five daughters. Ally knew that, some years previously, Ross had lost his other son to drug abuse, then his wife to heart failure shortly afterwards. Ally had been immediately attracted to him when they first met and, both independent characters, they now had an ideal relationship: time alone and time together.

That evening, Ally and Ross walked up from the malthouse to the castle, thus ensuring they could enjoy a drink or two. Or three probably. She felt apprehensive, not having any idea what to expect at the dinner, but as they turned the final corner of the drive, she gasped. The castle was floodlit! Ally had heard that it was only lit up at Christmas and New Year, so this confirmed it as a special occasion. In the dark evening it looked spectacular. Ross agreed and said that, in all the years he'd lived in Locharran, he'd only ever seen it lit up during the festive season. They both looked up in awe, and Ally dug out her phone to take a photo.

'He's obviously pulling out all the stops to impress this lady,' Ally said as they approached the massive oak door. Ross pulled the bell cord, which sent a deep, throaty 'bong!' into the depths of the castle and very likely for some distance around.

Mrs Fraser, the trusty housekeeper, opened the door, ushered them in, took their coats and said, 'The earl and his party are in the small drawing room, if you'd follow me, please.'

Mrs Fraser, who normally wore a pinny over a jumper and skirt of her own choosing, was tonight clad in a black dress, over which she wore a starched white apron and a starchy expression to match. Ally would have given a lot to know what this stalwart old retainer was really thinking, after serving the earl, without a countess's interference, for so many years. Could her position be about to be usurped? Mrs Fraser was not going to like anyone interfering with her authority.

FOUR

Her lips in a tight line, Mrs Fraser opened the door of the 'small' drawing room, the dimensions of which were at least the size of Ally's entire ground floor, revealing a tableau which Ally would always remember. There was the earl, in full Highland dress with green velvet jacket and green tartan kilt, standing in front of the roaring fire in the huge inglenook. His beard and hair were neatly trimmed, and he could easily have stepped straight out of the pages of a Walter Scott novel. Ally had never seen him look so attractive.

On the sofa alongside sat two women. One was small, plump, pretty and fair-haired, sitting back comfortably against the cushions. Her dark-haired companion was not as attractive and sat awkwardly on the end of her seat.

'Ah, come in, come in!' said the earl. There were introductions all round. 'This is Elena,' he said proudly, reaching out to clasp the hand of the blonde woman, 'and this is her sister, Magda.'

They all shook hands and, just as they were about to sit down again, the minister and his wife were ushered in.

The Reverend Donald Scott was a tall, gaunt, sombre-looking man, famed for his long, soporific sermons and his huge feet. His wife, by contrast, was small and well upholstered, with mousy hair and attractive blue eyes, dressed in a pink jumper and a tartan skirt.

Donald and Janet Scott were then duly introduced to the two sisters, and Ally was aware that everyone was sizing up everyone else. There was an awkward silence for a moment before Hamish said heartily, 'Drinks, everyone!' The sisters were each clasping a large glass of white wine, and Mrs Fraser was summoned to dispense drinks for the four incomers from an array of crystal decanters on a side table. Ally decided she badly needed a gin and tonic, and offered to help Mrs Fraser.

'No, no!' bellowed the earl. 'Mrs Fraser will manage fine!'

Ross, who'd also opted for a gin and tonic, sat down next to Ally on the sofa which faced the ladies and asked politely, 'How was your journey here? Did you fly?'

'Oh yes,' said Elena. 'I was planning to arrive yesterday, a day ahead of Mags, but my dress wasn't ready in time so we had to reschedule and travel together. But dear Hamey met us at the airport.'

Hamey! That was a new one, thought Ally.

Hamey, still standing, looked a little embarrassed but recovered quickly. 'Has everyone got a drink?' he asked, looking around. Some appreciative murmuring established that everyone did indeed have a drink. 'Right!' continued the earl, 'let's raise our glasses to my beautiful fiancée, Elena!'

Janet Scott gasped; this was plainly news to her, but her husband remained expressionless.

Then the minister spoke. 'Does this mean you intend to marry soon?'

His wife, her mouth open as she stared at the sisters, was clutching a small sherry.

'Oh, it does indeed!' Hamish replied heartily, plonking

himself down next to Elena and causing Magda to be squashed into the corner. 'As soon as possible!'

Donald cleared his throat. 'Well, Hamish, there's the small matter of—'

'No, Donald!' Hamish interrupted. 'I've made all the necessary arrangements so we can be married straight away. I've been planning this wedding for a month. And I'd like you to perform the ceremony in the castle chapel, next Saturday, after which we'll have a small reception in the castle here. No fuss, if you please! And *no sermon*! Just the necessary, and some nice music. A week today, Elena will be my Countess of Locharran!' He gave her a squeeze and raised his glass again, both he and Elena beaming. The minister was rendered speechless.

'How many people will you invite?' Ross asked. 'Surely this is quite an occasion?'

'Not many,' Hamish replied. 'Yourselves and Donald and Janet, of course, and probably my cousin and his family from London, if they deign to show up. My great friend, Simon Hartley-Knott, should be here tonight, but he's had to go to a conference in Zurich. One or two others. Oh, and Desdemona would be here, of course. She's been a wonderful friend over the years, but she's in London at the moment hosting an exhibition of her paintings. So exciting, and well deserved. She'll be back for the wedding though. Then, getting back to the wedding arrangements, later in the evening, we can throw it open to all the locals so they can party the night away if they wish. We shall probably retire quite early,' he added with a saucy smile.

His fiancée smiled at him fondly, while her sister remained deadpan. Ally wondered how she felt about her sister's engagement because so far she hadn't uttered a word or altered her expression in any way.

'I can't imagine what the village will say,' Donald said glumly.

'I should think they'd be delighted for us,' Hamish

retorted, giving Elena another squeeze. He cleared his throat. 'I shall be relieved to get my lovely fiancée married to me, especially after this terrible business with that poor woman in the loch.'

Everyone nodded in agreement.

'I can't believe she was that poor chap Ivan's fiancée – the coincidence is quite frightening,' he said, stealing a look at Elena as if to make sure that she was still there. 'I mean, I'd gladly have gone to meet this woman too, if I'd known she was coming.'

'Well,' said Donald, 'surely Ivan must have known she was coming, and surely he could have made arrangements to meet her?'

'Hasn't he got a car?' Hamish asked.

'Yes, he has,' piped up Janet, 'because I've seen him driving around in the village. Speeding, usually, and very likely way over the drink limit.' She sniffed to indicate her disapproval. 'And his car doesn't look too reliable either.'

'Actually, he wasn't able to go and get her because he was running the hotel for a couple of days,' Ally put in. 'Callum Dalrymple was away on a course or something.'

'Oh, I see. Perhaps that's the reason why he left her to get here on the bus then. Not that she was on the bus, of course.' Hamish turned to Elena. 'My dear, your glass is *empty*! We can't be having that! What about you, Magda?'

Magda hurriedly gulped what was left of her drink and handed the glass to Hamish, who made his way over to the decanters with an empty glass in each hand, which he then proceeded to fill with large measures of wine.

The sisters were eagerly attacking their refills when Janet asked, 'And what do you do, Magda?'

Magda took a large glug of wine as if preparing herself. 'I'm a nanny. I just finished working with a family in London but will be starting a new job after Elena's wedding,' she said.

Unlike her more striking green-eyed sister, she had attractive brown eyes but otherwise was somewhat dull looking.

'And you, Elena?' Ross asked. 'Hamish says you work in tourism?'

Elena nodded. 'Yes, I work for a company that organises luxury trips around the world. I'm based in London but travel all over.'

At that moment, Mrs Fraser reappeared. 'Dinner is served, sir,' she said without enthusiasm.

The earl got to his feet and, taking Elena by the arm, led the way, followed by Magda, then Ally and Ross, then the minister and his wife. Ally was relieved that they weren't to eat in the dining hall, which was enormous, cold and adorned on every wall with stags' heads. You could host a banquet for at least a hundred people in there. Instead, they followed the happy couple into a comparatively smaller room, oak panelled, stone floored and with another huge inglenook in which a fire roared. Ally was glad she'd put her thermal vest on underneath the green dress, because this room was never likely to warm up properly. The earl, for reasons best known to himself, had decided against central heating but most likely on account of the astronomical cost of installing any heating system in this enormous building.

In the centre of the room was a long, mahogany table, lit by dozens of candles placed along the centre, which delivered a glow and sparkle to the seven place settings, with their silver cutlery and crystal glasses. The whole effect was magical, high-lighted by the enormous chandelier overhead.

Ally was relieved to be seated close to the fire on one side of the table, next to Donald Scott, while Ross sat opposite, with Janet Scott on one side and Magda on the other. They exchanged amused glances as Hamish took his place at the top of the table and Elena on the opposite end.

Back came Mrs Fraser in her black dress and white apron,

looking for all the world like a waitress from the 1950s, ladling cock-a-leekie soup into delicate china bowls. Hamish seemed determined to initiate his bride-to-be into some typical Scottish cuisine. Before they ate, the minister stood up and gloomily thanked God for what they were about to receive, then everyone tackled their soup, the only noise that of Donald's loud slurping.

Then Hamish was on his feet, brandishing a wine decanter in each hand. 'From our cellars!' he said triumphantly. 'Been laid down for years, so should be good! Poor Mrs Fraser had to dust a mountain of cobwebs off the bottles!'

Poor Mrs Fraser, who had come in to clear the bowls, remained impassive. 'Would you like me to pour the wine, sir?' she asked.

'No, thanks, – that won't be necessary,' the earl said cheerfully. 'I can deal with that!' He waited until she'd left before he said, 'She always pours such awfully small amounts, you know. That must be fashionable, I suppose. Now, who's for Chablis and who's for claret? Or I've a further selection on the sideboard over there, from all the best chateaux!' He then proceeded to fill each glass to the brim. 'Saves having to top them up every five minutes.' He was in a very jolly mood.

The cock-a-leekie was followed by beef Wellington, with a selection of vegetables. Ally wondered if Elena had been offered the venison that the earl had suggested. She also wondered how much alcohol the sisters could handle. They'd obviously had wine before the guests had arrived, then large refills, and now both of them were already three-quarters through these. Ally began to feel sorry for them both. They were a long way from home, in a strange environment and obviously being weighed up. Were their parents still alive? she wondered. And they must know that they were being scrutinised, particularly Elena, as to her suitability to become a countess, in the space of one day, in a Scottish village in the middle of nowhere.

Elena smiled a lot but said little. Magda, on the other hand, remained expressionless and silent. Fortunately, the earl, the minister and Ross kept the conversation going, discussing local events, the spiralling cost of everything, particularly oil, and the ignorance of everyone in the Scottish Government as to what was going on in rural communities, particularly theirs.

As an aside, Ally asked Elena, who was seated at her end of the table, what she planned to wear for her wedding.

'I've brought my mother's wedding dress with me. Our parents were killed in a road accident five years ago. I'm so sad they can't be here,' Elena replied. 'Her dress is white and made of lace, but I'm a bit bigger than my mother, which is why it was being altered this week.'

'I'm sure you'll look lovely,' Ally said, noting the woman's beautiful skin and stunning green eyes. 'If you have any problems with anything, or need help, I'm just down at the malthouse – a ten-minute walk.'

'Thank you,' Elena said with a smile.

Glasses were refilled or topped up, and the earl got to his feet and raised his glass again. 'To my lovely bride-to-be!'

The lovely bride-to-be was already making short work of her wine refill. Though even she declined a dessert wine to accompany the whisky-laden Atholl brose which followed. This creamy, alcoholic dessert was apparently one of the cook's specialities.

By the time the cheeseboard was produced, Ally was beginning to feel uncomfortably full and very tipsy, and by the time they'd got to coffee and liqueurs, everyone was either in high spirits or half asleep. Donald, Janet and Magda fell into this latter category, but Ally felt that she, Ross, the earl and Elena were holding up very well.

By the time noises were being made about it being time to

go home, Hamish had Elena sitting on his knee, and was informing them all that he would be presenting his lovely fiancée to the estate and the village the very next day! They might even *go to church*!

At this, the minister woke up rapidly from his alcohol-induced stupor, announcing that he'd need to get up early in order to write a new, more appropriate sermon.

As they all took their leave, thanking their host effusively, Hamish murmured to Ally, 'Don't you think that Elena's lovely?'

Ally nodded, hoping only that the lovely Elena would make him happy.

As they walked down to the malthouse, hand in hand in the moonlight, Ross asked, 'Well, what did you make of *that*?'

'I'm still trying to digest it all!' Ally said with a giggle.

Ross gripped her hand more tightly. 'Now, what did you think of Elena?'

'I feel a little sorry for her, and I don't know why.'

'What about the sister?'

'Enigmatic. She certainly didn't have much to say.'

'There was something a little strange about her,' Ross said. 'She may not have said a lot, but I got the impression she didn't miss much, even when she was supposedly half asleep.'

'She didn't come across as particularly happy. Still, at least the earl was cock-a-hoop!'

'Elena's an attractive lady,' Ross said. 'What's not to like?'

'And she can certainly put away the alcohol!'

'Maybe she needs it to cope with Hamish in bed!'

'I thought Hamish looked very dishy tonight,' Ally said. 'She should have no trouble!'

Ross raised an eyebrow. 'Does that mean you could rather fancy him yourself?'

Ally smiled. 'No, it just means that he looked dishy. The minister didn't look particularly happy though.'

'The minister *never* looks particularly happy,' Ross said, laughing. 'I wonder what he'll put in his sermon for tomorrow? Don't think I'll be going!'

'And I don't think any of us will have much trouble sleeping tonight,' Ally said with a yawn as they entered the malthouse.

'I trust you're not going to send me home in this drunken state?'

'As if!' Ally said, giggling. 'Let's get to bed!'

She couldn't begin to imagine how the village was going to cope with this stupendous news.

FIVE

There was certainly lots of reaction in Locharran: disbelief; shock; astonishment; derision. Hot on the heels of the excitement caused by 'the lady in the loch', here was another young woman destined to wed a Locharran resident, but this one had at least arrived safely. And she was about to become a countess! Without any prior notice, if you please! How on earth had they met when she'd never been to Scotland before? It had to be the internet, which was surely no way to gauge anyone's suitability!

A company arrived on the Monday morning and strung bunting, in red, white and blue, from one lamp post to another, all over the village.

'Have ye seen all thae wee flags they're stickin' up all over the place?' asked Morag McConnachie when she arrived in the morning to do some cleaning. Morag, who was the wife of Murdo the postman, cleaned for Ally each morning when she had guests, and Ally had become very fond of the little woman. Morag was sixty years old, with permed, dyed blonde hair and pretty blue eyes.

'You mean the bunting?' Ally asked.

'Aye, buntin'. Ye'd think it was a royal weddin' or a coronation or somethin',' Morag shouted as she hung up her purple anorak on the peg inside the back door.

'The earl obviously thought it might be a joyous occasion for the village,' Ally said as Morag removed a newly laundered overall from her bag and wrapped it round her ample curves.

'What difference is it goin' to make if he has a wife or not? More likely she'll have all them fancy ideas and probably put up our rent!' With a snort, Morag went in search of the vacuum cleaner.

There was a similar reaction a little later when Ally visited the shop.

'I see yer friend, the earl, has found himself *another woman!*' exclaimed Queenie with great satisfaction. She shook her head sadly. 'Ye should've snatched him up while the goin' was good! We was just sayin' that, wasn't we, Bessie?'

There was no response, and Bessie was nowhere to be seen, but that didn't stop Queenie. 'And he had to go all the way to that London to find someone who'd take him on!'

'She's actually very nice,' Ally said.

'Mrs Fraser was sayin', only half an hour back, that the woman was hardly in the door when she was inspectin' the kitchen, wantin' this, and wantin' that, and tellin' them they needed a *uniform!* A *uniform!* She'll be full of them new-fangled ideas, so she will.'

Ally wondered what her friend Linda thought about all this. Linda was the owner of The Bistro, and Ally found her stuffing tablecloths into the washing machine. 'I had some customers last night,' she explained.

At least Linda was positive. 'It might just bring a few late tourists into the village,' she said hopefully. 'But Callum is apparently hopping mad because they've chosen this fancy caterer, and he's saying he could have done it just as well at the hotel and a bloody sight cheaper.'

Ally stayed for a cup of tea and one of Linda's delicious Danish pastries before making her way back to the malthouse, where Murdo was just pulling up in his red van. As he handed over her mail, he said cheerfully to Ally, 'This'll kill the old bugger! Havin' a young woman! He'll be havin' a heart attack before the week's over! And then *she'll* take over! Ye couldnae make it up!'

A little while before lunch, Detective Inspector Rigby appeared on the malthouse doorstep, and Ally could see immediately that this was not a happy man.

'Come in, Inspector,' she said, leading him into the kitchen, well aware that he never refused a cup of tea or a biscuit.

'Yes, I will come in because I need to speak to you, but I can't afford to stay long,' he said in a tone that indicated he was rushed off his feet.

'Cup of tea? I just made a pot.'

'Oh, I shouldn't really, but a cuppa would be very welcome. It's colder this morning.'

'It is,' she agreed, pouring the tea and handing him a mug. 'Shortbread?' She removed the lid from the box and passed it to him.

'Just one little piece then,' he said. 'Got to watch the figure, you know!' He patted his paunch affectionately, then took a large bite of shortbread and a gulp of tea before adding casually, 'Bad business this out at Loch Soular.'

'Horrendous,' Ally agreed with a shudder. 'I still keep seeing that poor woman's body when I close my eyes.'

'Now, Mrs McKinley, can we just go over some of this again? And do you mind if I record this conversation?' Rigby asked, somewhat apologetically, getting out his phone. 'You were just sitting by the lochside? Any particular reason?'

'It was a lovely day and it's such a beautiful wee loch. I'd walked Flora there and sat down to enjoy the scenery.'

'Do you go there often?'

'Since I've had the dog, yes.'

The dog in question was sitting, gazing hopefully at Rigby, her eye on the shortbread. So far he hadn't dropped a crumb.

'Have some more,' Ally said, wielding the box in his direction.

'Oh, just one more then,' he said, choosing another large piece. 'I need to go through this again with you: while you were sitting alone by the loch, did you see any activity on the opposite bank or anything at all suspicious while you were there?'

Ally racked her brains for a moment. 'Only the yellow object floating at the far end of the loch, which I later pointed out to the earl.'

'Ah, the earl.' Rigby frowned. 'Why do you suppose he came along at that very moment?'

'I've no idea,' Ally replied. 'He said he was hoping to see me, and he knows I like walking there with Flora.'

'So, he was looking for you? Why?'

'He wanted to tell me he'd found a lady he wanted to marry.'

'He did?'

'He did.'

'And the lady is...?' In his excitement, Rigby had dropped a couple of crumbs, which Flora guzzled at the speed of light.

'A lovely young woman called Elena. She recently arrived from London.'

Rigby froze. 'Another young bride-to-be! You know that the woman in the loch was coming to marry Ivan who works at the Craigmonie?'

'So I believe. It's quite a coincidence,' Ally agreed.

He leaned forward. 'Why would these two women be heading towards Locharran at the same time?'

'To meet their future husbands I should think,' Ally said.

'And that doesn't strike you as being a bit of an unlikely coincidence?'

'Not really, but coincidences do happen, Inspector.'

'And you'd seen no one at all around Loch Soular before the earl arrived – you're quite certain of that?'

'No one at all. It was bliss.'

'Hmm.' Rigby frowned. 'And when the earl arrived you suddenly saw the body?'

'I'd seen something yellow in the distance, at the far end of the little loch, but I'd no idea at that point that it was a body.. It looked like a yellow coat with something in it, but it was too far away for me to make out what it was. The earl had binoculars, and he was able to see what did appear to be a body, very slowly drifting in our direction, and that's when we phoned the police.'

'But neither of you had ever seen that body before?'

'No, Inspector. And it wasn't until later, when poor Ivan identified his fiancée, that we discovered who she was. Have you managed to find out any more about her?'

'Only what I can glean from questioning Ivan, which isn't much. I've been on to the bus company to check whether Kristina had been on the bus at any point, and they confirmed that she hadn't.'

'Ivan told me she'd missed the bus,' Ally said, 'but who could have got her here and then killed her?'

'That's precisely what I'm trying to find out, Mrs McKinley.' Rigby drained his tea. 'There's something funny going on round here,' he said ominously as he stood up to go.

SIX

What with the lady in the loch and the arrival of the earl's bride-to-be, the village was buzzing. Murdo, on his postal rounds, kept Ally in the picture with all the gossip. Queenie, apparently, had become so excited by these events that she'd had to lie down for a whole afternoon, leaving Bessie to deal with a long queue of supposed customers who'd only come in to mull over all this juicy gossip with Queenie. 'Among them were Mrs Jamieson and Mrs Fraser,' Murdo said. 'They're both aghast at these turns of events, particularly as the earl is plannin' to marry some woman less than half his age, and how is that likely to affect them? What does he think he's *doin*'? Has he developed dementia or somethin', do you think? You don't think he's plannin' on havin' children, do you?'

'I think that the earl would probably like an heir,' Ally said to Murdo.

'The way he's been putting it about, he's probably got heirs all over the place!' Murdo retorted.

'Perhaps so, Murdo, but if they're not legitimate, then they can't inherit the earldom or the estate,' Ally replied.

Murdo shook his head. 'Well it's all very strange if you ask me.'

Ally and Ross were invited to the wedding as a couple, along with the Locharran's retired GP, Doctor Murray; Desdemona, the sister of the earl's first wife; Hamish's London cousins, of course; and Simon his great friend and best man. They were the select few to be invited as proper guests and thus eligible to sit in the front pews. Villagers were invited to attend, but there was only so much room in the castle chapel, so first come, first served. And they were all to be seated further back. The atmosphere lightened somewhat when it became public that the earl would be inviting the whole village to a party at the castle in the evening and, crucially, would be paying for everything. Even the most suspicious villagers softened at that.

Preparations had been in full flow for several days. Two days before the wedding, the banker cousin from London duly arrived in Locharran along with his wife and son, all looking anything but happy. They'd refused the earl's offer of accommodation at the castle and booked themselves into the best suite at the Craigmonie where, it was rumoured, they were extremely demanding and generally unpleasant.

A florist was arriving on Friday to decorate the chapel, and specialist caterers were coming from Inverness.

'Bloody cheek!' exclaimed Callum Dalrymple, manager of the Craigmonie Hotel, when he called in at the malthouse on Wednesday. 'We could quite easily have provided the menu that the earl wanted. I reckon he's just showing off to impress this woman of his!'

Knowing that the Craigmonie had an excellent reputation for its food, Ally could only agree. Like everyone else, Callum was at a loss to understand why anyone as ancient as the earl would contemplate marrying again. What was the silly old goat *thinking* of?

The week passed. Ally, as always, wondered what to wear to this event. The weather was turning cooler, and she wondered if she could get away with wearing a summer dress, or would she freeze? There wasn't time to go gallivanting round the shops and, although there was a tremendous selection online, she couldn't be sure that anything she ordered would arrive on time. Or fit. So, out came the navy print silk dress which she'd only worn once before and, if it was cold, she'd wear her smart navy blazer on top. Then a hat? Did people still wear hats to weddings? Ally wondered. Up here they probably did.

It was Linda who came to the rescue.

'I've got a nice cream fascinator you can borrow, which would look great with that outfit!'

The wedding day dawned with beautiful sunshine. Morag had volunteered to look after Flora for the day. 'I'm nae bothered to go to that stupid weddin',' she said disdainfully.

As Ally got dressed, she wondered how many villagers would actually attend, if only to get a good look at the bride. The ceremony was to take place at eleven o'clock, and, at a quarter past ten, Ross appeared, looking very handsome in a smart dark-grey suit and immaculate white shirt with pale-grey tie.

'Wow!' he greeted Ally. 'Don't *you* look beautiful?'

'You look pretty tasty yourself,' Ally exclaimed. 'Now, do you think we should have a wee drink before we go?'

'Most definitely,' Ross agreed. 'I'm not sure I'm ready to witness this event without some form of stimulant.'

He settled for brandy and ginger, while Ally opted for a gin and tonic.

'This,' said Ross as they clinked glasses, 'is going to be most interesting.'

As they went outside, Ally noticed the Scottish saltire fluttering in the breeze from the castle flagpole. This, too, normally only happened at New Year, the Atlantic gales having shredded earlier flags after a couple of days. The church bells were ringing, the bunting was fluttering and half of the village seemed to be making their way up towards the castle. So many, in fact, that when Ally and Ross themselves walked up to the castle, they had to push their way through the throng which had gathered by the door and who were not permitted to enter until the invited guests had been seated.

The chapel was very small and very old, with a Celtic cross carved into the thick stone wall and rays of light filtering in through the elaborate stained-glass windows. There was a wonderful perfume emanating from the impressive white flower arrangements which were positioned all around. Ally thought it was jasmine but wasn't too sure. At the organ, an elderly lady was playing something unrecognisable and more suitable for a funeral.

As they sat down at the front, Ally looked around and recognised a few people by sight, including the lone woman with the long, dark, greying hair, wearing a multi-coloured kaftan and a load of wooden beads.

'Who's *that*?' Ross whispered, giving her a gentle nudge. 'Is it...?'

'Surely you recognise Desdemona,' Ally whispered back. 'Hamish's sister-in-law and the older sister of his first wife.'

'Oh yes, of course. I haven't seen her for years. Is she still living out in the wilds beyond The Bothy?'

'Yes, she is. I bought a couple of her watercolours earlier this year,' Ally said. 'The ones up in the bedrooms. You probably haven't seen them.'

'So she's still painting then? I remember she used to be quite good.'

'She certainly is. And she has the most amazing walled garden, growing herbs and things, some of which I've never even heard of.'

'I remember now. And wasn't her sister called Ophelia?' Ross chortled quietly.

'She was,' confirmed Ally. 'I believe her father was an English professor, and you know what the English are like about their Shakespeare.'

Casting her eyes around, Ally noticed the family of three sitting across the aisle from them. It could only be the earl's banker cousin and, for the moment anyway, still the rightful heir, along with his family. He was a distinguished-looking man, tall, dark, face like stone. His wife, designer-clad and wearing an enormous hat, looked equally disagreeable, along with a son who would possibly be in his late teens or early twenties and looked as if he'd rather be anywhere else on the planet than in this chapel. He was glued to his phone, until his mother rapped him on the hand and said something which caused him to roll his eyes heavenward and unwillingly put the phone in his pocket.

Then there was a ripple of sound from the crowd outside as the earl arrived, resplendent in full Highland dress and looking very debonair, making his way up the aisle, beaming at his guests. He was accompanied by an equally handsome man, presumably Simon, his best friend with the double-barrelled name – Ally kept forgetting it – also in full Highland dress, although in a different tartan.

Then the minister, Donald Scott, emerged from the vestry and stood with them both, looking towards the door. The public were now filtering in, and the organ decibels increased to cover all the shuffling and whispering.

After everyone was seated, and latecomers shepherded in to

stand at the back, the minister had a word in the ear of the lady organist, who immediately switched from 'Praise, My Soul, the King of Heaven' to Handel's 'Wedding March'.

Ally watched Hamish's face light up as he looked towards the door to see his little blonde bride in a very elegant, long, white-lace gown come slowly up the aisle on the arm of her taller, darker sister, who wore a long-sleeved claret number with a great many frills round the hem. Magda, having delivered her sister to the beaming bridegroom, then sat down with a thump and a sigh in the front pew, directly in front of Ally and Ross, and next to Desdemona, who looked at her with some distaste and moved further along the pew. The banker cousin was looking at them both with contempt and a raised eyebrow.

'Going to be an interesting reception,' Ross whispered with a grin.

The ceremony proceeded without a hitch. The bride looked up adoringly at her new husband as they set off down the aisle together, and Ally had never seen him look so happy. Perhaps, after all, this really *was* a marriage made in heaven!

SEVEN

The villagers were ushered out after the bridal party and guests, and they then got busy with photographing the happy couple and showering them with confetti, which got the minister tut-tutting away about who was going to have to clean it all up. Press photographers had arrived on the scene too.

'This will be all over the front pages tomorrow,' the earl said cheerfully, 'and I recognise that chap from *Tatler*.'

The happy couple were flanked on one side by the smooth, smiling best man, a somewhat glum-looking Magda, and the minister. On the other side was an even more glum-looking Randolph Sinclair, his wife with the hat, and the son. Everyone else had to gather behind, on the steps, and *smile* please!

The villagers dispersed as Hamish and Elena led the guests back into the castle and into the Sinclair Room, which was off the enormous Great Hall, with its stone walls and stags' heads. Ally had never been in the Sinclair Room before but was delighted to see blazing fires in the huge inglenooks at each end. The lower walls were oak panelled, and the upper walls had been papered in Sinclair tartan wallpaper. The mahogany table must have been twenty feet long, Ally reckoned. At one end were trays of champagne glasses, and ice buckets containing the finest champagnes. Then there was the most amazing array of luxury foods, hot and cold, all ready to be served by a line-up of waiters in white shirts, black trousers and Sinclair-tartan ties and cummerbunds. And everywhere were huge, exotic floral arrangements in white and green, and emitting the same wonderful perfume as in the chapel and which Ally now recognised as indeed being jasmine.

Hamish, holding his bride's hand tightly, cleared his throat and called for silence. 'We've decided to keep this informal, so do please help yourself to everything but, before you do, ensure you have a full glass of champagne for the toast!'

One of the waiters was already circulating with a silver tray of glasses, filled to the top with champagne.

'This certainly beats a pie and a pint at the Craigmonie,' Ross exclaimed, looking around and keeping a tight hold on his glass of Dom Perignon.

'Interesting that they've decided on a buffet,' Ally remarked, sipping hers. As she spoke, she spotted two new arrivals – Mrs Fraser, the housekeeper, in a pale-turquoise dress and jacket, with white high-heeled shoes on which she kept wobbling alarmingly, and with her was Mrs Jamieson, the cook, wearing a grey dress to match her grey, permed curls. Both ladies looked extremely uncomfortable.

'Everyone here now?' shouted the earl. 'Everyone got a drink? Jolly good! I would now like you to raise your glasses to my beautiful bride!'

Everyone raised their glasses and studied the beautiful bride, who blushed and nodded her appreciation.

'Right,' the earl continued. 'We hope you enjoy this little buffet, and I look forward to chatting with you all.'

At this point, Simon, the best man, called for silence. 'I've known Hamish for a very long time,' he said, 'and I know you'll join me in wishing him, and the lovely Elena, a long and happy life together!' Glasses were raised again. 'I, too, look forward to meeting you all!'

This was a cue for everyone to do some circulating, and Ally found herself next to Desdemona Morton. Not quite sure what she should say, Ally smiled and said, 'I do hope she makes him happy.'

Desdemona rolled her eyes. 'It'll be a bloody miracle if she does! I don't think Hamish was born to be monogamous.'

'Well, perhaps it'll be different now he's married? I mean, he was happy with your sister, wasn't he?' Then Ally wondered if she should have mentioned that, in view of the fact that Morag had told her that Desdemona herself had been in a relationship with the earl before he dropped her to wed her younger and prettier sister. Still, that was a long time ago, and he and Desdemona had obviously become friends again, if not lovers. Or *were* they lovers?

'Who's to know what goes on in a marriage?' Desdemona replied enigmatically.

'Do you not think your sister was happy with Hamish then?' Ally asked.

Desdemona shrugged. 'They seemed happy enough, but they were married for such a short time; they'd been married for less than a year when she died, so who knows what might have happened.'

'I'm beginning to think Locharran isn't the luckiest place for marriages, when you think of poor Ivan and his fiancée,' Ally said.

'Yes, I agree, but I've only just heard about the woman in Loch Soular.' Desdemona shook her head. 'I can hardly believe it because I think I may have given this woman a lift...'

'*What?* When?' Ally almost dropped her glass.

'Well, a couple of weeks ago, I had my cousin from London staying with me for a few days. And, when he left, I took him to the airport because he's quite old and I didn't want him to travel on any buses.' She looked around as if afraid someone might be listening. 'After I'd seen Harry off at the airport, I saw this distressed-looking woman with a backpack,' Desdemona continued. 'She was waving a piece of paper at the taxi drivers, but they were taking one look and shaking their heads. So I spoke to her and it turns out her flight was late arriving, she'd missed the bus to Locharran and she didn't know what to do. She didn't speak much English, and she was in tears. So I told her it was her lucky day and I could give her a lift all the way there. I've forgotten what her name was but off we go until we come to Cairn Cross – you know? The crossroad.'

Ally nodded.

'And my old Land Rover just stalled. No way could I get it started for about twenty minutes.' She sighed. 'It's always breaking down. Anyway, this woman phoned her fiancé again – she'd already let him know she was getting a lift – but there was no answer this time. I told her it wasn't far, only a mile, a mile and a half maybe, to Locharran, so she decided to walk. That was the last time I saw her.' She paused. 'I got the thing started again and made it home before I set off again for Fort William next day to get the train to London.'

Ally looked at her quizzically. 'Why on earth didn't you accompany the cousin on the flight to London?'

'I'm terrified of flying,' Desdemona said. 'Always have been, and there's a very good train service from Fort William to London, you know.'

'So you left the next day?'

'Yes, the next morning. I had an exhibition in a gallery just off Piccadilly and, over the next ten days, I managed to sell a lot of paintings. Just as well because I've had to pay that boy from The Bothy, the owner's teenage son, to go up and feed the dogs each day, and I have to admit I did have a few unpaid bills.' She shrugged, then smiled. 'So I'm solvent again, and hopefully now I can afford to get my Land Rover sorted out.'

'So when did you hear about the lady in the loch?'

'I didn't hear about that until earlier today, before I got dressed up to come here.' Desdemona played with some of her wooden beads for a moment. 'The boy from The Bothy told me.'

'Did he tell you who it was?'

'Just that it was some woman trying to get to Locharran from the airport to be married. That made me wonder if it was the same woman that I gave a lift to. Do you know what her name was?'

'Her name was Kristina Andris, and she was coming to marry Ivan, the barman at the Craigmonie,' Ally said.

'Oh my God!' Desdemona looked round for a seat to steady herself. 'That was *her!*'

Ally helped her into a nearby chair. 'Have you told the police?'

She shook her head. 'I've hardly had time to unpack yet!'

'You need to get straight on to them. The inspector is called Rigby, and he's been questioning everyone. I think you might have been the last person to see poor Kristina alive.'

Desdemona looked utterly shocked.

'This is urgent, Desdemona,' Ally said.

'It certainly is.' Desdemona hesitated. 'Nothing to do with me, I assure you. Someone must have seen her on that road to Locharran. Doesn't bear thinking about!' She turned away as the minister's wife approached her. 'I'm going to get out of here...'

There wasn't a lot she could say to that, and Ally was relieved to be distracted by the minister himself, who'd called for silence and decided he should say a few words too.

'I have been ordained by God,' he said piously, 'to join in holy matrimony our earl, Hamish Sinclair and his bride, Elena. I'd like to toast the new *Countess of Locharran!*' This raised a cheer and everyone clinked glasses and repeated, 'The Countess of Locharran!'

The banker's wife, frozen-faced, had appeared at Ally's side. She'd removed her hat, which she'd placed carefully on a chair. 'This is quite a charade,' she said to Ally, downing her drink in one and looking around for a refill. The waiter, with a white-linen-napkin-wrapped bottle appeared, as if by magic. 'I'm Lavinia Sinclair, by the way.'

Ally shook her hand. 'I'm Ally McKinley, a friend of Hamish's. Why do you say that this is a charade?'

'Well, we all know what the silly old fool's up to,' snapped Lavinia.

'Which is...?'

'Isn't it obvious? He plans to get her pregnant!'

'Oh, do you think so?' Ally asked, trying not to smile.

'We most definitely *do*! This is purely a ploy to deny Randolph, my husband, the heir to the earldom and the estate.'

'You don't think he might just have fallen in love?' Ally asked.

Lavinia regarded her with a look of sheer disbelief. 'Fallen in *love*? With some woman young enough to be his daughter? Are you *serious*?'

'Yes, I am,' Ally replied. 'And they both seem very happy, so I hope it turns out well.'

'Mark my words,' said Lavinia icily, 'it won't. At least he's got some decent caviar over there, so, if you'll excuse me...' And she was gone.

Ally noticed that the son had already helped himself to a heaped plateful of food and was sitting on a sofa, well away from everyone else, stuffing himself and tapping away on his phone. And Randolph Sinclair was going on at length about something with Ross.

Magda, in her frilly-hemmed claret dress, was standing alone, glass in hand, in front of the nearest fire. Ally felt sorry for this poor woman, with all the glory centred on her sister, and crossed to where Magda was standing. 'How are you, Magda? This is quite an occasion, isn't it?'

Magda nodded without enthusiasm.

'How do you like being in Scotland?' Ally asked.

Magda shrugged. 'Yes, it's beautiful here, but the castle is very cold, and it's not even winter yet. And those ladies don't want me helping in the kitchen!' She pointed at Mrs Fraser and Mrs Jamieson, who were busy piling up their plates, Mrs Fraser still wobbling precariously on her high-heeled shoes. 'I'm used to helping out, and I hate feeling useless.' She sighed.

Ally felt increasingly sorry for her. 'I think you said you'd be starting a new nannying job after the wedding?'

Magda nodded. 'I had a call from the agency I work for to say that there's a family that would like me to start in two weeks. They have a house in New York, so I'd be away a lot.'

Ally smiled encouragingly. 'That sounds exciting.'

Magda nodded again, a little glumly. 'I'm happy for Elena, but I am going to miss her when she's so far away from me.'

'I'm sure the earl will be more than happy to have you to stay any time you like,' Ally said consolingly.

'Yes, Hamish is so kind,' Magda said, gazing across at him with open admiration.

'Um, yes, I'm sure he is,' Ally said, wondering if Magda had become enamoured with the earl in the short time she'd been here.

At that moment, Elena appeared.

'I'm so happy!' she said, giving Magda's arm a squeeze.

'And you look very beautiful,' Ally said truthfully.

'Thank you, thank you.'

Ally moved round to give the sisters time to talk, to find herself face to face with Randolph Sinclair.

'Do you live in the village?' he asked without introduction or preamble.

'Yes, I do,' Ally replied, slightly taken aback.

'So what does the village think of all this nonsense?' he asked, pointing at Hamish.

'Nonsense? What nonsense?'

'This *marriage!*' he retorted. 'The old goat marrying a young woman. We all know why, of course. And we can only hope he's firing blanks at his late age.'

Ally was horrified at his candour. 'I don't agree. I think it's rather nice that he's found someone to love.' Her dislike of the man was increasing by the second. 'Will you excuse me?' She turned away to where the earl was standing alone.

'You've done us proud, Hamish,' she said. 'This is a magnificent setting, and the food is wonderful.'

'Thank you, Alison,' he said. 'I've always loved this room, and Elena has already said that she does too.' He looked around. 'I must introduce you to some of my old friends whom you won't have met before. They'll be fascinated to know you've bought the malthouse.' He pulled a face. 'Have you met my dreadful cousin and his ghastly wife?'

Ally nodded.

'Then I need say no more. Where's your Ross?' He looked around and groaned. 'Lavinia has him in her clutches, and he's doubtless being told what an old fool I am. You don't think I'm an old fool, do you, Alison?'

'No, I do not,' Ally replied sincerely. 'And I'm sure you'll be very happy.'

'Come with me.' He led her across to an elderly group who were standing a little apart and introduced her to the old retired doctor, and also to some other close friends of his whose names Ally couldn't later remember, and to Doctor Simon Hartley-Knott, the suave, handsome best man. He was dark, attractively greying, and bore a strong resemblance to Cary Grant.

'He is my greatest friend,' Hamish said, 'and a retired psychiatrist, so he understands me completely!' He laughed.

'We were at Cambridge together, and he was also best man at my first wedding to Ophelia.'

Simon Hartley-Knott proffered his hand to Ally. 'So wonderful to meet you, Mrs McKinley, especially on such a delightful occasion as this. Isn't it wonderful that my dear friend, the earl, has found happiness again?'

Ally shook his hand and said, 'I couldn't agree more.' She reckoned that the debonair best man must therefore be of a similar age to Hamish, although he didn't look it.

Simon Hartley-Knott continued to grasp her hand firmly. 'I'd heard that a lovely lady had bought the old malt store,' he said, gazing deeply into her eyes.

What an old smoothie, Ally thought, nevertheless enjoying his attention in spite of herself. He must surely have sent a few female hearts fluttering when he was in practice!

Then, Ross, having freed himself from Lavinia's clutches, appeared by her side. 'I see you've met Hamish's suave best man,' he said. 'A fine performance you put on today, Simon!'

'One does one's best,' said Simon modestly, still smiling at Ally. 'How are you liking Locharran?'

'Very much,' Ally replied. 'It's a beautiful village, and I fell in love with the malthouse at first sight.'

'And with Ross as well?' he asked, his eyes twinkling.

Ally felt herself blushing, just as Ross said, 'She fell in love with a Labrador puppy, and that's how we met. Now, behave yourself, Simon.'

Simon had no intention of behaving himself. 'You see,' he continued, still looking at Ally, 'I've had a go at marriage myself, but since my dear wife passed, I still appreciate meeting pretty ladies.'

'And chatting them up!' Hamish said from behind him.

At this point, one of his friends reappeared and said, 'I must talk to you, Simon, about that land you mentioned...'

Ross took her arm and led her away. 'Let's eat, Ally,' he said.

Ally gazed in awe at the sumptuous feast. There was, amongst other delights, caviar, smoked salmon, pâtés, poached salmon, lobster, prawns, beef, chicken and every salad imaginable. At the other end of the table was an array of mouth-watering desserts. As Ally began to load up her plate, she found herself alongside Mrs Fraser and Mrs Jamieson, who'd come back for refills. 'Isn't this an amazing buffet?' Ally said chattily.

There followed much eye-rolling and sniffing from the two ladies.

'*We* could have done this,' said Mrs Jamieson.

'And done it just as well,' added Mrs Fraser.

'Perhaps he wanted you to have the day off and to be his guests?' Ally suggested.

A snort from Mrs Jamieson. 'No, this was *that woman's* idea.'

'What woman?'

'The earl's woman,' said Mrs Fraser. 'That *Elena*! She wants *this*, she wants *that*!' She paused. 'And she's only been here five minutes.'

'She wants us to cook special recipes,' added Mrs Jamieson. 'Says she's concerned that our food isn't healthy enough. Gluten-free this, and low-carb that. His lordship has been perfectly happy with the food we cook, thank you very much!'

'Well, surely she's entitled to make some changes?' Ally suggested.

'She comes to Scotland, she should eat what we eat,' snapped Mrs Fraser.

'And she comes pokin' around in my kitchen,' added Mrs Jamieson, 'and that's even *before* she gets married!'

Mrs Fraser nodded in agreement. 'So what'll she be like now? A countess, if you please! And that sister of hers mooning around and getting in the way.' She sighed deeply. 'He should've stayed at home and not gone off down to London.'

'Aye, you're right,' agreed Mrs Jamieson, carrying her over-loaded plate back to where they'd been sitting earlier.

'Why couldn't he have married someone like yourself?' Mrs Fraser put in before she set off to join the cook. She looked at Ally doubtfully. 'At least you're Scottish.'

'I'm not sure if I've just received a compliment or not,' Ally said with a laugh, turning to Ross, who was standing beside her with a full plate.

'There's a definite lack of compliments round here,' Ross said gloomily. 'Let's find somewhere to sit and eat.'

They made their way across to a small table by the window, which was flanked by two antique chairs.

'For God's sake, don't spill anything,' Ally said, setting down her food, then sitting down carefully on the tapestry seat.

'Otherwise we'll have Mrs Fraser after us with a hatchet,' said Ross, grinning. 'How did you get on with those two harridans?'

'Elena hasn't exactly made a good first impression on them. Apparently, this spread, from the luxury caterers, was Elena's idea. Mrs Jamieson said they could have done it just as well.' Then Ally remembered Callum Dalrymple saying much the same thing.

'I doubt they could,' Ross said. 'They don't have the finesse. Anyway, did you get talking to Randolph Sinclair? What a bitter man! And his wife's not much better. They're certainly not happy.'

'Surely *somebody's* happy with these nuptials?'

'I think everyone's completely gobsmacked by the fact that all this has transpired within only ten days, and they just haven't had time to get their heads round it yet. Simon and Desdemona were about the only people told about the earl's intentions a month or so ago. But at least the bride and groom seem ecstatic. Did you know that he's taking her to Paris tomorrow for a week? And in a private jet, no less, from Inverness Airport.'

'That's *so* romantic,' said Ally.

'Perhaps we could go there in the spring? April in Paris? But I'm afraid you'd have to slum it with the standard airlines.'

'I'm very adaptable,' Ally said, thrilled at his invitation.

The reception continued until around five o'clock, when the guests began to leave. Ally and Ross walked unsteadily down to the malthouse, having drunk far too much champagne and wine, and where even the desserts had been laced with whisky, sherry or rum. They were certainly in no fit state to stay for the evening party.

'Well,' said Ross, 'and what did you make of *that*?'

'I'm not sure,' Ally admitted, 'but I heard something very interesting this evening.'

'Which was?'

'I got chatting to Desdemona, who's just come back from London. Before she left, she'd been seeing her cousin off at the airport and had noticed a girl in tears because she'd just missed the Locharran bus. She spoke to the girl and offered her a lift back.'

'Desdemona Morton gave a girl a lift back to Locharran? That doesn't sound like her.' Ross looked unconvinced.

'Well, she did until her old Land Rover broke down at the Cairn Cross,' Ally replied, 'and the girl then decided to walk from there to Locharran because it was only a mile or so.'

'This is unbelievable! Didn't Desdemona check to see if the girl arrived safely?'

'Apparently not. She took some time to get her vehicle moving again, and then drove straight home because she was getting the train from Fort William to London early the next morning. She had an art exhibition there.'

Ross frowned. 'Why the hell didn't she fly to London with the cousin then?'

'That's exactly what I asked her, and she said it's because she's afraid of flying.'

'So, when did she get back?'

'Yesterday, just in time for the wedding. The boy who was feeding the dogs while she was away told her about the lady in Loch Soular, but she didn't connect it with the woman she'd given the lift to until he said something about her having flown into Inverness that day. Anyway, I told her to get on to the police straight away. She seemed very distressed and wanted to escape from the reception and, presumably, contact the police.'

'Well, I'd say that could put her in the number one position as a suspect. Let's hope she *has* gone to the police.' He pulled her closer as they walked, and despite the warmth of her coat and his hand in hers, Ally shivered.

EIGHT

It wasn't a particularly cold evening, but when they got back to the malthouse, Ally decided to light the log burner in her little snug, so that she and Ross could watch some TV, or doze more likely, from the depths of her squashy old sofa.

'They'll be getting everything set up for the villagers' party now,' Ally remarked as she switched on the television.

'That's to be in the Great Hall,' said Ross, 'so let's hope everyone turns up because that is one *big* space to fill.'

'Callum is actually doing the catering for that,' Ally said, 'but he's had to hire staff to help with the bar because Ivan is still so traumatised.'

'Poor Ivan.' Ross cocked his head. 'What's that noise?'

'What noise? I can't hear anything,' Ally said, lowering the volume on the TV.

'There it is again,' said Ross.

Ally listened and could just about decipher some sort of low wail. 'Oh, no, Ross – don't tell me you think that's Willie!'

Ross grinned. 'Could be!'

When Ally bought the malthouse, she'd supposedly inher-ited Wailing Willie, the ghost who'd apparently occupied an upstairs storeroom, now the en-suite bathroom to Room 2. Wailing Willie, the local piper, had met his demise some two hundred years previously, by breaking into that room, where the finest bottles of whisky were stored, and drinking himself to death. He'd taken his bagpipes along for good measure, and the happier Willie got, so the livelier the music became, until he completely overdid it, when the music evolved into a series of wails. At least he'd died happily, with the reed still between his lips. And, according to local legend, Willie still wailed whenever a local death was imminent.

Ally was sceptical about the whole thing but had to admit that the noise had been heard by her guests during the summer months, and, purely coincidentally of course, there *had* been a death shortly afterwards.

The inevitable happened, and they both fell fast asleep. Ally woke first, at ten o'clock, to find the fire had gone out, the room was becoming cold and the TV was still blaring, halfway through some mystery drama. She nudged Ross. 'I think we should go to bed.'

That was the logical thing to do and had seemed a good idea at the time, but inevitably, they then both found themselves wide awake at 5 a.m.

'Shall I make us some tea?' Ally asked, getting out of bed and slipping into her dressing gown. Then, as she approached the window, she saw, in the near distance, the flashing light of what appeared to be an ambulance as it headed at great speed up the road towards the castle. 'Oh my God!' she exclaimed. 'Why would an ambulance be going up to the castle at this hour?'

'Somebody fallen over and broken something on the way back from the party perhaps?'

'The party would have finished hours ago.'

'So, I expect Hamish demanded his conjugal rights and gave himself a heart attack then,' Ross said with a grin.

'Ross, there's a *police car* now!'

'You're sure?'

'Yes, with blue flashing lights. Oh, you don't really think it's the earl, do you?'

'I've no idea. Do you want me to go up there to find out?'

'If you do, I'm coming with you,' Ally said, beginning to get dressed.

'Not sure what we can do exactly, but at least it'll put your mind at rest.'

They both climbed into their clothes, keeping an eye on the window to see if either vehicle was leaving. Then, just as they were about to leave the malthouse, the ambulance came back down the road slowly, with no lights flashing.

'Looks like it was a false alarm,' Ross said.

'I still think we should go up there to find out and see if we can help,' Ally said.

As they approached the castle some ten minutes later, they noticed that the police car was still there, and the castle door was wide open. Ally and Ross exchanged glances, shrugged and walked in through to the Great Hall, still brightly lit, with evidence everywhere that a party had taken place; glasses and plates abandoned on every surface, a half-eaten buffet, squashed food on the floor, half-empty bottles.

At that moment, an ashen-faced Mrs Fraser came towards them. 'I need to shut the door,' she said, staring expressionlessly behind them.

'We only came in because the door was open and...' Ally began hesitantly.

'And we were worried because we'd seen an ambulance and police car coming up here,' Ross added.

The housekeeper looked dazed. 'We've had a tragedy,' she said, just as Detective Inspector Rigby emerged from what Ally thought was the Sinclair Room, where, only hours earlier, they'd enjoyed the wedding reception.

Rigby looked at them questioningly, and Ross repeated their concerns.

'You were both guests at this wedding?' Rigby asked, looking from one to the other.

They nodded.

'And what time did you leave the reception?'

'About five o'clock,' Ally replied.

'Hmm,' said Rigby. 'Have either of you felt unwell, been sick or had any strange symptoms?'

'Only a bit of a hangover,' Ross said, 'but otherwise no.'

'What's happened?' Ally asked. 'Is the earl all right?'

Before Rigby could reply, a hoarse male voice called out from within the Sinclair Room. 'Is that Alison and Ross out there? If so, let them come in.'

Ross led the way, Ally following.

The earl was sitting, hunched, in an armchair, in blue-and-white striped pyjamas, pale as a ghost and in tears. Sitting close beside him, a comforting hand on his knee, was an equally tearful Magda.

'What on earth has happened, Hamish?' Ally asked, crossing over to where he was sitting and crouching down beside him.

'It's Elena,' he said, wiping his eyes. 'She's dead.'

NINE

Ally could not believe what she was hearing. How could this be? 'Can you tell us what happened?' she asked gently.

The earl blew his nose and, in a voice thick with emotion, said, 'She didn't feel well...'

'When the evening party began,' Magda put in, her voice wobbling.

'What – at seven o'clock last night?' Ross asked.

Hamish nodded. 'We were both going to appear briefly at the party at around eight, just to welcome everyone, you know? But Elena wasn't feeling too good and only wanted to go to bed. To sleep,' he added.

Magda wiped her eyes. 'I stayed with Elena while Hamish made a speech to the guests. And then she was sick, very sick.'

'When I got back, I wanted to call the doctor,' Hamish continued, 'but she felt a little better by then and didn't want to make a fuss. "Not on my wedding night!" she said.'

'So she went to sleep for little while,' Magda said.

'Then she woke up with tummy pains,' Hamish continued. He looked at Magda. 'What time would you say that was? Around eleven?'

Magda nodded. 'I think near midnight.'

'Then she seemed to sleep again,' Hamish said, 'so I told Magda to go to bed. I stayed with Elena in the bedroom, dozed in the armchair.' He shuddered. 'When I woke up, she seemed peaceful. Too bloody peaceful! I couldn't hear her breathing. I panicked then and tried to wake her up...' His voice cracked, and he shook his head.

'So you called for an ambulance?' Ross prompted.

'Yes. I had only ever called 999 once before in my life, and I'd hoped never to have to do so again.'

Ally guessed he was referring to his first wife, Ophelia, who'd died of some food allergy. *A food allergy*! Could this be a repeat? Had lightning struck twice? No, no, no, she thought, far too much of a coincidence surely?

As if reading her thoughts, Ross asked, 'Could she have eaten something she was allergic to?'

Hamish shook his head sadly. 'I don't know,' he said, looking at Magda.

'No, she doesn't have any allergies,' Magda replied.

'Then could it have been something wrong with the food? Food poisoning? Botulism or something?' Ally asked, wildly searching for an explanation.

'She only ate what we all ate,' Hamish said. 'We won't know, I suppose, until later in the day, if any of our other guests were ill.'

'So the ambulance arrived?' Ally prompted.

'They were wonderful. So efficient, so caring, but' – his voice wobbled – 'it was too late.'

'Oh, Hamish,' Ally said. 'I'm so sorry.'

The earl nodded and blew his nose again. 'They asked us lots of questions but didn't seem happy about something, and called the police.'

'Because it was an unexplained death?' Ross asked.

'I don't know,' Hamish replied. 'They only said something

to the effect that, from what we told them, there could have been some form of poison involved, and they decided to call the police before they took Elena's body away.'

Ally could only think about Rigby's concerns. Another visiting bride-to-be. Another death.

Magda removed her hand from Hamish's knee. 'My little sister is dead!' She wept, cupping her hands over her face.

Ally felt desperately sorry for her and moved across to give her a hug.

'All this way to marry and then die!' Magda removed her hands and looked around. 'What am I going to do now?'

'We will work something out,' Hamish said, wiping his eyes and patting her hand. 'Now you need to sleep. And I need to sleep. I have some strong sleeping pills.'

'Then I think you should both take one now and get a few hours' rest,' Ross said. 'Ally and I will be ready to help in any way we can, but I think now we should leave you in peace.'

'Thank you for coming,' Hamish said, struggling a little to stand up. 'You are truly wonderful friends.'

Ally and Ross didn't speak for a few minutes as they walked back to the malthouse. The early morning silence felt quite eerie, almost as if this part of the world had died too.

Ally broke the silence. 'I cannot believe this.'

'Neither can I,' Ross said.

'It's just too much of a coincidence if Elena had some sort of allergy – despite what Magda said – when that's what killed his first wife.'

'We won't know until they do a post-mortem,' Ross said.

Ally's thoughts had returned to Rigby and how he'd said, "There's something funny going on round here." He was right. These were two women, both coming to Locharran to get married and both dead in suspicious circumstances, all in a period of about ten days.

Ally doubted that Rigby would be getting much sleep.

TEN

To say that Locharran was in shock would be a serious understatement. Shock and horror! Because only a week ago, no one had ever *heard* of the earl's bride, so the wedding was a shock in itself. And now this, as well as the shock of the lady in the loch!

Elena, Countess of Locharran for less than twenty-four hours, would, after her body was released, be interred in the castle crypt after a brief, private ceremony. So the bunting had to be hastily removed, and the flag lowered to half mast the very next day.

Most of the villagers had to digest this news on top of raging hangovers, since everyone had overindulged at the earl's expense. The media went mad; within twenty-four hours, the village was swarming with reporters, photographers and camera crews.

Jamie, Ally's son, phoned from Edinburgh the following day. 'We just can't believe what's going on in Locharran,' he said. 'Are you *sure* you made the right decision in going up there? Neither Liz nor I have had a wink of sleep worrying about you.'

Ally refrained from mentioning that she wasn't sleeping too well herself.

Then daughter Carol, who lived down in Wiltshire, rang up to suggest that her mother should abandon this hotbed of Highland crime and come down to stay with them in civilisation until all the fuss was over.

Ally appreciated their concern but politely declined their offers. Both her kids meant well, had supportive partners and responsible jobs, and she could see no point in upsetting their routines, particularly as she now had this lovely relationship with Ross. And the earl had become a friend, a friend who was going to need support at this tragic time. In addition, although she hadn't been in Locharran for a year yet, it already felt like home.

She and Ross spent the rest of the day quietly together, having phoned the castle at lunchtime to offer any help needed and to be told by Mrs Fraser that the earl wanted no callers today.

On Monday, when Murdo delivered the post and the gossip, he told Ally that the snooty Sinclair family were extremely unhappy at not being permitted to leave Locharran.

'Yesterday,' he said, 'Callum tells me they're all up and ready to go, luggage in Reception and all that, before Rigby arrives and tells them they're no' goin' nowhere.'

'Well, at least it appears they weren't ill,' Ally remarked. 'And so far as I know, none of the other guests were either, so it was only poor Elena.'

'She'll have been poisoned then,' Murdo said matter-of-factly.

'Who would want to poison Elena? It must have been an allergy.'

'Allergy my arse!' exclaimed Murdo. 'Someone at that fancy weddin' didnae want her around, and my money's on that banker or whatever he is, the cousin at the Craigmonie. He'd be next in line, ye see, and he widnae be wantin' a bairn, that's for sure!'

Ally had been thinking along similar lines. 'Well,' she said, 'poor Rigby will have his hands full, what with this and the lady in the loch!'

'And poor Ivan's goin' off his head,' Murdo went on cheerfully. 'Callum's tryin' to calm him down. What a bloody business!'

Ally dreaded visiting the shop, that hub of local gossip, but she needed some bread and milk, and so steeled herself as she walked down to the village shortly after Murdo had left. As she suspected, the shop was full of chattering groups, and she had to edge her way up to the counter, where Queenie, in her usual position, was holding court with a bunch of excited women.

'Ah,' said Queenie, 'here comes one of the honoured guests!'

A woman Ally didn't recognise, who had a long red nose, said, 'Wiz it *you* who spiked her drink?'

There followed some snorts and giggles, and someone said, 'Och, ye shouldnae be sayin' that, Betty.'

Ally ignored them. 'I'll have a small loaf and two pints of milk, please, Queenie.'

'Ye're keepin' well yersel?' Queenie asked solicitously.

'Yes, I'm very well, thank you,' Ally replied.

'And is yer boyfriend all right?' Queenie asked, causing further giggles.

Ally resisted the urge to roll her eyes. 'If you mean Ross, then yes, he's fine.'

'Mrs Fraser says you wiz up there at five in the mornin', before the poor woman wiz barely cold,' said a thin woman with shifty eyes in a very accusatory way.

'Because we, er – I – saw the ambulance and the police going up to the castle.'

'And Mr Patterson would be with ye?' Queenie gave Ally a wink.

Ally didn't reply.

'The minister and Janet are fine too,' said the thin woman, 'and so is them awful relations of the earl's, the ones stayin' at the Craigmonie.'

'Mrs Fraser's sayin' that the sister's fine too,' said Betty, her nose red as always. 'Sittin' real close to the earl, very pally.'

'Well, *somebody* wanted that woman gone,' the thin woman said ominously. 'Now, who else was there?' They all looked enquiringly at Ally.

'Oh, just some old friends of the earl,' Ally said. 'I didn't know them all.'

'What about that Desdemona Morton?' a woman in a green beret asked. 'Was *she* there?'

'Och, she's a funny one, her,' said Queenie. 'It wiz *her* sister that died last time the earl tried matrimony.' Then, turning to Ally, she added, 'Just as well ye've settled for the vet and not the earl!'

This caused some further suppressed giggles.

'Just the bread and milk, please, Queenie,' Ally repeated through gritted teeth.

Ally had just got back from the shop when Rigby was at her door again. What did he want this time? she wondered as she ushered him in.

Yes, he'd love a cup of tea, he said, but he was really here on very serious business. *Very serious*, he repeated.

'Has Desdemona been in touch with you, Inspector?'

Rigby frowned. 'Desdemona?'

'Desdemona Morton. It seems she gave Kristina, the lady in the loch, a lift from Inverness Airport, but her car broke down at

Cairn Cross, and Kristina decided to walk to Locharran but never arrived.'

Rigby looked outraged. 'Nobody's told me *this* before. How come I'm only hearing about it now? So why hasn't Desdemona been in touch? Where's she been all this time?' Rigby was shaking his head in disbelief.

'She was in London,' Ally replied, 'and only got back the day before the wedding. Knew nothing about it.'

'Let me get this straight,' said Rigby. 'This woman just happened to be at the airport, just happened to see Kristina, just happened to give her a lift most of the way, supposedly let the girl walk to Locharran, and then she goes tootling off to London?' He paused for a moment. 'Didn't she call a break-down service?'

'She has an old Land Rover which is always breaking down and she managed to get it going again herself.'

'So this girl, Ivan's fiancée, began walking to Locharran? Didn't she have a mobile phone? Couldn't she have contacted Ivan, who was presumably waiting for her?'

'Well, apparently she had phoned him after they left the airport to tell him she'd missed the bus and got a lift. When they broke down, she phoned him again, but there was no answer. But her English wasn't good, so Desdemona couldn't quite work out what she was saying.'

Rigby threw up his hands. 'For God's sake!'

'Listen, Inspector, there's no point in questioning me. I told her to report to you the very next day, but she obviously hasn't done so.'

'Is she the artist woman who lives out somewhere near The Bothy? Where *exactly* does she live?'

Ally nodded. 'She lives way out beyond The Bothy, a couple of miles along the track that continues along the lochside. She's a bit of a recluse, paints beautiful pictures and grows vegetables and things in a walled garden, including some very unusual herbs and spices.'

'Does she now?' Rigby made a note in his book. 'And how well do you know her?'

Ally shrugged. 'Not well at all, really. I bought a couple of paintings from her once, and we spoke briefly at the wedding reception.'

'Well I need to see her, that's for sure.' Rigby took a big gulp of tea from the mug in his hand. 'Now, I hate to mention this, Mrs McKinley,' he continued, 'but you were present for the discovery of Kristina Andris's body, were you not?'

Ally shrugged, having a good idea what was coming next. She nodded cautiously.

Rigby went on. 'You'll appreciate that you and the earl were the only two people we're aware of to see Kristina Andris in the loch. You rang the police, did you not?'

'Yes, I did.'

'Now,' he said, looking increasingly uncomfortable, 'no one else was present at the scene and so we only have your word for it that this was the first time you'd seen something that later turned out to be a woman's body as it floated towards you.'

So he *did* suspect her. Ally wasn't going to be offering him shortbread today, that was for sure. 'Are you suggesting that I had something to do with her death?'

'I'm not suggesting anything, only pointing out that you *could* have killed her and dumped her body in the loch before the earl arrived on the scene.'

Ally stared at him in disbelief. 'Why, in God's name, would I want to kill a woman I'd never seen before and who was coming to marry Ivan?'

'You tell me,' said Rigby wearily. 'Perhaps it was a case of mistaken identity. You knew the earl was getting married and perhaps you wanted her out of the way?'

'But I *didn't* know he was engaged! He only told me about Elena moments before, when he first arrived at the loch.'

'I only have your word for that,' said Rigby.

'Don't be ridiculous!' Ally was becoming increasingly angry. 'You could easily verify that with the earl. And even if I *had* known, what would be my motive?'

'Jealousy,' replied Rigby, scratching his nose. 'I've heard you and the earl were close soon after you came to Locharran, and that you remain close now. Maybe you were jealous that he was looking for a younger woman, a *much* younger woman.'

Ally stared at the detective in shock and astonishment. 'I simply cannot believe my ears,' she said, sinking into the nearest chair.

Rigby shrugged. 'Well the fact is, like it or not, that you were present at, or around, the time of death of these two women.'

'*Two* women?'

'You were at the earl's wedding reception just some hours before the unfortunate death of the bride, and you could – I only say *could* – have doctored her meal or spiked her drink.'

Ally was dumbstruck for a moment. As she regained her composure, she said, 'So could *any* of the other guests at the reception! You can't honestly be suggesting—'

'As I said before, I'm not suggesting anything,' Rigby cut in. 'I'm only pointing out that you were present around the time when both these women met their deaths.'

'As was the earl.'

'The earl arrived at the loch *after* you, and he was hardly likely to want to kill his new wife,' Rigby said.

Ally was becoming increasingly alarmed. 'You know perfectly well what sort of reputation Hamish Sinclair has got when it comes to women, and his charms have never worked for me in that direction, although I like him very much as a friend. We are *friends*, Inspector, nothing more. I'm sure you're aware that I'm in a relationship with Ross Patterson, who was with me the entire time at the reception. And I was delighted that Hamish had found someone to marry and to settle down with and who would hopefully provide him with an heir.'

Rigby nodded, almost apologetically. 'I hope you understand that I have to ask these questions, Mrs McKinley.'

'I understand, but I didn't kill either of them!' Ally was aware that her voice was beginning to wobble.

'There are just too many coincidences if you ask me,' said Rigby. 'There has to be some connection between these two deaths. Two young women, both travelling to meet their fiancé, both dead within less than two weeks of each other.' He got to his feet. 'Anyway, thanks for answering my questions, Mrs McKinley, and I hope not to have to question you again.'

'I sincerely hope you don't,' Ally muttered.

But Rigby wasn't finished yet. He cleared his throat. 'I'm told that the earl was married once before.'

'So I believe,' Ally replied, 'but quite some time ago. I think he and his bride were both in their twenties or thirties.'

'Hmm, and I understand that his first wife suffered a similar fate?'

'I believe she had an allergy of some sort,' Ally said.

Rigby was making notes. 'But an almost identical incident?'

'His first wife died after nearly a year of marriage,' Ally retorted, 'so not exactly an identical incident.'

'Another coincidence nevertheless.' Rigby looked uncomfortable. He cleared his throat again. 'Mrs McKinley, I have to ask you, since we're both comparative newcomers to the area and you know Hamish Sinclair better than I do, would you say he was capable of murder?'

Ally was confounded for a moment. 'I've read that *everyone* is capable of murder if they're pushed far enough, Inspector. But if you're asking whether I think Hamish would be likely to do such a thing, or things, then no, I definitely do not.'

Rigby didn't look particularly convinced. 'Can you think of any reason why he would want to kill both his wives? I'm told he was quite a ladies' man. Perhaps he got bored within the confines of marriage?'

Ally stared at him in disbelief. 'How could he possibly have got bored with *this* marriage? They'd only been wed for a few hours, for God's sake!'

Rigby nodded slowly. 'I suppose you're right,' he admitted grudgingly.

'He was also really excited at the idea of having a family with Elena, so he was unlikely to murder his bride before the marriage was even consummated!'

'Well, I have to ask these questions, but I'll leave you in peace now.' With that, he made his way towards the door. 'I'm going to find this Desdemona woman. Thank you for telling me about that. I wonder why the hell she hasn't contacted me?'

After he'd gone, Ally sat down, shell-shocked. She was plainly a suspect too! And purely because she'd been in the wrong place at the wrong time. No one in the village probably believed that her relationship with the earl was purely platonic.

The only way to get herself out of this mess was to find out who *did* kill these women.

ELEVEN

'Well,' said Morag, removing her purple anorak and plonking herself down on one of the armchairs, 'what do ye make of all this, eh?'

Ally sighed. 'I've no idea what's going on, Morag, but it's all very worrying.'

Morag ran her fingers through her badly dyed locks and squinted at Ally through narrowed eyes. *She's about to tell me something*, Ally thought, having seen this expression before.

'I've been told somethin' very interestin'.'

'And what was that?'

Morag opened her blue eyes wide. 'The bride was *poisoned*!'

'I'd guessed she might have a food allergy, but...'

'*Poisoned*, Ally, *poisoned*!' Morag nodded and narrowed her eyes again to emphasise the point. 'Murdo overheard Rigby talkin' on the phone.'

Knowing Murdo's love of gossip, Ally reckoned he'd hidden himself away in a corner of the police station somewhere.

'Ye see,' Morag continued, accepting a large mug of tea from Ally, 'Murdo was needin' a pee, cos he keeps bein' taken short these days. I'm thinkin' it's his prostate or somethin'. Well, he was at the polis station, see, and asked the man at the door if he could use their lavvy. That man often has a drink in the Craigmonie so he knows Murdo, and he says, "OK, Murdo, but dinna be long, cos I'm no' supposed to let anyone in." And when Murdo's just about to come out of the lavvy, he hears Rigby pacin' up and down the corridor and gabbin' into his phone.'

'And what did he overhear?' Ally asked, visualising Murdo with his ear pressed against the toilet door.

'Somethin' *very* interestin',' Morag said, sipping her tea and plainly enjoying keeping Ally in suspense.

Ally was determined not to sound too keen to know what Murdo had overheard, so there was silence for a moment or two before Morag could contain herself no longer.

'Do ye know what he was sayin'?'

'No,' said Ally. 'Tell me.'

'He was sayin' to somebody, "I canna believe this! Surely ye must know what kind of poison it was that killed her?" Then, the next thing he said was, "Well, how soon will it be before ye can identify it?" Then he heard Rigby shout, "In the meantime, I've got two bloody women bein' murdered on my patch!" *That's* what he said.'

Although Ally had had her suspicions, she was nonetheless shocked. 'That's awful.'

Morag leaned forward. 'And I was talkin' to Mrs Fraser this mornin'. She was tellin' me about the sister.'

'What, Magda?'

'Aye, the bride's sister. She won't go outside the door – terrified of gettin' killed!'

That was hardly surprising, Ally thought, when Magda's own sister plus another woman had both been murdered in the space of a couple of weeks. If someone was out there killing female visitors to Locharran, Magda certainly wouldn't want to be the third.

'Aye,' Morag continued, 'and she's that frightened to eat anythin' in case she gets poisoned. Mrs Fraser and Mrs Jamieson are goin' potty – don't know what to feed her with! And the earl's no bloody help because he's shut himself away and doesnae want to see anyone.'

'Poor Magda,' Ally said quietly. 'Who on earth would have it in for these poor, innocent women?' She changed the subject, knowing that Murdo had likely been at the Craigmonie the night before. 'And how is poor Ivan?'

Morag shrugged. 'No' very good. Still weepin' away every five minutes for the fiancée he wasnae able to get away to Inverness to meet, and the rest of the time he's knockin' back the Scotch like there's no tomorrow!' Morag paused. 'Which there just might *not* be!'

Ivan had been knocking back Scotch for years, and Ally wondered how he was fitting in many more drinks when she'd never seen him without a glass in his hand. 'But he's still working at the Craigmonie Bar?' she asked.

'Oh aye, he is. Everyone's buyin' him drinks, but it doesnae seem to affect him much.' Morag shook her head admiringly. 'Anyway, I thought ye'd like to know the latest.'

'Yes, thank you for the news, Morag.'

'Ye havenae any guests?'

'Not at the moment. The last one left the other day."

'Ye'll let me know if ye need any cleanin' done, won't you?'

'I certainly will,' Ally replied.

After Morag had departed, Ally wondered how long it would take the earl to recover and to be back in circulation again. Then her thoughts returned to poor Magda, and how she must be feeling. Here she was, having lost her parents in an accident, now in a strange place, her sister murdered, marooned in an enormous castle and in fear of her life.

Magda needed a friend. Ally decided she must try to help.

.   .   .

Ally was mystified as to why Desdemona hadn't contacted the police. She'd seemed only too eager to do so at the reception and had even left early. That was why Ally had assumed she'd left anyway.

For some time, Ally had been toying with the idea of buying another of Desdemona's paintings. She'd already put one in two of her bedrooms, but there wasn't one in Room 3, mainly because she couldn't afford a third one at the time she'd bought the others. This was as good a reason as any to make the trip out to Loch Trioch. Desdemona's ramshackle house was by the side of the loch about a ten-minute drive past The Bothy restaurant and involved a bone-shaking journey on a rough track with a grass ridge in the middle. She drove her silver Golf very slowly and carefully, and arrived at Desdemona's in a hail of stones and a cacophony of barking from the half dozen or so dogs that she kept.

Desdemona emerged from the garden wearing a conglomeration of mismatched items, topped with a huge purple cardigan. Not for the first time Ally wondered how someone with such bizarre taste in her outfits could produce such exquisite, understated paintings.

She looked at Ally quizzically. 'What brings you here?'

Ally smiled. 'How about a painting?'

Desdemona gave a deep sigh. 'Well, I'll have to wash my hands before I show you any paintings, because I've been working in the garden.'

She disappeared into the house while Ally stood surrounded by dogs. The first time she'd come here, she'd been a little afraid of those dogs of all shapes and sizes, but in this case, their bark was worse than their bite, and they were more interested in Flora's scent on her clothes than they were in her.

Desdemona reappeared and led the way into the studio,

which was a former farm building but had been beautifully and sympathetically restored. As far as she could see, Ally reckoned this was the only building which had been restored. There were skylights in a row along the roof, along with other windows, flooding the studio with light. The walls and floor were of stone and, on the ledge around all four walls, Desdemona had stacked and displayed her artwork. But on the easel at the far end of the studio was a painting she was currently working on of a gaggle of geese flying over what looked to be Loch Soular, complete with the little boathouse.

'Oh, that is beautiful!' Ally exclaimed.

'It's not finished yet,' Desdemona said. 'I'll need a while longer to complete it.'

Ally took a deep breath. 'Before we go any further, did you not contact the police about the woman you gave a lift to?'

Desdemona actually looked puzzled for a moment. 'Oh, *that*! I should have done, I suppose. I've been meaning to, but I've been very busy.'

'I think you'll get a visit from Detective Inspector Rigby any time now,' Ally said.

'Oh, I don't suppose he'll find this place very easily. If the Land Rover will start' – here she rolled her eyes – 'I'll make a trip down to Locharran, because I need to get some diesel anyway. They've opened up a temporary police station in the village, I hear.'

'Yes, they have.' Ally nodded, wondering why Desdemona considered this murder to be of so little importance.

They discussed money and agreed a price for the painting, and Desdemona said she'd bring it down to the village sometime in the next few days. 'If I remember,' she added.

'You *will* get in touch with Rigby, won't you?' Ally asked.

'Yes, yes, I will.' Desdemona paused. 'I may as well tell you that the reason I've been avoiding him is because of my Land Rover. It needs a lot of work done to it, so it hasn't got an MOT certificate, and so I can't tax it.'

'So you're not insured?' Ally asked, horrified.

'No, but I'll get it all sorted out soon now that I have some money. In the meantime, do come to see my garden,' Desdemona said, as if she really wanted to change the subject. 'I've got some lovely leeks, parsnips and pumpkin already picked and, as a good customer, you can take what you like.'

Ally had wanted to be on her way, because she'd thought of calling in on Linda when she got back, but knew it would be rude to turn down such a generous gift.

As Desdemona led her outside to her vegetable patch, Ally decided that it was time to broach her other reason for visiting. 'Have you heard about Elena?'

'Elena?'

'Hamish's bride. She died on her wedding night, just hours after the reception. Hamish is absolutely distraught.'

Desdemona looked shell-shocked. '*What*? Oh God, I've got to go to him!' She paused for a moment. 'How did she die?'

'I believe it may have been poison. I'm not sure they know yet exactly what killed her.'

'But that's what happened to Ophelia...' Desdemona looked uncharacteristically close to tears.

'So as you'd expect, Locharran is in uproar,' Ally said. 'We've now had two recent murders, and nobody's quite sure whether they should be looking for one or two killers.'

As they walked into Desdemona's walled garden, for a moment, Ally's attention was diverted. Growing profusely along one of the borders was a plant with long feathery leaves that she was sure she'd seen only once before, when she had been doing research for a TV murder mystery in her life before retirement. It had been a good fifteen years ago, but she could swear it was identical to a plant called monkshood. It wasn't much to look at, but it was poisonous. Very, very poisonous.

TWELVE

The afternoon had turned cool and blustery when Ally popped in to see Linda at The Bistro on her way back from Desdemona's house. Linda was English, widowed and a wonderful cook. She was also blonde and petite, which made Ally even more aware of her towering five feet ten inches.

'Good to see you, Ally,' Linda said, leading the way into her little sitting room. 'Would you like some tea or something stronger?'

'I'll settle for tea, please,' Ally said, glancing at her watch. 'Ross is coming over later and I've no doubt we'll see off a bottle of wine.'

'So, how's life?' Linda asked.

'Interesting,' Ally replied. 'I heard some gossip today which could well be true.'

'Tell me when I bring in the tea,' Linda said, heading towards the kitchen.

A few minutes later, she reappeared with a tray of tea and some chocolate cake. 'I'd like to know what you think of this,' she said, 'because I've put some Baileys into it.'

Ally laughed. 'I love the way you always manage to get some alcohol into your concoctions!'

The cake was delicious, and after she'd been congratulated on her prowess, Linda asked, 'So, tell me. What have you heard?'

Ally told her about Morag's visit and the information she'd imparted. 'I just feel so sorry for poor Magda,' Ally said. 'She's come all this way for her sister's wedding, and now Elena's been murdered, as has Ivan's fiancée. And the poor woman is stuck in a freezing-cold castle, terrified of being the third victim of some maniac.'

'That's horrendous,' Linda said, refilling their cups.

'I'm planning to go up to see her as soon as I can and ask her down to the malthouse for tea, if she'll trust me not to poison her!'

'Tea and sympathy,' Linda said. 'I must admit to feeling a bit nervous here in the evenings on my own. I mean, you don't know who to trust, do you? And you must feel the same, stuck up there in that big, old house all by yourself.'

Ally didn't consider herself to be a nervous type, but she did lock up everything securely at night, including her bedroom door.

'And what does the lovely Ross think about all this?' Linda asked with a smile.

'Well, I haven't told him this latest gossip yet. I'm saving that for later. But I've no reason to doubt Morag, or Murdo, for that matter. He usually gets the facts right.' Ally took another bite of cake. 'God, Linda, this is delicious!'

'I'm glad you like it,' Linda replied.

'And how about you? Do you have any news for me?' Ally asked.

Linda grinned, then cleared her throat. 'The only news I've got is that Callum Dalrymple has asked me to go out to lunch with him tomorrow.'

'He *has*? Wow!' Ally had always liked Callum, the manager at the Craigmonie Hotel, and had been won over by his beautiful blue Paul Newman-ish eyes. She'd quite fancied him at one time, although he was considerably younger than she was – and probably a fair bit younger than Linda too.

'Yes, we're going to Seascape,' Linda said.

'Oh, that's lovely!' Ally exclaimed. 'Ross took me there on our first date, and it's got fantastic views and great seafood. You'll love it!'

'I mean it's probably just his way of thanking me for making the desserts for the hotel.'

'I think it's much more likely that he likes you! I mean he doesn't have to take you to an expensive restaurant like Seascape if all he wanted to do was thank you for a few puddings. Do you like him?'

'He's about ten years younger than me,' Linda said.

'So what?'

'I know, but...'

'You didn't answer my question. Do you *fancy* him?' After she'd spoken, Ally thought she detected pinkness across Linda's face. So, she *did*!

'No, no,' Linda said hurriedly. 'It's just that he's been so nice to me since I started doing the desserts. I didn't really know him before that.'

'Those gorgeous blue eyes!' Ally teased.

Linda grinned but said nothing.

'I used to fancy him a bit myself before I met Ross,' Ally admitted. 'Can't believe he's still single.'

'I think he was married once,' Linda said, 'but I don't know the details.'

'I'm sure you'll find out,' Ally said, 'and I'll want a full report!'

As she walked home a little later, Ally reckoned that Seascape was a good omen. It had certainly brought herself and

Ross together. Then she had a disturbing thought: could Callum be a suspect? Could it be that he hadn't wanted Ivan's impending wedding upsetting his staff arrangements at the Craigmonie? And he'd made it plain to anyone who'd listen that he was angry at being passed over for the catering job at the earl's wedding reception, and it had been *Elena* who'd refused him. But those reasons could hardly be considered motives. Could they?

Ally quickened her step, shook her head and took a deep breath to expel her ridiculous thoughts. Surely she was seeing demons where none existed? It was just that, with there being no obvious suspects, there were so many people who could have committed the crimes. If she wasn't careful, she'd be suspecting Ross next!

Ross appeared at half past six with a large bag of groceries, a couple of bottles of wine and Ebony, his seven-year-old black Labrador, who Flora adored. After they'd chased each other around the kitchen for a minute, the two dogs settled down together in front of the wood burner.

'You're to sit back and not interfere,' Ross commanded, 'while I make us a curry.'

'I'll happily leave you to it,' Ally replied. 'But, first, would you like to hear some interesting news?'

Ross did. He unpacked his ingredients and poured them both a glass of wine.

Ally told him.

'Poisoned? She was *poisoned*? Is that definite? Who the hell would want to kill two women? Two *brides-to-be*?'

'Perhaps there were two different killers?' Ally suggested.

'Two? Are you saying they had a killer *each*?'

'I don't honestly know what to think,' Ally admitted. 'But you must agree that it's a weird coincidence that these two women were murdered in the same area within ten days of each other. And now poor Magda's terrified to go out of the door or even eat!' She thought for a moment. 'I must try to do something to help, and I have an idea, which I'll tell you about after the curry!'

Before she retired, Ally had been a researcher for a TV company in Edinburgh. It helped that she was nosy by nature because it involved finding out, in depth, about people, history, geography, not to mention food, furnishings, facts and fashion. She'd excelled at probing and analysing, generally by setting out all of her findings on a large wall board. Since an incident a few months earlier, Ally had found a way of setting out her thoughts using the back of a large, wooden still-life painting which hung in the kitchen. And it was invisible to any visitor when it was hung back in its normal position, showing an array of oranges, lemons and grapes.

It was a couple of hours after Ross's delicious lamb curry, when the dogs had given up hoping for scraps from the table that, as they were draining their coffee, Ally stood up and removed her still-life from the wall. Ross made no comment but raised an eyebrow as she placed the picture upside down on the table, with the back facing upward.

'Now I'm going to need some paper and some Post-its,' Ally said, rummaging in the dresser drawer.

'You have a fruity solution?' Ross asked, continuing to look mystified.

'Not exactly.' Ally tapped on the board. 'We just post our clues on *there*.'

'And *that*,' said Ross, looking at her in disbelief, 'is going to solve these crimes?'

'It could help. I need to stick some paper on the surface, on which we draw a couple of circles, like clock dials. We put the name of the victim in the centre of the imaginary clock dial, and all around it we stick on the names of the likely suspects, ensuring the main suspect is placed right at the top.'

'At twelve o'clock, you mean?'

'That's right. Then the next most likely subjects would be positioned either side at eleven o'clock and one o'clock.'

'So presumably the least likely suspects would be placed around the bottom of the dial?' asked Ross.

'You've got it!' Ally confirmed.

Ross looked worried. 'Ally, I know you mean well, but—'

Ally stopped him. 'It's worth a try.'

Ross sighed. 'OK. So one dial for Kristina, and one for Elena?'

Ally drained her coffee. 'Yes, though I have a gut feeling there's only one killer.'

'We can't count on gut feelings,' Ross said firmly. 'You're going to need one of your clock dials for each victim.'

Ally grabbed a dinner plate and drew two circles, side by side. 'There's plenty of room.' With that, she stuck one Post-it with 'Elena' written on it in the middle of the first circle, and then one with 'Kristina' on it in the other. 'So, beginning with Elena, who shall we have as our chief suspect?'

Ross shook his head. Then, after a moment, he said, 'The banker, I suppose – Hamish's cousin.'

'Just what I was thinking! Or even his nasty wife.' Ally stroked her chin. 'Therefore I'll put Randolph Sinclair at twelve o'clock and Lavinia Sinclair at one o'clock.'

'Is that it?'

'No, it isn't. How about Mrs Fraser and Mrs Jamieson? Neither of them were at all happy about Elena arriving on the scene. She'd been interfering in the kitchen and asking for special meals for Hamish's health.'

'It seems quite reasonable,' Ross said, 'that she would want to be involved in what the kitchen served at the castle, as the new countess. I can imagine those ladies having their noses a bit put out of joint, but it's hardly an excuse to kill her.'

'Nevertheless, I'm putting Mrs Fraser up at number eleven, and Mrs Jamieson at number ten.'

'I can't think of anyone else at the reception who'd be likely to doctor Elena's food, unless one of the caterers had been well paid to do so,' Ross said.

'Good point. I hope Rigby's been questioning the caterers.'

'Then there's Magda, of course,' Ross added.

'Magda?'

'Perhaps Magda was jealous of her sister?' Ross suggested. 'Perhaps she didn't want to be here, playing second fiddle to Elena? After all, we don't know their history, do we, or anything about them? Perhaps she wants Hamish for herself?'

'Oh, that's *ridiculous!*'

'Not a great deal more ridiculous than any of your other suspects. I know you feel sorry for Magda, but you can't entirely rule her out. This business about being afraid to go out or to eat anything could all be an elaborate act! Remember how she had her hand on Hamish's knee?'

'Hmm. OK, I'll put her down at the bottom of the dial. She wasn't even here when Kristina met her fate, so she can't have anything to do with *that*! Now, how about Kristina?'

'Since we know so little about her, we can hardly speculate,' Ross said.

'Ivan might be able to provide a clue if we could get him at a relatively sober moment,' Ally suggested.

Ross pulled a face. 'He's hardly likely to have killed his own fiancée, is he?'

'He could have had a change of heart, I suppose.'

'I shouldn't think there are many occasions when there's more blood than alcohol in his veins,' Ross retorted. 'And if he had a change of heart, he could just have sent her packing, paid her return fare or whatever. Why on earth would he go to such extremes and probably end up sentenced for her murder?'

Ally sighed. 'In that case, the only other suspect could be some unknown maniac who preys on female visitors to Locharran. Or Desdemona, who admitted herself to having given Kristina a lift and then supposedly left her at Cairn Cross.' She continued scribbling on the Post-its.

'So what are you going to do? Place "unknown maniac" at twelve o'clock?' Ross asked.

'No, I shall put Ivan at twelve o'clock,' Ally replied, 'and Desdemona at eleven. As far as I'm concerned, Desdemona gave the girl a lift and left her in the middle of nowhere. And who knows what happened to Kristina after that? And I'm going to put *myself* at six o'clock!'

'*What*?' Ross almost choked on his coffee. 'Why would you do that?'

'Because Rigby reckons I'm a suspect too. Don't forget that I was at the loch, alone, before Hamish arrived – just me and Kristina's corpse presumably. And I *could* have doctored Elena's food at the buffet, I suppose. So I *was* around for both murders.'

'That's ridiculous! I was with you all the time at the buffet, just for a start! And what possible motive could Rigby dream up?' Ross exclaimed.

Ally pulled a face. 'Don't forget that half the village think I was having an affair with their precious earl! They probably think I wanted to eliminate the competition.'

'But Kristina had nothing whatsoever to do with the earl! I cannot believe that Rigby could begin to suspect you.' He frowned. 'Why didn't you tell me this before?'

Ally shrugged. 'I don't know. I suppose it just seemed so bloody ridiculous. Usual story, I suppose: wrong place, wrong time. But do you know what? If I put myself on the board as an unlikely suspect, then I can have the pleasure of eliminating myself, because I damn well did not kill either of them. And there's great satisfaction in being able to eliminate a suspect!'

'Well.' Ross yawned. 'As much as I've enjoyed this window into your process, it's getting late.' He nodded to where the dogs were both fast asleep in front of the log burner. 'Let's go to bed because I've got to be up early in the morning. The guests in Heather Cottage are leaving at eight to catch a flight from Prestwick later in the day.'

Ally nodded, hung her still life back on the wall – with the fruit facing outward of course – and led the way upstairs. One killer? Two killers? Should she have placed the earl somewhere? Would she ever be able to sleep tonight?

THIRTEEN

Ross left at half past seven next morning. He had a busy couple of days ahead, helping out his son at the veterinary practice, and dealing with guests at his lodges.

Ally had a clear day ahead before a couple of hill walkers were due to arrive the next day. As she sat with a cup of tea after Ross's departure, she wondered how long it would take for the earl to recover sufficiently to emerge in public again, and how she herself could best approach Magda.

Therefore it was quite a shock when, two hours later, she answered the front door to find none other than the earl himself standing there, looking haggard and exhausted.

'Oh, *Hamish!*' Ally couldn't prevent herself from giving him a big hug. 'I'm so pleased to see you! Come in!'

Hamish followed her into the kitchen and sat down on the chair vacated by Ross earlier.

'Would you like some tea?'

The earl nodded. 'Tea would be lovely. How are you, Alison?'

'*Me?*' squeaked Ally, pouring the tea and handing him a

mug. 'I'm fine. It's *you* I've been worrying about! How are you feeling?'

He shook his head wearily. 'Oh, you know... it's all been such a bloody shock, and it's the first day I've felt like coming out and facing everyone. I can't seem to get my head round what's happened.'

'I'm not surprised. I hardly know what to say,' Ally admitted. 'How's Magda?'

'That's one of the reasons why I wanted to come to see you,' he replied. 'Magda has, naturally enough, taken this very badly, and she's shut herself away. She seems paranoid that someone is out to kill her next, and I don't know what to do. I wondered if, when you have a moment, you could possibly come up and try to chat to her? She needs to talk to someone she can trust.'

Ally wondered what he would think of her if he knew of Rigby's suspicions – this wasn't a good time to mention that the detective had considered her a suspect for both murders.

'Unfortunately, it's a bit of a coincidence that these two brides-to-be were killed so close to each other,' she said.

Hamish waved his hand, almost spilling his tea. 'But what had my poor Elena ever done to upset anyone? She'd only just *got* here, for God's sake!'

Ally doubted that Mrs Fraser would have told him about Elena making her presence known in the kitchen. 'I hear it was definitely poison?'

'Yes, something deadly, although they haven't yet analysed exactly what it is. But it must have been slipped into her food or drink sometime at the reception.'

'I cannot believe anyone at the reception would have contemplated doing such a thing. We were all so happy for you.'

He blew his nose. 'Not everyone. There was Randolph, my cousin, who, as you know, is heir to the earldom. Not to mention his ghastly wife and son, both of whom would love to get their hands on all this.' He waved his arm around again.

'You don't honestly think...'

'I *do* honestly think, Alison, and I've told Rigby of my suspicions, so he's prevented them from leaving until this whole ghastly business is sorted out. I hear that they're not well pleased and are making life hell for everyone at the Craigmonie. I did suggest they stayed at the castle when I invited them for the wedding, but they refused. God knows why. However, in the circumstances, I have to say I'm very glad they opted for the Craigmonie.' He gave a ghost of a smile. 'Consider yourself fortunate that they didn't decide to stay here!'

Ally had been thinking exactly the same thing. Then another thought occurred to her – Rigby's idea about Kristina's death being a case of mistaken identity.

'Hamish, when did you tell your cousin about Elena? I presume you told him before you told me, what with him being family...?'

'Yes,' Hamish said, still looking distracted.

'So when did you tell him?'

'Oh, I suppose about a month or so before I told you.'

'Did you tell him much about Elena?'

Hamish shook his head. 'None of his damn business really. I told him I was getting married, I told him she was very beautiful, with lovely blonde hair and gorgeous green eyes. I told him when the wedding would be.'

Ally thought hard. 'And your sister-in-law? Desdemona, I mean?'

'About the same time, I suppose,' he replied, shaking his head as if he was bothered by a wasp. 'Now, getting back to Magda,' Hamish said. 'Might you have time in the next day or two to have a chat with her? She's contacted the agency she works for in London and cancelled her next job, and I want her to stay here for the moment, until she feels confident enough to face the world again.'

'I'd be more than happy to chat with her this afternoon,' Ally replied. 'Of course, she may not want to talk to me.'

'She liked you,' Hamish said, 'so I think she would.'

'I'll pop up around three o'clock then,' said Ally.

'I've been neglecting the estate of late, since...' Hamish's voice tailed off sadly. 'I must get to grips with everything again, so I may not be there when you come up. But I'll tell Mrs Fraser to expect you.' He drained his tea and patted her briefly on the hand. 'You're a good friend, Alison. Thank you.'

As she accompanied him to the door, Ally felt unexpectedly moved by his words. It was only months ago that he'd been doing his utmost to add her to his list of sexual conquests and she'd told him firmly that she was only prepared to be his friend – a platonic friend; that it was possible to have *friends* of the opposite sex. It seemed to have worked.

After he'd gone, she wondered what type of little gift she should take to Magda. Probably anything edible would be out of the question if Magda was paranoid about being poisoned. Flowers might be safest, and there was a tiny garden centre down by the river which usually had flowers and pot plants for sale.

It was a cold, grey day, and Ally wore her warm faux-fur-lined winter coat as she and Flora made their way down to the village. There hadn't been much sunshine since the day of the wedding, and it almost felt as if the whole village was in mourning. Fortunately, the plant section had some tiny miniature roses in pretty pots, which probably wouldn't last long but at least it would be a gesture. Ally decided on a pink one.

She took Flora home, wrapped up the rose and set off for the castle, wondering what reception she was likely to get, if any. She was now becoming used to approaching the massive oak door, pulling the cord for the bell, and had stopped panicking about the din it made.

Mrs Fraser, who'd returned to her usual uniform of jumper,

skirt and pinny, came to the door and gave Ally a trace of a smile.

'Good luck with this one,' she said ominously, leading the way along a labyrinth of corridors, up a stone staircase some-where in the middle of the castle, along yet another corridor before finally stopping outside one of the oak doors. 'I'll wait until she answers,' added Mrs Fraser, 'because if she doesnae want to see you, ye'd never find yer way back again.'

This came as a relief to Ally, who'd been thinking precisely the same thing. Nervously she knocked on the door. 'Magda?'

There was no reply. She looked hesitantly at Mrs Fraser, who rolled her eyes. Ally knocked again. 'It's me, Magda – Ally. Ally McKinley. Can I come in, please?' She was gratified to hear some movement behind the door. '*Please* can I come in? I only want to see if I can help you.'

Ally heard a bolt being removed, and Mrs Fraser whispered, 'Ring the bell on the wall inside when you want to leave,' before hoofing it rapidly along the corridor and down the stairs.

The door opened a crack. 'Yes?' Magda said.

'I'm Ally – remember me? Can we have a little chat, please, Magda?'

Magda opened the door a fraction more. 'Yes, I remember you.'

The door then opened a little wider to reveal a pale, wan Magda.

'I won't stay long,' Ally reassured her, terrified of the door being shut in her face.

Magda's eyes alighted on the pink rose, peeking out of its wrapper. 'Is that for me?'

'Yes,' Ally confirmed. 'I bought it for you.'

Magda opened the door wide. 'I love roses.' She gave a faint smile.

Ally followed her into a large, cold bedroom, with half-panelled walls, shiny wood floors, and a meagre square of carpet beside a huge four-poster bed. One tiny fan heater was doing its best to warm up a few square inches next to a chintz-covered armchair where Magda had plainly been sitting. She was wearing at least a couple of sweaters, as far as Ally could see, and a black winter coat on the top.

'It's *freezing* in here!' Ally exclaimed.

Magda nodded. 'I think the room is too big.'

'You can't stay holed up in here,' Ally said, looking around the large space. 'Why don't you sit downstairs in Hamish's sitting room with the open fire?'

Magda shrugged. 'I'm afraid.'

'Oh, Magda!' Ally laid the plant down on a small table alongside the one and only chair. 'You have no need to be afraid.'

'My sister is dead,' Magda said, wiping her eyes, 'and that lady they found in the loch is dead. What if I'm next?'

'No, no!' Ally protested. 'Both Kristina and your sister were coming here to get married, and it seems that, for some reason, someone wanted to make sure that they *didn't*.' She paused. 'Magda, everyone is feeling so sad for you, to be here, without your family, having to deal with this tragedy all on your own. Please come down to the malthouse with me, and we can have something to eat in my lovely warm kitchen.'

She could see Magda hesitating. 'You can't stay in this horrible great room. The weather is getting colder all the time, and you'll freeze. There must surely be a smaller, warmer room near the front of the castle. I'm confident Hamish wishes you no harm. In fact, he came down to see me to tell me how worried he is about you.'

Magda smiled. 'Hamish is kind, I know. But those ladies in the kitchen...' Her voice tailed off.

'Why would they want to hurt you?'

'Because they didn't like Elena! They didn't like that she

was going to be the new countess and take over running things. Who has more access to my food than them?'

'Well, they haven't poisoned you so far, have they?' Ally said.

Magda looked mutinous. 'They bring me food, but I don't eat it.'

Ally sighed. 'Magda, you *have* to eat.'

'I eat things I can open myself – things they don't touch. Little packets of biscuits, cereal bars, that kind of thing.'

'This won't do. You need hot food and a warm bedroom.' Ally thought for a moment. 'If it comes to it, I have a free bedroom with a nice radiator in it. Let me have a talk with the earl. In the meantime, why don't you come home with me, and have some tea and a snack, and I will eat exactly the same thing as you, so if someone's trying to poison you, they'll get me too!'

For the first time Magda smiled. 'You're very kind, Mrs McKinley.'

'Ally, please. Now, switch that silly little heater off and come with me.' Ally made her way to the bell pull on the wall and gave it a good tug.

Several minutes later, Mrs Fraser put her head round the door. 'You ready to leave?' she asked Ally, completely ignoring Magda.

'Yes, and Magda's coming with me,' Ally replied firmly. 'I'm going to take her back to the malthouse, give her something to eat and contact the earl later.'

'She won't eat whatever it is,' Mrs Fraser said. 'She'll think you're going to poison her.'

'No, she won't. And perhaps you could find a smaller, cosier bedroom for Magda nearer the front of the house? With a lock on the door and a nice fire, perhaps?'

'We don't *have* any bedrooms at the front with bolts on the doors,' Mrs Fraser snapped.

'Well, I shall have to tell the earl to have a lock installed then. Can you lead us out now, please?'

With a grunt and a sigh, the housekeeper led them back to the front of the castle. 'What am I supposed to tell his lordship?'

'You tell him that Magda is with me, so he'll know where to find her.'

As they arrived at the main door, Mrs Fraser sniffed loudly. 'Well, best of luck with *that*,' she snapped as she closed the door behind them.

FOURTEEN

Magda came alive when she set eyes on Flora, who was in a particularly playful and amenable mood.

'Oh, I love dogs!' she informed Ally, playing with Flora's silky ears.

'Then you must have one,' Ally stated. 'Hamish will get you a puppy.'

Magda didn't look particularly convinced but, nevertheless, settled herself comfortably in the armchair beside the log burner with a mug of tea, and a dog on her knee.

The doorbell rang. It was Hamish.

'Is she here?' he asked Ally, looking around, worried.

'Yes, she is,' Ally said, leading the way into the kitchen. 'And here she stays until you can find her a warmer bedroom somewhere nearer the front of the castle, with a fireplace and a lock on the door.'

'Oh, Magda!' He bent down and pecked her on the cheek; Ally noted that she looked up at him with shining eyes. Surely not? she thought. *Surely* she wasn't falling for the earl's undoubted charms? Then, once again, she remembered Magda's hand on Hamish's knee on the night that Elena died...

Hamish sat himself down on one of the kitchen chairs. 'I'm so grateful to you, Alison,' he said, accepting a mug of tea. 'And I wanted you to know that I've been in touch with Simon, my best man, you know?'

Who could possibly forget that suave, dapper charmer? Ally wondered.

'I know he's an elderly country gentleman now,' Hamish said, 'but Simon Hartley-Knott was an eminent Harley Street practitioner, a top-notch psychiatrist.' He drank some tea. 'We were at Cambridge together, you know, and we've been best friends ever since. Then he got married, had a couple of kids, and they came up here to stay with me every year on holiday. His dear wife Elizabeth died some years ago, but Simon continued to come up each year and eventually bought a lovely old lodge out near Clachar, with wonderful sea views. He's mostly retired now, of course, but still consults sometimes and is often called on to speak at conferences.' He drained his tea. 'He was my best man on both occasions, Alison,' he added sadly.

Ally didn't reckon that his presence on either occasion had actually brought the earl much matrimonial luck.

'Now,' said Hamish, 'he's coming to see me tomorrow, and he's going to have a nice little chat with Magda here. I'm sure he'll be able to help alleviate the problems she's been suffering from since Elena's death.' He turned to Magda. 'I didn't realise that you didn't like your bedroom.'

'I'm sorry I didn't tell you myself, Hamish. It's just that it's so big and cold,' Magda said, sipping her tea and looking at him adoringly.

'Right!' said Hamish. 'I will instruct Mrs Fraser to find you a smaller room, with a fireplace, Magda, and I shall have a lock put on the door. And we shall eat dinner together tonight, serving ourselves from the same pots, so you can be assured that no one's out to poison you.'

'She'd like a dog too, Hamish,' Ally added as she watched Magda stroking Flora's fat little tummy.

'She shall *have* a dog,' said the earl, thumping his fist on the table and standing up to further emphasise the point. 'We can find you a nice puppy if you decide to stay here in Locharran.' He turned to Ally. 'In the meantime, I'd like Magda to come back to the castle with me. I will look after her, I promise.'

Magda stood up without argument.

As she accompanied them to the front door, Ally wasn't sure whether to be relieved or worried.

After they'd gone, Ally sat down and had a think. She'd been a little alarmed, if not altogether surprised, by Magda's very positive reaction to the earl. She needed to give Magda more thought. She hadn't seemed terribly enthusiastic about Elena and Hamish's engagement when they first met. Maybe Magda had always been a little jealous of her younger, prettier sister? Particularly as she'd managed to snare an aristocrat! And when Magda arrived for her sister's wedding, had she fancied Hamish for herself?

Ally sighed, hating herself for thinking along these lines. Nonetheless she stood up, removed the oranges and lemons from the wall, and laid the still-life face side down on the kitchen table, relieved to see that all the Post-its had remained firmly in place.

Of course there was no obvious link between Magda and Kristina unless, of course, they'd known each other at some time in the past, which seemed extremely unlikely. But it certainly couldn't be denied that perhaps – just perhaps – Magda's sisterly love had evaporated over the years and her feelings had come to a head when, not long after arriving at this majestic castle, Elena had had the world's attention focussed on her, she'd married a lord, an earl, and so become a countess overnight. Furthermore, she might just have married a man that Magda wanted for herself!

Ally took a deep breath. This was *ridiculous*! She reconsidered — no, it wasn't *entirely* ridiculous. Ally moved Magda further up the dial. Then she replaced the painting onto the wall, feeling a little guilty.

She really needed to get to know some of the other suspects and not keep concentrating on poor Magda! Her main suspects were, after all, the obnoxious banker and his avaricious wife. And even more so since Hamish had told her that Randolph had known about Elena a month before Kristina was killed. Rigby could have hit on something for once, and poor Kristina was indeed a case of mistaken identity. But first impressions weren't always accurate, so perhaps she should give them the benefit of the doubt. What did they do all day, apart from upset the staff at the Craigmonie Hotel? Not for a minute could she imagine them in the Craigmonie Bar, with Ivan and all the locals, so she supposed they'd have their pre-dinner drinks at the cocktail bar in the hotel. And they would almost certainly eat in the hotel dining room. She couldn't see them at Linda's bistro or, even more unlikely, Concetti's fish and chip shop. Takeaways? It was difficult to imagine them opening greasy takeaway boxes in their hotel suite and devouring pizzas or fish and chips. She'd check with Callum to see if they ate in the hotel dining room each evening. And if so, then she'd suggest to Ross that it might be an idea to have an evening meal at the Craigmonie Hotel.

The phone rang and cut off her thoughts. It was Jamie.

'Mum, we're all so worried about you! Carol's been on the phone to me for two nights running, nagging me to come up to Locharran to try to talk sense into you! She, like us, would be more than happy to have you stay for a few weeks until this killer is found!'

Ally sighed. 'Jamie, I know you're concerned but, honestly,

I'm absolutely fine, and I'm happy to stay right here. You really don't need to worry about me so much. I also have guests booked in.'

She could hear him tutting, and could visualise him rolling his eyes and shrugging at Liz, his wife.

'We worry for your *safety*, Mum.'

'I know you do but, honestly, I'm OK.'

'Well, I hope that vet guy is keeping an eye on you?'

'Yes, he is, and I feel like I'm more of a villager now.'

'Mum!' Jamie interrupted. 'That makes you even more vulnerable if there's some maniac roaming the streets taking potshots at single women!'

'Both these women were coming here to get married,' Ally said, 'so that certainly lets me off the hook.'

'They might think you're going to marry the vet.'

Ally guffawed. This conversation was going from bad to worse, and it took several more minutes to persuade her son that she was perfectly fine and that she had no intention whatsoever of leaving Locharran. Or marrying Ross.

Ally felt exhausted when she cut the call. She poured herself a generous glass of wine, fed herself and Flora, and then settled down for an evening watching TV before having an early night.

Her guests were due the following afternoon, and so, in the morning, Ally made her way down to the shop to stock up on groceries. And who should be standing at the counter, in deep conversation with Queenie? None other than Mrs Fraser.

She turned round rapidly when Ally arrived. 'I've just been telling Queenie here about that *madam* up at the castle!'

'What madam?' Ally asked, unable to imagine they were talking about Magda. She was quite amused that, just for once, she was almost being treated as a local and not as an outsider.

'Yes,' said Mrs Fraser, 'yer wee friend, Magda.'

'Why do you call her a madam?' Ally asked.

Mrs Fraser pursed her lips. 'First of all, on the first night, she wants a room as far away as possible from the bride and groom.'

'Perhaps that's understandable?' Ally suggested. 'Perhaps she didn't relish being next door to her sister on her wedding night?'

Mrs Fraser looked mystified for a moment before rolling her eyes heavenward. 'So then she goes on about being cold and so I get her a nice wee heater.'

Ally recalled the tiny fan heater facing a losing battle with the chilly air in the large room.

'And *then*,' Mrs Fraser continued, 'she thinks we're planning to *murder* her!'

'I bet you felt like it,' muttered Queenie.

'I did, Queenie! I was glad enough to see the back of her sister! So now this little madam won't eat anything unless it's in a sealed box or somethin'. What a palaver.' The housekeeper was rapidly warming to her subject, encouraged by a wide-eyed and open-mouthed Queenie. 'And *now* she's got Mrs McKinley badgering the earl to get her room changed!'

Both sets of eyes rounded on Ally.

'Yes, Mrs Fraser, *I* was the person who thought she should have her room changed,' Ally said. 'That room was huge – and icy.'

'It was *her* choice!' Mrs Fraser snapped.

'Well, now that her unfortunate sister's no longer with us, I think it's time for a move,' Ally said, trying to remember what it was she'd come in here for.

Eggs, that was it. 'Could I have some eggs and—'

'And what about that lassie in the loch?' Queenie put in, licking her lips in the hope of more gossip.

'That'll be Ivan,' said Mrs Fraser confidently. 'He's likely changed his mind about gettin' wed. And as far as the other one's concerned, I wouldn't put it past that Magda to have finished off her own sister.'

'Oh my!' said Queenie. 'But why would she want to do that?'

'Cos the earl's bride was nicer and bonnier and, between you and me' – here she leaned across the counter to Queenie – 'I'm thinkin' she fancies the earl herself!'

'Aye, but they wiz *sisters*,' Queenie said, frowning.

'But even sisters can still get awful mad with each other sometimes.'

Queenie's eyes swivelled round to where Bessie was busy unpacking tins of baked beans. 'Right enough,' Queenie said, plonking a dozen eggs on the counter for Ally.

'And I'll have some sugar,' Ally said, helping herself to a packet off one of the shelves.

'Well, I'll be off then,' said Mrs Fraser, placing her items in her shopping bag and heading towards the door.

As she disappeared, Queenie said in a hushed, reverential tone, 'Mrs Fraser's awful clever, isn't she? I bet she's right about who did them killin's too!'

No need for any police round here, Ally thought, with Mrs Fraser solving two murders single-handed. No need at all.

On her way home, Ally decided to call at The Bistro. Linda was clearing out a kitchen cupboard. 'One of the jobs I never get round to doing,' she explained. 'Coffee?'

'No, thanks, I'm not stopping. I just wondered how your date went?'

'Oh, very well,' Linda replied, looking a little pink. 'We're going out again on Friday.'

'Good for you!' Ally said, then added, 'And I wondered if you could do me a favour? If you could ask Callum something?'

'Like what?'

'Like does he have any idea where the Sinclairs from London normally dine? Is it in the hotel dining room, or do they go elsewhere?'

Linda widened her eyes. 'Ally, these people are horrible! Why do you want to know about them?'

'Because I want to book a table next to them on Saturday evening and get chatting with them,' Ally said, 'because I'm trying to do some detective work.'

'Oh my God! Be careful! You don't really want to get involved in all this!'

'But I *am* involved! Rigby is already suspicious of me, and the only way I can prove my innocence is by finding out who *did* do these killings.'

'Well, I'll see what I can find out,' Linda said doubtfully.

'Thanks, Linda. Give me a call.'

When she got home and unpacked her groceries, she thought she should inform Ross of her plan since he'd be accompanying her.

Ross answered after the first ring. 'I was just thinking about you,' he said, 'and wondering where we could go for a bite on Saturday evening, for a change.'

'Well...' Ally then proceeded to tell him about her plan to 'accidentally' meet the Sinclairs over dinner. 'The thing is, Ross, I know they're not very nice, but I really want to get chatting because that's the only way we're likely to get any clue about them. And, hopefully, they'll have been drinking so might not be too careful about what they say.'

'You're becoming a right wee sleuth!' Ross exclaimed.

'Ross, I'm five foot ten!'

She'd hardly hung up when her phone rang again.

'Ally, I've just been having a chat with Callum,' Linda said, 'and he tells me that the Sinclairs have booked a taxi to take them to The Bothy and back on Saturday evening, where they've booked a meal for eight o'clock.'

'Linda, you're an angel!'

'That's true,' Linda agreed, laughing.

A few minutes later, Ally was back on the phone to Ross to inform him of this information. She could only hope he would agree and that her idea might be worthwhile. Would she possibly be able to extract any useful clues or information out of the horrible pair?

FIFTEEN

When Ross had arrived a few hours later, he was looking rather pleased with himself. 'Not only have I booked us a table,' he said, 'but I had a chat with Euan the manager, who I've known for years, and he's arranged for our table to be next to the two Sinclairs. And, before you ask, they *are* the *only* Sinclairs who've booked this evening.'

'That's great, Ross. You did say *two* Sinclairs?'

'Yes, just two. I imagine the son has opted out,' Ross replied.

When Saturday came Ally asked 'Remind me whose turn it is to drive tonight?'

They'd devised a system where one of them would abstain from alcohol for the evening when a drive was involved. And a drive generally was involved, unless they were eating in Locharran itself.

'My turn,' Ally said, 'so why don't you get yourself a drink while I finish getting ready?'

At the beginning of their relationship, Ally had been quite nervous driving Ross's big, black Mercedes after her own little VW Golf, particularly on these narrow, one-track roads. But, over the months, she'd got used to it. They set off at half past seven in torrential rain. They were often spared snow in this part of the world, but there was no avoiding rain, which blew in horizontally from the Atlantic.

The Bothy, a long, low stone building, had once been a tiny shelter from the elements for anyone who'd got lost on the moors in the mist. This was long before the roads were built and there were certainly no mobile phones to inform anyone of your whereabouts. It had mainly catered to farmers and shepherds marooned on the moors.

There was a proper road leading to it now, although it continued onward as a rough track round the loch, leading eventually to where the elusive Desdemona Morton lived, painted, and grew her herbs and vegetables. The original bothy had been extended several times and had been transformed into an excellent restaurant, complete with tartan carpets and stags' heads. The bar was stocked with countless varieties of whisky, and, best of all as far as Ally was concerned, there were roaring fires in huge stone fireplaces at each end of the building.

She'd only eaten there once before, with the earl, shortly after she'd taken up residence in Locharran. That had been at lunchtime in the spring when the whole setting had been sunny and picturesque. Tonight it was dark and lashing rain and, as Ally and Ross raced from their car into the warm shelter of the restaurant, Ally could imagine the horror of being marooned out here on a night such as this.

Half of the tables were already occupied as Ross's friend, Euan, directed them to a table for two where, during the day, there would be a beautiful view of the loch and the surrounding hills. There was no sign of the Sinclairs yet, but the table for two next to them had a 'Reserved' sign on it.

'We'll spend some time with our faces hidden behind the menu,' Ross said with a grin as Ally took her seat facing into the restaurant, where she could keep an eye on the door. 'So that, when they arrive, they won't recognise us straight away. In fact, they may not recognise us at *all,* but we can make out we've just recognised *them* later when, hopefully, they'll have had a few drinks and generally be more talkative and amenable.'

Twenty-five minutes later, Ally, who was about to tackle her main course, caught sight of them being escorted in. She picked up the drinks menu and held it in front of her face until they'd sat down, wondering if all this subterfuge was really necessary since they'd only met once – and briefly.

Ross was right: the son had opted out. Randolph and Lavinia had their coats hung up, complained at length about the weather to the hovering waiter and then argued about who was going to sit where. They both appeared to be designer-clad, and Lavinia had enormous rings on her bony fingers.

'It's not as if there's a *view,*' Lavinia snapped, 'other than blackness and rain lashing against the window!'

'All right,' said Randolph with a sigh, 'sit where you like.'

Lavinia did. She sat down facing out into the restaurant, while Randolph faced the stormy blackness, which meant he was also facing Ally at the next table. However, he was so busy ordering cocktails and wines that he hadn't even glanced in their direction.

Ally, having had a smoked salmon starter, was now enjoying her sea bass, rationing herself to one small glass of white wine. Ross had settled for lobster bisque, followed by venison, which was the speciality of the house.

Carefully avoiding any eye contact with the next table, they chatted about their day. Ross had been called out to stand in for his son again at the veterinary practice, because Will had had to deal with the breech birth of a Highland calf. Ally told him about her latest guests: a young German couple who'd arrived the previous afternoon and who had retired to bed very early and got up very late. 'I don't think it was lust that kept them in bed,' Ally remarked. 'They'd been camping, hadn't slept properly for nights and looked utterly exhausted. I don't think they realised quite how rough the local terrain is. They're here until Monday.'

The Sinclairs, in the meantime, were barely speaking to each other apart from arguing about which wine they should order with their chateaubriand. There were several other older couples dining, and Ally couldn't help but notice that they too seemed to have little to say to each other. Not for the first time she wondered why some elderly married couples appeared to run out of things to talk about; she couldn't recall herself and Ken ever sitting in complete silence.

It was while Ally was trying to decide between the crème brûlée or the lemon posset that she caught Randolph's eye. He stared at her for a moment with a 'where have I met this woman?' look on his face before Ally whispered to Ross, 'Here we go.'

'I think we've met before,' Ally said to Randolph.

He frowned. 'Yes, I thought I recognised you from somewhere.'

With that, Lavinia turned round and studied them both. 'Hamish's reception, darling,' she said to her husband.

'Oh, so it was,' said he.

'It was such a lovely day,' Ally continued, 'but with such a tragic ending.'

'Wasn't it *just!*' exclaimed Lavinia, topping up her wine glass.

'Randolph Sinclair!' her husband boomed by way of introduction, leaning in their direction. 'And this is my wife, Lavinia.'

'Ross Patterson, and this is my friend, Ally McKinley. We had a brief chat at the reception, if you remember?' Ross said.

Randolph frowned. 'Weren't you a doctor?'

'A vet,' Ross replied, 'and Ally here has recently bought the old malthouse and has transformed it into a very lovely B&B.'

'Oh!' Lavinia exclaimed dramatically, raising her eyes to the ceiling. 'We should have come to you instead of that *ghastly* hotel!'

Thank goodness you didn't, Ally thought. 'The Craigmonie has a very good reputation,' she said.

'Not with us!' snapped Lavinia. Then, leaning towards Ally, she said, 'Of course, we are accustomed to the very best. We stay in The Ritz or Claridge's when we have to go up to town, you know.'

'Yes, well, I don't suppose the Craigmonie is in *quite* the same category,' Ross admitted, 'but it's a nice wee Highland hotel with, as Ally said, a very good reputation.'

'We're not exactly nice wee Highland types,' Lavinia admitted, dabbing her lips with a napkin.

'Nevertheless,' Randolph said, looking around, 'this is where we may well end up.'

'Is it?' Ross asked.

'Indeed,' Randolph replied, 'because we are the Earl of Locharran's only relatives and, should we perish tomorrow, our son would still inherit. Doesn't want to be here, of course – he's had a pizza delivered to his room, would you believe!'

'*None* of us want to be here!' snapped Lavinia.

'So why *are* you still here?' Ally asked, abandoning the menu.

'Because we're not *allowed* to leave,' Lavinia said petulantly.

'Oh, that's a shame,' Ally said. 'Let's hope they find this killer soon.'

'They should call Scotland Yard in,' Lavinia said, taking a large gulp of wine. 'They'd soon find out what happened to the woman.'

'Her name was Elena,' Ally said, 'and she was very sweet.'

There was silence for a moment.

'I think she was a fortune hunter!' snapped Lavinia dismissively.

'I don't think she was,' Ally protested.

'I think you're being rather rash,' Ross added, 'and extremely unfair. I mean, you didn't really know her, did you? And you seem to forget that Hamish *invited* her here.'

'I've not the slightest doubt she wheedled him into doing just that!' Lavinia said, taking an enormous gulp of wine.

Ally was becoming more and more annoyed by this woman. 'I don't think for one minute that that's true,' she said.

'Well,' said Randolph, 'she certainly didn't waste any time getting him to the altar when she *did* get here.'

'And it's wrecked everything for us,' Lavinia wailed. 'Randolph had some very important business meetings in London, didn't you, darling?' She turned briefly and solicitously towards her husband. 'And that awful policeman with the Birmingham accent' – she shuddered – 'won't let us *leave*.' She drained her wine glass and then refilled it to the brim.

'I rather fear we're all suspects,' Ross said calmly. 'But something was obviously put into Elena's food or drink at the reception. Apparently, she was so excited about everything that she couldn't eat any breakfast!'

'Well, *we* had nothing to do with it!' snapped Lavinia.

Randolph cleared his throat. 'They'll point the finger at us, of course, because Hamish plainly got himself entangled with this woman...' He paused while Lavinia interjected, 'Young enough to be his *daughter*...' as Randolph scowled at her and continued, 'Hamish wanted that woman to bear his child because it's common knowledge that he hates the prospect of us inheriting. So, of course, that's why *we're* suspects!'

'And why *shouldn't* Randolph inherit?' Lavinia asked loudly, imbibing half a glass in one gulp. Her dark red lipstick had completely worn off. 'Hamish Sinclair has had years to produce an heir, so what's stopped him? This whole thing has become utterly ridiculous.'

'And do not forget that *two* young women have been murdered in the space of a few weeks,' Randolph retorted.

'Don't think I can manage a dessert,' Ally said to Ross as the Sinclairs attacked their main courses.

'Me neither,' Ross agreed. 'Let's just have an espresso and head home.'

There had been no further conversation and, as they left, Ally and Ross had politely wished them goodnight.

'Well, what did you make of that?' Ally asked as they got into the car. The rain was still lashing down.

'Not sure,' Ross admitted. 'I don't like either of them much, but she's particularly obnoxious.'

'Insufferable woman!' Ally exclaimed. 'She's going to have a sore head tomorrow the way she was knocking back that wine.'

'She's definitely the boss in that marriage,' Ross said. 'There's little doubt she fancies being the next Countess of Locharran.'

'So do you think she'd be more capable of killing than him?' Ally braked sharply as a large fox stood in front of them on the road, dazed by the headlights. It took a few moments for it to move.

'If I had to choose between them then, yes, I'd say she was more likely to be a killer,' Ross replied.

'I'm not surprised the son chose to stay behind at the Craigmonie with a pizza,' Ally said.

'Of course, it might have been *him*,' Ross said. 'He kept himself to himself at the wedding, and I didn't speak to him at all. Did you?'

'No, I didn't, but I must say he looked thoroughly bored.

Don't quite know how we can get to meet him. Wonder what he does all day?'

'No doubt you'll find out!' Ross said, giving her knee an affectionate squeeze. 'But I'd put money on the fact that he probably plays video games in his room and avoids his parents.'

Ally sighed. 'You're probably right.'

She'd give it some thought but, in the meantime, she needed a word with Ivan.

SIXTEEN

Ally thought carefully about how to approach Ivan. He'd recovered sufficiently to be back behind the bar, but she didn't fancy going in there in the evening when it would be full of locals and Ivan would be at the peak of his alcohol consumption.

What was needed was an excuse to go in during the afternoon when the locals would still be at work. With a notebook in her shoulder bag, Ally wandered down to the Craigmonie and headed towards the adjoining bar.

The bar had been something of an afterthought, added on mainly for tourists and villagers, whereas the hotel guests generally used the cocktail bar next to the restaurant. Ivan had arrived from Lithuania some five years previously, had fallen in love with Locharran and, in particular, the whisky, just as Callum was looking for a new barman, and had no hesitation in accepting the job. He was a popular barman, although no one could recall ever seeing him completely sober.

Ally cautiously opened the door and was relieved to see Ivan sitting behind the bar, half asleep behind the *Daily Mirror*.

The place was empty apart from one young couple at the far end of the bar, so the setting was ideal.

Ivan jumped up and folded the newspaper away. 'Mrs McKinley? Nice to see you.'

'That's me. Could I have a small shandy, please, while I pick your brain?'

Ivan looked a little confused. He placed the shandy on the counter, frowned and said, 'My brain?'

'I just want to ask you a question,' Ally said, getting out her notebook. 'I had some American guests staying during the summer and one of them asked if I could make a Manhattan. Now, I know it should be rye and sweet vermouth with bitters and ice, but I didn't have any rye so I substituted Scotch. He said it was good but never asked for a second one, so I'm not sure I got it right.'

Ivan shrugged. 'Because I have here the rye, so I've never made it with whisky. Did you use a cocktail shaker?'

'No, I don't have one,' Ally replied. 'Do you think it makes a difference?'

'Definitely,' said Ivan. 'You shake, like so.' He picked up a cocktail shaker with both hands and shook it around with a flourish. 'Then you strain it into the glass with ice, and a cherry.'

Ally scribbled a few notes, although she had little intention of buying a cocktail shaker for a drink she had no intention of making.

She gave it a moment and then said, 'I'm so very sorry for your tragic loss, Ivan.'

Ivan's eyes filled with tears. 'I still cannot believe someone could do this to my poor Kristina. I blame myself for not meeting her at the airport, but I am in charge of the hotel because Callum is away! *In charge*! I am not a manager; I am a barman! I was going crazy, and no way could I go anywhere.'

Ally nodded.

'So I think it better she get bus to Locharran and I meet

her right here.' He pointed vaguely out of the window towards the bus stop. 'But the plane was late and she missed the bus. So she phoned me and told me that a nice lady had said she would give her a lift all the way.' He blinked. 'Then she called again and left a message to say that the lady had a very old car and it had broken down and that she'd decided to walk to Locharran because the lady told her it was not far.' He sighed. 'It was the artist lady with the wreck of a Land Rover.'

Ally nodded. 'Yes, she was going to London the next day. She wasn't here when the body was found but got back a week or so later.'

'She is the killer,' Ivan said loudly. 'Who else could it be?'

'I don't know, unless someone found Kristina walking along the road to the village here.'

'But who could that be? No one knew who she was! It's crazy!'

'Yes, it's crazy. I don't know what to think,' Ally said, draining her shandy. 'Well, I guess I'd better be off.' Then, remembering the supposed reason for the visit, added, 'Thanks for your advice about the cocktail shaker.'

When she got home, her mobile rang. It was Ross.

'What have you been up to?' he asked her.

'I just had a chat with Ivan, but I'm not sure I'm any the wiser about anything.'

'How about I come up tomorrow evening and you can fill me in on everything?' he asked. 'Let's get a nice takeaway pizza from Concetti's.'

'I'll look forward to it,' Ally said.

Not long after she returned home, someone knocked at the front door. Ally was astonished to find Magda standing there in the pouring rain.

'Magda! Come in.' Ally stood to one side to let Magda enter. 'I was just going to make some coffee.'

Magda nodded, stepping inside and taking off her coat. 'Thank you, Ally.'

For the first time, Ally saw Magda's sad brown eyes properly, free of any make-up or being awash with tears. There was something very appealing about those eyes.

'You said I should come here if I needed help?' Magda asked as she sat down beside the stove.

'Yes, and I meant it,' Ally said, spooning coffee into the pot.

Magda looked around her. 'It's so cosy in this kitchen.'

'Yes, I'll be spending most of the winter in here,' Ally said with a smile.

'I have a much nicer room now,' Magda said. 'It's small, and the heater works. I'm so grateful to Hamish – he's been so kind to me.'

'I'm pleased to hear it.' If her room was better, and things between her and Hamish were good, what was the problem then?

Magda liked her coffee black with one sugar, took a sip and proclaimed it was perfect. Then she said, 'I've cancelled the job I was going to after the wedding, and I'm going to stay here for the time being, until I'm certain about what I want to do. Hamish has said I can stay at the castle for as long as I wish, but he worries about how Elena's murder has affected me.' She paused. 'Can you come to the castle later?'

Ally had planned to call in to see Linda, as she was keen to know how she'd got on with her date with Callum. But that could wait. 'Well, yes, if you'd like me to,' she said, offering Magda the biscuit tin.

'There's a man coming to talk to me,' Magda said, accepting a custard cream.

'A man?'

'I think he was Hamish's best man at the wedding?'

'Oh, you mean Simon,' Ally said. 'Yes, Hamish mentioned that. I think he wants to help you, as you've been so shaken up by Elena's death and because you were afraid someone wanted to kill you,' Ally reminded her.

Magda smiled faintly. 'I don't think I'm so afraid someone wants to kill me now. I'm not afraid of Hamish, and I don't go anywhere else, except here.'

'Maybe in time you can come with me when I walk the dog?' Ally suggested.

Magda rubbed Flora's head. 'I'd like that. So you'll come?' She looked anxious. 'He's coming at three o'clock, and I think I'd like to meet him if you were there too.'

Ally smiled. 'Of course I'll be there, Magda.'

'She insisted on having you here,' Hamish told Ally as he met her in the Great Hall at quarter to three. 'I hope you don't mind?'

'Of course not. I'm glad she trusts me. In fact, she's notice-ably more confident already.'

Hamish nodded. 'She insisted she wanted to go down to the malthouse by herself, but I did worry a bit because we don't really know if there is someone out there taking potshots at ladies. Not that it would be likely on a wet day like this, particu-larly as no one would know she was going to see you.'

Hamish ushered Ally into his sitting room, where Magda was sitting by the fireside, her face breaking into a smile when she saw Ally.

'Simon should be here any minute,' Hamish said, 'after which Mrs Fraser will bring in some afternoon tea.'

Ally knew, from her first visit to the castle, what afternoon tea was like here, and she was pretty sure there would be a similar spread today. In the distance, she could hear the 'bong!' of the doorbell, and a few minutes later, Simon Hartley-Knott was ushered in. He was casually, and expensively, dressed in designer jeans and a black roll-neck cashmere sweater and was, of course, groomed to perfection. He gave Magda and Ally dazzling smiles as they all shook hands.

'I didn't realise it was to be a tea party,' he said to Hamish with a grin. 'I thought I was having a one-to-one session with Magda?'

'Well, things have improved,' Hamish replied, sitting down next to Magda. 'Magda is slowly regaining her confidence, and Alison here is a good friend to her.'

'That's wonderful,' Simon said, sitting down opposite them both and next to Ally. 'Lovely to meet you again, Alison!' He gave her hand an affectionate squeeze.

I'm not going to suggest that he calls me Ally, she thought. *Hamish insists on calling me by my full name, and so can he.*

After the weather had been remarked upon, Simon asked, 'Are you beginning to feel at home here now, Magda?'

Magda gave a wan smile, and again Ally noted what sad eyes she had. 'Yes, I think so.'

'You're happier?' Simon enquired, just as Mrs Fraser trundled in with the tea trolley, laden with sandwiches, scones, cakes and two pots of tea.

'Will you stay to pour the first cup, Jean?' Hamish asked. 'Then we'll manage fine after that.'

Mrs Fraser dutifully did as she was bid, asking who would like Assam and who would like Earl Grey? She dutifully poured Assam for everyone except Simon, who chose the Earl Grey. Then she left them to it.

Ally decided she might as well play hostess, so she handed round the sandwiches and plates, and added that she would leave them to fetch their own scones because she wasn't prepared to be responsible for putting the jam on top of the cream, or the cream on top of the jam, which she knew was a bone of contention between Devon and Cornwall.

Magda was piling sandwiches on her plate with gusto. Ally reckoned she was almost certainly thinking that no one could poison her here if they didn't know what she'd be eating.

'Delicious!' proclaimed Simon, helping himself to a scone.

He even manages that elegantly, Ally thought, as she watched him in fascination. He didn't even drop a crumb. She couldn't imagine him ever becoming ruffled. Was that due to his training, or was it just the way he was?

Simon, patting his mouth neatly with a napkin, turned to Ally. 'How wonderful that you've made friends with Magda.'

'Everyone needs someone to turn to, whoever they are,' Ally replied. 'But when they've experienced such a terrible tragedy, well...'

'That's exactly what I'd recommend,' said Simon. 'Who wants to talk to an old fool like me when you can share your worries with a friend?' He looked approvingly at Ally before turning back to Magda. 'You've had a very traumatic experience, Magda.'

Magda nodded, starting on her third sandwich.

'We all have,' Hamish added sadly.

'That's true,' Simon agreed, smiling kindly at his friend before turning back to Magda. 'And am I right that apart from Elena, you don't have any other family?'

Magda nodded again. 'Our parents were killed in a car crash. We have some cousins in Australia,' she said, 'but apart from that, I don't have anyone.' Her voice cracked.

'What about friends?' Simon persisted.

Magda shrugged. 'I have some friends in London, but being a nanny makes it hard to make friends or see people. I had a boyfriend, but... it didn't work out.'

'Oh, I'm sorry to hear that.' Ally smiled sympathetically. The poor girl.

Magda shrugged. 'We were engaged actually. I thought I was going to get married, build a life together. But it was for the best really. He… wasn't kind to me. And he left me for someone else.'

Hamish looked shell-shocked. Ally wondered why he'd never asked Magda this himself. She was beginning to understand the sadness in Magda's eyes. For that matter, why hadn't *she* herself thought to ask? Probably because everyone was so busy trying to assuage her grief.

'You've had so much to deal with, even before this tragedy,' Ally said. 'I'm so sorry that you lost Elena too.'

Magda's eyes filled with tears, and she began to cry. 'I miss her so much!'

'Of course you do, my dear!' Hamish soothed, patting her hand. '*You've* had your whole life with her, whereas I only knew her for a short time.' He withdrew a large, pristine white handkerchief from his jacket pocket and handed it to Magda.

'So what's next, Magda? I think Hamish said you had another nannying job lined up?' Simon asked.

Magda gazed into the fire. 'No, I've cancelled my next job. This place, this wedding…' She gestured to Hamish. 'It made Elena so happy, and I… can't leave the place where she was so happy. Not yet.'

'You can stay with me as long as you like,' said Hamish. 'I really want to make it up to you for such an awful thing happening in Scotland. It is so out of keeping because this is usually such a hospitable country.'

'I can try to find a job,' Magda said, still gazing into the fire. 'I want to pay my own way.'

'No, no, no!' Hamish said vehemently. 'As long as I have breath in my body, you will not pay anything for your accommodation here.'

There didn't seem to be a great deal to say after that, and they all stared into the fire. The conversation then turned to which was considered to give out the best heat: peat, coal or wood. On this occasion, Hamish was burning logs, and they were being swallowed up very quickly in the large fireplace.

'You should see Simon's huge hearth,' Hamish said. 'He feeds in tree trunks, one at a time, some of them ten feet long, and you have to be careful not to fall over it as you go in the door! Then he kicks the log in as necessary and, by the end of the evening, most of it has been shoved in. Just a heap of ashes there in the morning. New log needed for the next evening. Fortunately, he has a stone floor, as you wouldn't want to be lying half a tree trunk down on your best carpet!'

'The later you come the better,' Simon said, 'because by then I've kicked most of it into the fire!' He grinned. 'My Elizabeth wouldn't have let me do things like that, of course, so, in that sense, I rather like being single again.'

'But you must miss your wife terribly?' Ally said.

'Of course,' Simon said, smiling fondly. 'I miss her every day, but she's been gone several years now. It was all very sudden – her heart, you know.'

'Oh, I'm sorry,' Ally said. 'That must have been so difficult.' Then she got to her feet. 'I've had a lovely tea, thank you, Hamish, but I must go as Flora will be needing to go out.'

Simon decided he should go too and offered her a lift home. Ally declined.

'No, thank you, Simon – it's only a ten-minute walk, and I need the fresh air,' she said as she waved goodbye. Simon was very personable, stylish and refined, but there was something about him that Ally couldn't quite put her finger on. He was plainly flirty, and she wondered if this was natural, or did he do it to win Magda over and set her at ease? Probably something to do with his psychiatry training, she thought.

SEVENTEEN

Just as Ally got in the door, Linda rang. 'Are you doing anything tonight?' she asked.

'No, I'm not,' Ally replied. 'I've been chasing around all day and feel like a quiet evening. Ross is coming up tomorrow night.'

'In which case why don't I come up with a bottle of wine and lasagne?'

'I can't think of anything nicer,' Ally said truthfully. 'And I'm longing to hear about your date with Callum!'

While she waited for Linda to appear, her thoughts kept returning to Ivan and Desdemona, particularly Desdemona. Had Rigby finally come face to face with her? Had he got to the bottom of why she had apparently 'forgotten' to contact him? Surely she was the last person to see Kristina alive? But what about a motive? Could it be her feelings for the earl? Rumour had it that Desdemona was still sweet on the earl, even after all these years. If she was still in love with Hamish and thought that Kristina *was* his bride-to-be, could she have killed her out of jealousy? It was a very disturbing thought, but Desdemona was certainly a very strange woman. Then Ally felt guilty for feeling that way because, after all, she hardly knew Desdemona.

When Linda arrived, Ally was glad to be able to think about something else. She put the oven on to heat the lasagne, and opened the bottle of wine and, when they each were holding a large glass, Ally asked, 'Well? Are you going to tell me about this date or not?'

'It was nice,' Linda said, her eyes mischievous.

'Nice? Come on, Linda – you can do better than that! Are you seeing him again? I've been longing to know.'

'As a matter of fact, I am,' Linda replied. 'I've invited him to my place because I'd like to cook him a meal.'

'Very cosy.'

'Thing is, he eats hotel food every day, restaurant food. All very nice, of course, but I thought he'd like a meal cooked just for him in a normal house.'

'I should think he would. But did you *like* him?'

'Yes, I did. Apart from those hypnotic blue eyes he's quite an interesting character. He was married for a short time, now divorced. His ex couldn't take the long hours he had to work, but that's catering for you.'

'Yes, I guess it is,' Ally said, thinking how fortunate she was to only be doing bed and breakfast.

'But he's nine years younger than me. He's only fifty-six.'

'What does that matter? You don't look any older than him.'

Linda shrugged. 'I suppose it's convention. It's expected that you'll go out with someone your own age, or a couple of years older.'

Ally pulled a face. 'And that's ridiculous in this day and age! How come it's OK for a man to go out with a woman decades younger? I mean, look at the earl! There was forty years between him and Elena! So why shouldn't a woman go out with a man ten or twenty years younger?'

'You're right,' Linda said. 'Anyway, it's not as if I'm about to marry him, for goodness' sake! We just enjoy each other's company. How about you and Ross?'

'Ditto. We enjoy being together, but we need time apart too. And *he's* nine months younger than me!'

'OK, point taken.' Linda laughed. 'But poor Callum's going through quite a time of it with Ivan at the moment. He's afraid he'll lose him. Yes, I know he drinks a lot, but he's a good barman and very honest. And some barmen are not. And he's also very popular with the locals. I think Callum was particularly worried about Kristina's arrival because he thought Kristina might tempt Ivan to leave Scotland. Ivan had confided that Kristina was coming to stay for a couple of weeks, but she'd wanted their marriage to take place back home where all their relatives could attend, whereas he was perfectly happy to have a quiet ceremony here. The last time Ivan went home on holiday, Callum had the devil's own job trying to find a replacement barman and ended up running the bar himself, which meant neglecting some of his management duties. He didn't want to go through all that again.'

'No, I don't suppose he did,' Ally said, wondering if she should add Callum to her Post-it board.

Later, when Linda had gone home after they'd eaten the lasagne, drunk the wine and watched some old episodes of *Friends*, Ally was tempted to take the painting down from the wall. Then she decided she'd do it with Ross the following evening. They had quite a bit of catching up to do. In the meantime, her thoughts kept going back to Desdemona.

Ally badly wanted to question Hamish about his relationship, if there was one, with Desdemona over the years. But she had no idea how to get him on his own, or how to diplomatically probe into his past love life so soon after this tragedy.

When Morag arrived next morning to do a couple of hours'

cleaning, Ally decided to try to tap in to her store of gossip from years past. After Morag had finished upstairs and they were having a cup of tea, Ally asked casually, 'What do you think of Desdemona Morton?'

Morag looked at her in surprise. 'Well, she's always been odd. Of course, she's *English*. Did you know her parents came up here to live off-grid, grow their own vegetables and all that? All the rage these days, I suppose, but it wasn't then. Everyone thought they were crazy. Her father was a brilliant gardener, and he built that walled garden.'

'I wonder how Desdemona managed to meet the earl?' Ally mused.

'She used to come down to the village here, on Wednesdays, to sell her fruit and vegetables. She was quite pretty, I suppose. Long, dark hair.' Morag sniffed loudly. 'She'd been home-educated too, so when the earl came across her, he probably reckoned she was a cut above the rest of us.' She leaned forward and narrowed her eyes. 'We all knew she was spendin' nights up at the castle. Mrs Fraser said that the father would come down every so often and read the riot act to the earl, but Desdemona paid no heed. She was in her twenties by then anyway. Then both the parents died within a few months of each other.'

'So she was with the earl for quite some time?' Ally asked.

'On and off for years. He had plenty others, believe me. Then the sister, this Ophelia, comes home from university or somewhere. Pretty girl she was, and the earl fell for her hook, line and sinker!' Morag rolled her eyes. '*Men!*'

'And did the locals resent Desdemona seeing the earl regularly, her being English and all?' Ally asked.

Morag shook her head. 'I don't think the locals ever thought the earl was ever that serious about her, to be truthful. At one time he even told Angus, his gamekeeper, that she was visiting the castle a bit too often, and he wanted to get rid of her. Then he met the sister.'

'Ophelia? And he fell for her? And married her?'

'He did.'

'Poor Desdemona.' That must have been tough, Ally thought.

'Yeah. Desdemona went down to London for a bit and came back shortly before her sister died.'

'Did she indeed?' Ally's mind was working overtime.

'Aye, she did. There was a lot of bad feelin', and she never even went to Ophelia's funeral.'

'And did she resume her relationship with the earl after Ophelia died?' Ally asked.

Morag shook her head. 'No one knows for sure. He was chasin' women all over the place by then, so it's hard to tell, but there were rumours that she never got over him.' Morag paused. 'That's nice shortbread, Ally. Did ye make it yersel'?'

'Yes, I did,' Ally admitted proudly. She'd begun baking only since she'd come to Locharran and was proud of her prowess.

Morag was carrying her mug and plate over to the sink. 'Well, I'd better be off,' she said.

Ally knew she wasn't going to find out more about Desdemona from Morag today. But from everything she'd learned over the past week or so, it was certainly time to promote Desdemona up to replace Ivan as the most likely suspect for Kristina's murder, and put her somewhere near the top of the list for Elena's murder too. Sadly she'd have to fit Callum in there somewhere as well.

She'd do nothing now. She'd already decided that she'd wait until Ross came round in the evening. He was a good sounding board and was good at reining in her somewhat extravagant imagination. So she'd wait.

EIGHTEEN

After they'd eaten in the evening and cleared everything away, Ross said, 'I bet you're itching to get that picture down from the wall again, aren't you?'

'Yes, I am,' Ally admitted. 'I have a few names to add and to move around.'

Ross stood up and carefully removed the oranges, lemons and grapes from the wall and laid it, picture side down, on the table.

Although Ross had phoned every evening, usually from the veterinary practice where he seemed to be doing endless late shifts, and she'd given him a rundown of her day, she'd not given him the finer details.

'Let's begin with Kristina's murder,' Ally suggested, 'because I now need to make Desdemona the chief suspect.'

'Well, she's at eleven now,' Ross said.

'I think she should be at twelve. I'm going to move Ivan down to eleven and I also need to put Callum Dalrymple in somewhere,' Ally said.

Ross looked puzzled. 'Where does Callum Dalrymple come

into all this? I thought he was away on a course, leaving Ivan in charge, which was why Ivan couldn't go to pick Kristina up?'

'Well, that's what everybody thinks, but we have no proof that he was actually there, do we? And wouldn't it be the perfect alibi if he was intending to sneak back and kill Kristina?'

'What's put this idea into your head?' Ross asked.

'Something that Linda said to me.' Ally told him about Linda's visit the previous evening. 'Did I tell you that Callum had asked her out to lunch?'

'No, you didn't. They'd make a good couple though.'

'He took her out to Seascape and they had a great meal. He was telling her that this Kristina wanted Ivan to go back with her to Lithuania to get married.'

'Which is understandable,' Ross said. 'That's where all the friends and family would be.'

'Callum didn't see it that way though. He seemed to think she could persuade him to stay over there. Ivan's an excellent barman, and Callum has problems finding replacements whenever he's away. Ends up having to run the bar himself.'

'I can understand that might be an inconvenience,' Ross replied, 'but do you really think Callum would spend all day driving along the road to Cairn Cross – when he was supposed to be in Glasgow – on the off chance of meeting Ivan's fiancée?'

'Well, I think it could be possible, if he was that worried about losing Ivan,' Ally replied.

Ross wrinkled his nose. 'I'm not so sure. Yes, of course it would inconvenience him if Ivan left the Craigmonie Bar, but surely not enough to want to kill the poor woman?'

Now that Ross said it like that, Ally was beginning to have doubts herself.

'Why don't we keep him as a suspect but place him at six? Alongside yourself,' Ross suggested as there was already a Post-it at six with Ally's name on.

'Oh well, perhaps I'll remove myself now!' Ally said. 'But I do think Desdemona is the favourite.'

'From what you've told me, I agree,' Ross said. 'But, then again, Desdemona isn't really of this world, you know. She's spent most of her life in the middle of nowhere, alone since her parents died. She's arty-crafty, back-to-nature and in her own world. Would she think it was particularly important to go straight to the police after she realised she'd given the lady in the loch a lift? You or I would, but her mind was probably elsewhere.'

'I was questioning Morag about her. She told me that she thinks Desdemona's always had a soft spot for Hamish. They were lovers long before Ophelia came on the scene, and there are rumours that they might have continued their relationship in the years afterwards. Possibly still going on to this day, the villagers think, and of course they hear all the gossip from Mrs Fraser and the others up there.'

'So, you think Desdemona bumped Kristina off because she thought she was coming to marry the earl?' Ross asked. 'Mistaken identity? But surely she knew enough about Elena to know that when she met Kristina, she wasn't Hamish's bride-to-be?'

That was the thing with Ross – he was a little more logical than she was, more grounded. Ally considered. 'If she's as airy-fairy as you were suggesting, then she might well have forgotten what Hamish had told her about Elena. They were due to arrive at Inverness Airport at about the same time on the same day, but Elena had to delay her journey because of her dress fitting. I mean, how many pretty blonde women would be likely to be landing at Inverness Airport at that time and heading to a fiancé in Locharran?'

Then she remembered the monkshood. 'One more thing, Ross. When I went up to visit her at her studio, she gave me some vegetables straight from the garden before I left, and, while I was there, in among her herbs and things was something that looked like monkshood. Identical, in fact.'

'What's monkshood?'

'It's a very poisonous plant. In my previous life, I once had to research poisons for a crime thriller, and I spent a fair bit of time researching plants that could be used to kill people. It's very, *very* poisonous, you know.'

'But can you be *sure* it was monkshood?' Ross asked.

'I'm more or less convinced it was. Ninety per cent anyway. It gets its name because the flower resembles a monk's cowl, did you know? The flowers were beginning to die off, but they were the same vivid purple colour. Now, why would she be growing *that*?'

Ross raised an eyebrow. 'To be ready to annihilate anyone who looked like snaffling her part-time lover?'

'Ross, be serious! You must admit it *could* be possible. In which case she could be the chief suspect for Elena as well.'

'I agree it *could* be possible, but I don't somehow think she did do it. If you want my money, I think it's still more likely, when it comes to poor Elena, to be the evil Randolph and Lavinia, who you currently have as your most likely suspects on that dial. And what about your new friend, Magda?'

Ally shook her head. 'I'm moving Magda from six to five, though I don't think she'd kill her own sister to get her hands on Hamish, when she'd only met him a week or so before the wedding. I really don't.'

Ross yawned. 'Are we done?'

'No, we aren't. I really feel I have to place Desdemona as chief suspect on Elena's board too, because if Kristina was a case of mistaken identity and Desdemona did kill her out of jealousy, then surely she'd want to finish the job to kill the intended victim – which was Elena.'

'Well, I can see your reasoning.' Ross watched as Ally wrote a new Post-it for Desdemona and added her to Elena's board.

Ally put Desdemona at eleven and moved Mrs Fraser down to ten, alongside Mrs Jamieson. 'Now let's go to bed, Ally.'

When Ally had finished, Ross hung the picture back on the wall and let the dogs out for five minutes, while Ally made them both a hot chocolate. Ross had brought Ebony with him, much to Flora's delight. When he arrived, they'd romped round the garden and then settled down together in the kitchen in their respective beds. Ross had learned early on that he needed to bring Ebony's basket with him, because the animals were far too big to fit into Flora's. While the dogs settled down, Ally and Ross decided it was time to do the same.

They were planning to spend most of the next day together, although Ross had agreed to do a couple of hours in the surgery in the late afternoon. In addition to his duties as Locharran's vet, his son, Will, and his wife, Hannah, often had to ferry their five girls in five different directions to after-school activities, such as sport, music, dance and Girl Guides, meaning that Ross, who was supposedly retired, frequently ended up volunteering to take a shift to help out.

The next morning, Ally woke up first, snuggled against Ross's back and thought, for the umpteenth time, how lucky she was to have met this man. It was all down to Flora, of course. If she hadn't acquired the dog, their paths might never have crossed. What was unusual was that they were both such independent people, and always had been, even during their long marriages. Much as she'd loved Ken, Ally had often yearned to spend some time on her own. She'd felt extremely guilty about this because none of her friends seemed to feel quite the same way, although they'd all loved a girls' night out. It wasn't until she met Ross, so many years later, that she found a truly kindred spirit. He, too, said that he'd sometimes dreamed of freedom, taking off to look after lions in Africa or something, but his wife would never leave Scotland. He'd never admitted this before, he told Ally, because it didn't mean that he hadn't loved Barbara. Ally understood completely. And so, as long as they were able to, they'd continue to keep their own abodes.

When they'd finished their breakfasts, they decided to take the dogs for a good walk across the moors, then take them back to the malthouse, before strolling down to the Craigmonie Bar for some lunch. It was when they'd been walking for about half an hour and were sitting on a large boulder to get their breath back that Ross said, 'Did I tell you that Hannah's pregnant again?'

'No, you did *not!*' Ally exclaimed. 'Oh, Ross, that's wonderful news! Perhaps this time...?'

'Don't say it!' Ross rolled his eyes. 'If it does turn out to be a boy, can you imagine what a spoiled little brat he's going to be, fussed over by five big sisters?'

'He could become a vet though and carry on the family name,' Ally suggested.

'Well, my eldest granddaughter, Lauren, wants to be a vet, she says. And she probably will because she's a very determined type. Furthermore, she has no intention of changing her name even if she does get married. Doesn't see why she should. Says that women don't these days if they don't want to – so the name may well continue.'

'Are Will and Hannah pleased?'

'Not altogether sure about that. I don't think it was planned exactly. I mean, *six* kids...?'

'It's quite a lot in this day and age.'

'Hannah has the girls well trained though, and, for the most part, they kind of look after each other. I guess as long as the baby's healthy, we can't ask for much more.'

'I think it calls for a celebration! My treat today at the Craigmonie.'

'There's no need for you to treat me. I had nothing to do with it...'

'Maybe not, but I insist. A new, little life – what's not to celebrate?'

'OK then, I guess a guy knows when he's beaten,' Ross said with a sigh. Then, laughing, he said, 'Christmas becomes more expensive every damn year! How about you? You hardly ever talk about your grandchildren, and I know next to nothing about them.'

'Well, there's Fiona in Edinburgh,' Ally said. 'Jamie and Liz have just the one. She's eighteen and wants to be a nurse. I guess I'm closer to her than Carol's three, due to the distance.'

'Remind me about your daughter's family?'

'Well, Carol's married to an airline pilot, and they live in Salisbury in Wiltshire. She's kept pretty busy with her kids because he's away such a lot. And, as I think I might have told you before, she runs her own greeting cards business from home. Always been artistic.'

'Wow, she can't have much free time!' Ross exclaimed. 'I mean, Hannah might have five kids, but she's not got a paid job as well. She's a full-time mother, and it looks like she's going to stay that way for the foreseeable future.'

Hand in hand they made their way back to the malthouse, the dogs chasing each other round in circles.

'I love this view,' Ally said, squinting in the autumn sunshine at the village below.

'It's a bonny wee place,' Ross agreed, 'particularly now with all the autumn colours and the heather blooming.'

By the time they'd dropped the dogs off at the malthouse, and changed out of their boots and Barbours, it was two o'clock before they got to the Craigmonie Bar. As they ordered their lagers and sandwiches, they could hear raised voices which seemed to be coming from the hotel reception. Ivan, who was pulling the pump for the draught lagers, raised his eyes to heaven.

'Whatever's going on?' Ally asked.

'Callum is arguing, again, with the Sinclair people,' Ivan replied, pulling a face. 'They're horrible people, always causing trouble.'

'What are they arguing about now?' Ally asked. She could hear a woman's shrill voice.

Ivan shrugged. 'I think Callum's finally had enough and wants them to go somewhere else. But Mr Sinclair is saying that he paid to the end of the week and he is refusing to go anywhere until Saturday.'

'In which case the earl will have to accommodate them after that,' Ross said firmly. 'Like it or not, they're *his* relatives!'

'Callum's training says you should never argue with the guests,' Ivan said with a wry smile, 'but he's doing plenty arguing now!'

'Oh yes, was that the course he was on in Glasgow when you were looking after the hotel and couldn't go to meet Kristina?' Ally asked.

Ivan nodded. 'Yes, for hotel managers. He was away for three whole days.' He sighed, looking down at the bar. 'If he'd been here, I could have gone to meet Kristina.'

'So when did Callum leave for the course?' Ross asked.

'The day before my Kristina is due to arrive.' His eyes filled with tears momentarily. 'And he came back the day after she disappeared.'

Ally and Ross exchanged glances.

Again they were interrupted by the raised voices in the reception area, which were growing even louder.

'Where the hell are we supposed to go?' a woman's hysterical voice demanded. It could only be Lavinia.

'I'm sorry. I really don't know,' she heard Callum say, 'but you could always try The Auld Malthouse. I know Mrs McKinley normally has three rooms to let.'

Ally felt her blood run cold. She did indeed have three available double rooms with bathrooms, and not a guest in sight for more than three weeks. Surely these snobby Sinclairs would want something much grander than what *she* had to offer! Perhaps Rigby would agree to them staying in Inverness or Fort William? Or else *surely* the earl could accommodate them in that enormous castle of his? She tried not to think about it while she and Ross sat munching their sandwiches and sipping their lagers.

Ross took her hand. 'You don't have to be a mind reader to know what you're worrying about,' he said. 'But my bet is that they'll opt for a smart hotel in Inverness or somewhere.'

'We can only hope,' said Ally.

'And, if not, they can have one of my barns and look after themselves.'

'Thank you, Ross,' she said, feeling some sense of relief.

She did not want these people under her roof.

NINETEEN

Hamish arrived on her doorstep the very next morning at nine o'clock.

'I have a bit of a problem,' he said.

Ally knew what he was going to say as she ushered him into the kitchen.

'It's to do with my cousins,' he said, 'at the Craigmonie Hotel. They're causing problems.'

'I know all about their problems at the Craigmonie, and no offence, Hamish,' she said firmly, 'but I do *not* want them here. Ross has kindly said that they could have one of his barns.'

'Yes, Ross rang me this morning with the offer, and I put it to my cousins, but they flatly refused. They like to be looked after, you see, and I know I can depend on you to do a good job.'

'Oh, Hamish...!'

'They're my responsibility – I *know* that,' Hamish said sadly, gazing out of the window as he sat down. 'The problem is Magda.'

'Magda?'

'She's convinced that it was Randolph and Lavinia who

poisoned Elena, and she's terrified at the thought of them being anywhere near her.'

'Perhaps Magda could move down here then?' Ally asked, hoping he couldn't hear the desperation in her voice.

'Possibly,' Hamish said with a sigh. 'But I feel responsible for her, and she should be under my roof. She likes her new room, which you kindly arranged for her, and she's become fond of the castle. She's even become more friendly with Mrs Fraser and Mrs Jamieson, and I feel the very least I can do for Magda is keep her safe. Now she would like a dog and, in the meantime, she's helping Angus out at the kennels. He says she's very good with the dogs, and she's happy when she's there.'

Ally nodded but said nothing.

'The thing is that Rigby wants the three of them to stay here in Locharran. I'd hoped he'd let them stay in either Fort William or Inverness, but no such luck.'

'I hoped the same as you, but I really don't want them here,' Ally said firmly.

He stroked his beard. 'They'll only be here for bed and breakfast, and you wouldn't have to bother with them for the rest of the day. Have you any bookings over the next few weeks?'

Ally shook her head. 'It's not that—'

'I know it's not that,' Hamish interjected, 'and I know they're not very nice people. But, Alison, I'm going to pay you top price for two rooms for them. Summer rates. For as long as it takes.'

There was no doubt about it, this was tempting. She had a few bookings over Christmas from relatives of families in the village, but otherwise the holiday season had come to a close. And she could do with some money to see her through the winter. But *the Sinclairs?*

Hamish had sensed her hesitation in replying. '*Please,* Alison!'

Ally recalled how kind Hamish had been to her since her arrival in Locharran, how hospitable he'd been. He'd even given her Flora, a free pedigree puppy! It would be churlish and ungrateful to refuse him a favour now. And particularly as she could do with the money.

'Let's hope it won't be for long then,' she said after a moment. 'Do you know when I should expect them?'

'Callum wants rid of them, but they've paid up until the end of the week,' Hamish replied, looking at her with pleading eyes. 'So they'd need to come to you on Saturday.'

'OK then,' Ally conceded, wondering if she was to be accommodating a family of killers. She supposed, if nothing else, it would give her the opportunity to suss them out at close quarters. Possibly even pick up a clue in their rooms?

She might as well make the best of this.

Ally was surprised, a couple of hours after Hamish had left, to find Magda on the doorstep.

'I need to speak to you,' Magda said. 'Can I come in?'

'Of course you can come in,' Ally said, standing to one side to let her enter. 'It's just a short time ago since Hamish left.'

'He was here?'

'Yes. He made a booking for his cousins to stay here.'

'Oh, thank God!' Magda sat down on a kitchen chair. 'I was afraid they would come to stay at the castle.'

'Hamish knew you wouldn't want that,' Ally said, filling the kettle.

'So they're coming here – you're certain?'

'Yes, probably at the weekend,' Ally replied with a sigh. 'I owe Hamish lots of favours, and I have no other guests.'

Magda frowned. 'But it means I won't be able to visit you.'

'Why not? Most likely they'll be out most of the time. I don't do lunches or dinners,' Ally reminded her.

Magda shook her head. 'I think they killed my sister, and I do *not* want to see them. Will you be able to come to see me at the castle?'

'Of course I will,' Ally said.

'Because I'm happy there now.' Magda gave a little smile. 'Doctor Simon has been to see me a couple of times and we talk for thirty minutes, sometimes more. He's very kind and is helping me to think about starting a new life here in Locharran.'

Ally was pleased. The old smoothie was obviously good at his job because she could see Magda's confidence growing day by day.

'Hamish is also very kind to me.' She paused. 'He's a good man.'

'Yes, he is,' Ally agreed. 'And, of course, you can phone me any time, you know.'

Magda pursed her lips. 'I hate having to ask to use the phone.'

'Haven't you got a mobile, Magda?'

She shook her head sadly. 'I think I must have left it on the plane. I wasn't worried when I first arrived in Scotland because my sister had a phone I could use. I was planning to buy a new one when I got back to London, but the police took Elena's phone as evidence.'

'Oh, that's a shame. I tell you what: one of these days we'll have a quick trip to Inverness or somewhere and get you a new one. How about that?'

'That would be wonderful,' Magda said. 'Thank you! I can buy some more clothes while I'm there too.' She smiled. 'Hamish has said he'll help me buy new things to wear until I find my feet here.'

Thinking of the large Marks and Spencer store in Inverness, with its large department of ladies' clothes, Ally said, 'Good idea! How about tomorrow?'

'Oh yes, please, Ally! Thank you.' Magda was almost

jumping up and down. Ally had never seen her so animated. She'd expected she might be pleased but hadn't anticipated this level of enthusiasm.

'I'll pick you up at nine o'clock then,' Ally said.

The road from Locharran to Inverness wound its way through the mountains and passed three lochs before it arrived at Loch Ness, near Fort Augustus. On the way Magda chatted non-stop, mainly about dogs. She was helping Angus at the kennels, and she was going to have one of Mona's puppies, when he'd had all his inoculations. She loved Labradors, and she was going to have one of her very own, for the first time in her life, and he was going to be called Benjamin, because that had been her father's name.

From Fort Augustus they drove up the stunning lochside road, past Drumnadrochit and Urquhart Castle, with Magda in a high state of excitement at the remote prospect of seeing the Loch Ness Monster.

'This is the loch with the monster, isn't it?' she asked Ally with almost childlike wistfulness, refusing to take her eyes off the water.

'So I believe,' Ally replied, 'but very few folk have ever set eyes on it.'

'But that doesn't mean it's not there,' Magda persisted, continuing to keep her eyes on the loch.

'Of course it doesn't,' Ally replied. 'Perhaps it'll surface on the way back and then you'll be able to take a picture of him with your new phone – and make a fortune! And you'll be sitting on the lochside of the car.'

'Maybe it's a lady?' Magda suggested.

Ally laughed. 'Perhaps it is. No one's ever got close enough to tell!'

·   ·   ·

Inverness was busy, and it took some time to find a parking space. When, finally, they emerged into the shopping precinct, Magda hardly knew which way to turn. It struck Ally that perhaps she wasn't accustomed to having much time to herself with her busy job caring for families. 'When did you last spend a day wandering round the shops?' she asked.

'I can't remember!' Magda replied, her eyes like saucers.

'Well,' Ally said, 'we have all day here, so you'll have plenty of time to look at everything. But let's get your phone first, and then we'll have coffee.'

Within minutes, they'd found a shop selling every conceivable type of electronic equipment, and with a young, very enthusiastic salesman. Ally had prewarned her not to tell anyone that she was the sister of the now famous 'murdered bride of the earl', which had dominated the media. Apart from anything else, they hadn't asked Rigby's permission to leave the village, which Ally supposed they should have done.

A phone was chosen, followed by a lot of personalising, and some paperwork. By the time they left the shop, they were more than ready for coffee. As they drank these, Magda added everyone's numbers to her phone and took a couple of photos of passers-by to ensure that the camera worked. She even sent an email to Ally. It read, *Thank you so much, Ali.*

Then they hit the shops. Magda had clearly not been shopping for herself in years. She hardly knew which way to turn in Marks and Spencer. Hamish had obviously given her quite a bit of money to spend because she'd already bought her phone, and none of the prices of the clothes she gathered up to try on seemed to faze her.

By the time they sat down to lunch, they were lugging around six large carrier bags. While they ate, Ally studied Magda. She'd never seen the woman look so happy – not that Magda had had much to be happy about since she'd arrived in Scotland.

'Magda,' Ally said hesitantly, looking at the woman's shoulder-length, rather straggly, brown hair, 'why don't we try to find a hairdresser while we're here?'

Magda ran a hand through her hair and pulled a face. 'D'you think I need it?'

'I think you deserve a bit of pampering,' Ally confirmed.

They finished their salads and made their way back to a couple of salons that Ally had noticed on the way. It was almost certain they'd be fully booked, but it was worth a try. The first one was fully booked, but the second one wasn't, only because Pierre's customer had, much to Pierre's annoyance, 'managed to break her leg'. He sat Magda down in a chair and looked at her locks with disapproval. 'When was this done last?'

Magda shrugged. 'Months ago. I haven't had much time for myself lately.'

Pierre rolled his eyes. 'That probably explains it,' he said.

'I'll come back in an hour,' Ally said to Magda before setting off to do some shopping for herself in the nearby supermarket.

On her way round, she paused at all the ranges of cosmetics and the bewildering array of reasonably priced make-up on offer. Should she choose some for Magda? She had never seen her wear very much, even at Elena's wedding, but wondered if this, too, was a symptom of not having had much time to look after herself lately. She'd give it a try.

Ally spent a good ten minutes choosing some smoky-coloured eyeliner and eyeshadow, mascara and lipstick in a shade she hoped Magda would like, and then had to rush back with her trolley to her car. Then she bolted back to the hairdresser, ten minutes later than she intended. Not that it mattered because Pierre was only just putting the finishing touches to a transformed Magda.

'Wow!' Ally said, hardly able to believe this new Magda smiling back at her in the mirror. What a decent haircut could do for a woman! Pierre had got it shining, cut beautifully in layers which revealed the natural chestnut glints in her hair.

'Magda, you look beautiful!' Ally exclaimed truthfully.

Magda looked at herself in the mirror as if she could hardly believe it. 'I think... I look good.'

'It's more than good! It's transformed you.'

Pierre looked pleased. 'Come back in six weeks' time,' he ordered. 'Why don't you make the appointment now?'

While Magda did as she was told, Ally paid the bill. She wanted to pay for something, and Magda had obviously already spent a great deal of Hamish's money because she'd been shelling it out, left, right and centre until now.

As they made their way back to the car, Ally said, 'We'll go back to the malthouse, so you can change into some of your new clothes, and maybe put on a little make-up before I deliver you back to Hamish.'

Ally noticed that Magda's face had become alive, even without the make-up that she'd bought. The day in Inverness had been worth every penny.

It could only have been improved if the Loch Ness Monster had decided to appear on the way back.

But, of course, it didn't, though shortly after they left the city, something else occurred.

Ally had been aware for some miles of a muddy Land Rover driving far too close behind.

Then Magda saw something floating on the loch. 'Oh, what is that? Is it the monster?' she asked excitedly.

Momentarily distracted, Ally slowed down a little, hoping at the same time that the damned Land Rover would overtake and get out of the way.

Instead she felt, and heard, the awful sound of crunching metal as the Land Rover drove up alongside and deliberately rammed into the side of her car, causing it to veer sharply to the left and stop with what had to be only inches before they'd have crashed directly into the loch.

'What the hell?' Ally gasped, watching the Land Rover gather speed and zoom round a bend before she had time to get the registration number. Only two digits stuck in her mind: an X and a nine.

Magda was sobbing. 'Oh, Ally, it's my fault...'

'No, it isn't,' Ally said. 'That Land Rover deliberately rammed into *me*. They've been looking for an opportunity to do so for some miles.' Her own eyes were now swimming with tears as she tried to open her door to see how much damage had been inflicted. The door wouldn't open so had obviously been caved in. She'd have to get out of the front passenger door and, unless she fancied an unplanned dip in the loch, it didn't seem like a good idea to move around much on the nearside.

Fortunately, the engine was still running, and Ally managed to reposition the Golf back onto the road and put on the hazard warning lights. Magda got out, Ally climbed across and, her heart in her mouth, walked round the car to study the damage. There was a small dent on the rear wing, but the car was crumpled along the driver's side. This would necessitate at least two new doors.

Ally was trying very hard not to cry as she tried to work out who would inflict this sort of damage. *Who?* It had been done deliberately without a doubt.

'Oh, Ally, I'm so sorry...'

'So am I, Magda. Somebody hoped to injure us, I think.' She'd been so fond of her silver Golf, even if it was eight years old.

'Because of me?' Magda asked, wiping her eyes.

'No, not because of you.' Ally sighed. She was certain it was she herself who had been the target. Had she been asking too many questions? She studied the damage and tried not to think of the insurance claim. She could decipher a streak of green paint in one of the deeper dents. Would that yield a clue, along with her X and her 9? Probably not. Most Land Rovers round here were painted some shade of green.

At least the car was driveable, and Ally wasn't about to get stranded here.

'We're not going to let this ruin our day out,' Ally said more confidently than she felt as she crawled back into the driving seat. 'So we're going home.'

'What about your poor car?' Magda asked anxiously as they pulled up in front of the malthouse.

'I'll deal with that later,' Ally said as she switched off the engine and ushered Magda inside.

Ally unloaded their shopping, and then dug out the make-up she'd bought. Magda, in the meantime, was studying her chic reflection in the hallway mirror. Pierre had certainly done her proud. Not only had the pixie haircut actually managed to make her look pretty; it had also made her look younger.

'Shall we try a little make-up now?' Ally suggested.

Magda turned away from the mirror and frowned. 'I haven't any.'

Ally smiled. 'But I do! Shall we try? Come up to my bedroom.'

'OK,' said Magda with a shrug.

Ally hadn't bought her any foundation or skin products, but she had a drawerful of mistakes she'd made over the years. Stuff she'd bought without checking the colour properly. She should, of course, have thrown most of them out months ago, but it was a well-known fact that, if you hung on to something long enough, it would probably come in useful. Hopefully this might prove the point.

Ally was no make-up artist, but she was longing to have a go at completing Magda's new look and made her sit down on the dressing-table stool. One of these foundations just had to suit Magda. She got to work, added a modest amount of eyeliner, shadow, mascara, and finished off with the lipstick before she permitted Magda to look in the mirror. Then, 'Voila!' she said and swivelled the stool around so that Magda could see herself.

Magda gasped. 'Is it really me?'

'I don't see anyone else in here,' Ally said, laughing. 'You look so pretty.'

Magda shook her head in disbelief. 'I don't think I've ever been pretty.'

'You were pretty without the make-up, Magda, but you look even prettier with it. Why don't you put on those nice jeans and one of your new jumpers, and I'll drive you up to the castle?'

In something of a daze, Magda obeyed, catching glimpses of herself in every reflective surface and smiling.

It did something to compensate for her dented car.

Ally insisted on driving Magda back to the castle because she wasn't confident enough that Pierre's hairdo, or her own attempt at make-up, could withstand the horizontal rain that was now lashing against the windows. They'd set out in brilliant sunshine in the morning but, typically of the region, the weather had changed dramatically in the course of the day.

Umbrellas raised, they dashed out to the car, and Ally, after clambering into the driving seat again via the passenger side, drove the short distance up to the castle. As they ran into the Great Hall, they saw Hamish peering up into the vast heights of the fireplace chimney.

'Do you know,' he muttered to no one in particular, 'I do believe there's still birds stuck up there.' He turned round slowly. 'Oh, hello, Alison, how nice to see you.' He looked across at Magda. 'And who do we have here?'

Ally couldn't believe that he hadn't recognised her.

'It's me, Hamish. Magda!' Magda said with a huge smile.

Hamish blinked as he walked towards her. 'My God, Magda, you look utterly beautiful!' He turned to Ally. 'What magic have you come up with here?'

Ally smiled, said nothing, but watched with some foreboding as Hamish put his arm round Magda's shoulders and continued gazing at her.

Then he suddenly remembered Ally was still there and said, 'Oh, do come in.'

'No, thank you, Hamish, I won't. I still have a load of shopping to unpack, not to mention a half-wrecked car to sort out.' Seeing Hamish looking at her questioningly she added, 'Magda will tell you.'

As she got back into her car, she began to wonder at her wisdom in encouraging Magda's transformation. She'd recognised the light in Hamish's eye.

What had she done now?

An hour later, Hamish arrived on her doorstep. 'Magda has told me what happened,' he said, 'and I am so very sorry. I just wanted you to know that I will pay for your car to be fixed, so please don't go worrying about the insurance.'

'No, I can't be having that. I'll phone the insurance company in the morning, but, to be truthful, I still feel a bit shaken at the moment from the experience.'

'You don't have the driver's particulars,' he said, 'so the insurance will load your next premium. I feel responsible because I do think this has to do with Magda.'

Ally shook her head. 'No, I think that attack was directed at me. I've been asking too many questions, I think.'

'Nevertheless,' Hamish continued, 'I insist on sorting out the damage. I have a great garage where I get my Jag and my Range Rover serviced, and they'll do me a good deal. But surely you should go to the police? This could well have been the murderer. Could you see who was driving? Did you get the registration number by any chance?'

Ally shook her head. 'No, I *think* it might have been a man driving, but I really couldn't be sure. It all happened so fast, but there was an X and a nine in the registration somewhere.'

'Mercifully neither of these digits are in my Land Rover registration, so you can count me out,' Hamish said, smiling.

'I didn't think for a moment it was *you*!' Ally exclaimed.

'I'll have them here tomorrow morning to tow your car away,' he said as he made his way out.

TWENTY

Ally had one day to herself before Randolph, Lavinia and the son arrived on her doorstep.

Hamish, true to his word, had her Golf towed away and promised that they would fix it as soon as they could. She then spent the morning dusting, vacuuming and airing the rooms and had even gone so far as to buy a bunch of flowers to put in the Sinclairs' room. Then she wondered if they would choose a twin-bedded or double-bedded room. There was no way of knowing so she left the flowers in the dining room for the moment. Next, she phoned Morag to see if she could resume her cleaning duties from Sunday onward. Fortunately, Morag could.

'Aye, I'm workin' at the Craigmonie from one to three, but I could do you every mornin' nine to eleven while they're stayin' with you, if that's OK? I could do with the extra money for Christmas.'

With a sigh of relief, Ally replaced the phone and concentrated on the next item on her list: some shopping. She'd bought most things in Inverness, but she was definitely going to need a few last-minute bits and pieces. What did these people eat for breakfast? She hoped it was nothing obscure, and for a minute she wondered if she should phone Callum to find out, and then talked herself out of it. Damn it, they could eat what she offered them, and she'd had no complaints so far!

As Ally made her way down to the shop, she wondered if Queenie had got news of the Sinclairs' move yet. She was hardly through the door when Queenie, stretched across the counter as usual, called out loudly, 'I hear ye're goin' to be gettin' some visitors then!'

Well, *that* hadn't taken long to get around, Ally thought. 'Correct,' she said, 'so I'm going to be needing a few extra bits and pieces.'

Queenie and Bessie liked lists, so Ally had written one out. As usual Queenie gave it a quick glance, then hollered 'Be-ss-ie!' at the top of her voice, and, also as usual, Bessie appeared from the dark depths of the storeroom, nodded at Ally, picked up the list and disappeared again.

'Ye're goin' to have yer hands full, Mrs McKinley!' Queenie continued cheerfully. 'I'm hearin' that they was a pain in the a— er, backside at the Craigmonie. Callum Dalrymple can hardly wait to get rid of them!'

'You certainly know how to cheer me up,' Ally remarked drily.

'Aye well, truth be known, we're all feelin' a wee bit sorry for ye,' Queenie said with what could almost have passed for a smile. 'Ye'd have thought the least the earl could do would be to put them up himsel'. He's got plenty of rooms, that's for sure, and they're *his* relatives! Mind you, Mrs Jamieson and Mrs Fraser are awful glad they're no' goin' to be goin' up there! They're still that mad at the earl for no' tellin' them about that Elena comin' until *the day before*! The day before! One day's notice, can ye imagine? And then she was a bit of a madam! Mrs Fraser was sayin' to me that she was glad that Elena was got rid of. But the sister is much nicer, or so she says.'

The phrase resonated in Ally's mind... '*She was glad that Elena was got rid of...*'

'Yes, I daresay,' Ally replied, feeling distracted as Bessie laid her purchases on the counter.

As she rummaged in her bag for her purse, Queenie added, 'Next time we see ye, ye'll likely be lookin' for goat's milk or somethin'!'

'And would you be likely to have any?' Ally asked as she turned to go.

'Oh aye,' Queenie said. 'This isnae the backwoods, ye know!'

When she got home and sat down with a cup of tea, Ally thought again about Queenie's comment that Mrs Fraser was glad that Elena 'was got rid of'. It was obvious, even at the reception, that the ladies at the castle didn't care for Elena. But could they possibly care for Elena so little that they'd poison her? Ally somehow doubted it, but nevertheless, there was no way she could remove them from her suspects. Not yet anyway.

She phoned Ross.

'How was Inverness yesterday?' he asked.

'Very good. We had an extremely successful day, until we started driving home.'

'What happened?'

'A Land Rover, driving right up my arse, pushed me off the road, dented the whole side of my car and shot off at a hundred miles an hour!'

'Oh, Ally, are you OK? Why didn't you phone me? I'd have come straight over! Have you rung the insurance?'

'Hamish has insisted on dealing with it all, and he's already had the car towed away. He reckoned it's all to do with Magda, but I think it was directed at me. I've probably been asking too many questions.'

'That's very generous of Hamish. But, Ally, I'm so worried about you! You could be making yourself a target. You must lie low for a while. Leave it to the police.'

'I'm not going to let this get to me, Ross, because we had a lovely day up to then.'

'So, was it a successful day otherwise?'

'Well, I encouraged Magda to beautify herself; new hairdo, new clothes, new make-up.'

'She certainly needed brightening up,' Ross remarked.

'She did, but when I delivered her back at the castle, I was a bit worried at the way Hamish was looking at her.'

Ross laughed. 'She's old enough to look after herself.'

'I'm not so sure. She's not very worldly, and she's been hurt before. I'm going to keep an eye on her. Anyway, this is my last day of freedom, so I'm looking forward to seeing you later.'

'You know I phoned Callum and offered the Sinclairs one of my barns? But they didn't want to know. I'm really sorry.'

'Yes, Hamish told me. That was so kind of you,' Ally said. 'Thanks for trying.'

'We'll go out for a nice dinner tonight,' Ross said, 'and, if you like, I could be with you when they arrive tomorrow.'

'That would be great.' Ally sighed with relief. 'They're most likely the type of people who'd try to run rings round a woman on her own but might behave better if they think there's a man around the place.'

'I promise to appear to glare at them in a manly, no-nonsense fashion any time it's necessary,' Ross promised. 'In the meantime, you need some cosseting after your awful experience.'

Later, after they got back from a delectable – as usual – meal at Seascape, Ally pondered over whether or not they should make some adjustments to her suspects for Kristina's murder.

'I'm beginning to think I should remove Callum,' Ally said.

'I don't think he should ever have been on the dial, considering he was on that course in Glasgow,' Ross reminded Ally as he lifted the picture down from the wall.

'Do we know that for sure?' Ally asked. 'Could he just have pretended to be there?'

'Are you saying then that he invented the whole course so that he could hang around in Locharran waiting for the chance of finding Kristina and doing away with her?' Ross asked. 'Do you really believe he'd go to such lengths just to hang on to a barman?'

'I must admit I'm coming round to your way of thinking, and I agree it seems unlikely. But, Ross, this is only relevant *if* Desdemona was telling the truth.'

'What do you mean?' he asked.

'Well, we only have Desdemona's word for it that she broke down at Cairn Cross. No one saw her there, did they? She didn't call out any breakdown service, did she? She could just as easily have driven Kristina on somewhere quiet, killed her and then dumped her body in the loch before driving on home.'

'So you're becoming more convinced that Kristina's death was a case of mistaken identity?'

'I think I am,' Ally replied thoughtfully. 'If we could eliminate Callum, then all the others could go onto one clock face – with just Ivan on the side, as I don't think he had a reason to kill Elena – and that would make everything a lot simpler.'

'OK,' Ross said, 'we could eliminate Callum by finding out if he really was at this meeting, or course, or whatever it was. Let me try to find out tomorrow.'

Ally nodded, wondering if she'd get a wink of sleep tonight.

Ally did sleep, eventually, although it took her some time to drop off.

In the morning she got up but couldn't settle to do anything much except wander around flicking a duster at imaginary dust, angry with herself for being so nervous. She certainly hadn't been as nervous as this even when she'd awaited her very first guests!

The Sinclairs arrived just after eleven.. Randolph, a suitcase in each hand, came through the doorway first, followed by the son, also carrying a couple of suitcases, and then Lavinia, carrying only a designer handbag and sighing audibly.

'Welcome to The Auld Malthouse,' Ally said cheerfully.

Randolph laid down his suitcases and nodded. At this point, Ross appeared from the kitchen.

'Let me show you to your rooms,' Ally said as Ross asked, 'Can I help you with your bags?' at the same time picking up one suitcase from Randolph and one from the son. Without further ado, they all made their way upstairs.

'I wasn't sure which bedrooms you would prefer,' Ally said politely, 'but as all three are available, I'll let you pick whichever you'd like.'

Lavinia was peering through each door. 'Have you any other bookings?' she asked.

'Not at present,' Ally replied, fervently wishing she had.

'In that case,' said Lavinia, 'we'll take all three.'

'All three?' Ally repeated, recalling that Hamish had specified only two rooms.

'All three,' confirmed Lavinia, laying her handbag down on the king-sized bed in Room 1.

'But—' Ally began.

'But nothing,' snapped Lavinia. 'He won't have us at the castle because of that trollop of a sister, so he can damn well pay the price here!'

There was silence for a moment, and Ally realised that neither of the other two were about to argue.

Obediently Randolph settled for Room 3, while the son

shrugged and made his way into Room 2. There was little Ally could do; it was a problem between the Sinclairs and Hamish.

She cleared her throat and said, 'Can I just give you the Wi-Fi details and the breakfast times, please?'

No one appeared to be listening, but she stood in the landing anyway and called out the details as loud as she could. Ross, having deposited the bags in the appropriate rooms, emerged onto the landing and nodded that they should go downstairs.

Back in the kitchen, Ross said, 'Well, we can see who's boss in *that* family!'

'The boy didn't utter a word.'

'I have a feeling he doesn't get asked his opinion very often,' Ross remarked. 'And did you notice what they were *wearing?*'

'Not high street,' Ally agreed.

'Like him or not, that guy must be making some money,' Ross added.

An hour or so later, they heard footsteps in the hall and, peering out, saw Randolph and Lavinia heading towards the front door. No sign of the boy.

'He obviously likes to be rid of them,' Ross said, 'and who could blame him? Leave him to settle in and see how it goes.'

It was during the afternoon, when Ally had let both Flora and Ebony out into the garden, that she heard a male voice somewhere outside.

'Who's that?' she asked Ross.

'No idea,' Ross said, looking up briefly from the football match he was watching on TV.

Ally ventured out through the back door and wandered round to the main part of the garden to find the Sinclair boy throwing a chewed-up old tennis ball in the air, laughing at the two dogs racing manically around trying to catch it.

'They're quite competitive,' Ally remarked with a smile.

'Yeah,' the boy said.

Ally studied him. Now she had a chance to look at him more closely, he wasn't as old as she'd first thought, probably around seventeen. He was quite tall, dark like his parents, with brown eyes and hair shaved up the sides but with a long line of thatch across the top. He'd be good-looking if he grew his hair normally, she decided.

After a minute, the dogs came back, Ebony with the ball, which she deposited at the boy's feet. He laughed and threw it again.

'I'm Ally,' she said casually.

'Giles,' he muttered without taking his eyes off the dogs vying for the ball.

'Welcome to The Auld Malthouse, Giles,' Ally went on. 'We haven't been introduced, have we?'

He shook his head. 'Are they your dogs?'

'Flora is. She's the smaller of the two. The larger one is Ebony, and she belongs to Ross, my friend.'

'I always wanted a dog,' he said wistfully.

'You don't have one then?'

He shook his head slowly. 'No, my parents won't have one. Anyway, they're both out all day.'

Ally nodded. 'It's not fair to leave a dog on its own all day.'

'We have a live-in housekeeper,' he retorted, 'and a gardener.'

'Yes, well, you can enjoy the dogs while you're here,' Ally said, feeling sorry for this lad with the sad brown eyes.

He nodded, prised the ball from Flora and threw it to the far end of the garden for them to retrieve again.

The day passed uneventfully. Randolph and Lavinia didn't

return until about seven o'clock and left again about an hour later, taking Giles with them.

'Presumably they've gone out to eat somewhere,' Ally said to Ross as she popped a fish pie into the oven.

Ross was uncorking a bottle of Sauvignon Blanc. 'My guess is that it won't be the Craigmonie,' he said with a wry smile. 'What time are they having breakfast?'

'No idea,' Ally admitted. 'I'll just have everything ready to go and wait for them to appear. Morag's coming in at nine and will hopefully get their rooms done while they're having breakfast, and before she leaves at eleven.'

'You must be firm with these people,' Ross said, waving a finger. 'This is *your* establishment, and *you* call the tune. You tell *them* the time you serve breakfast. This is not a hotel.'

'I did make a speech about all that when I took them upstairs,' Ally said.

'But they weren't listening, and they haven't given you a time.'

'I know, I know.' Ally sighed. 'I must become more assertive. I'll tell them in the morning.'

Ross looked concerned as he handed her a glass of wine. 'I don't like this, Ally; they could well be killers. Please be careful.'

Ally promised she would. She had been relieved to see, when they arrived that morning, that they were driving a dark-green Jag and not a Land Rover.

TWENTY-ONE

Morag arrived at nine o'clock sharp. 'So, where are they?' she asked as she removed her purple anorak.

'Still in bed presumably,' Ally informed her, 'and in three separate rooms.'

'You're havin' me on!' exclaimed Morag.

'No, I'm not! They wanted a room each, if you please, and God only knows what Hamish will say because he's footing the bill.'

'He can afford it,' Morag said dismissively. 'But ye need to be gettin' them up at half past nine, ten at the latest, because otherwise how am I goin' to be gettin' their rooms done before I go at eleven? Tell me *that*!'

'I'll try to get the times and everything else sorted out this morning,' Ally said, just as Ross came in through the back door, having taken both the dogs for a walk across the moor.

'They still in bed?' he asked, pointing a finger skyward.

'Well, it's Sunday morning,' Ally said, 'but I'll have to make half past nine or ten the deadline from now on.'

In the dining room next door, she'd set up the long sideboard with all the usual cereals, fruits, yoghurt, sauces and jams, and in the kitchen, she had all the ingredients for full breakfasts lined up alongside the hob, sausages already cooking slowly in the oven. She hadn't the faintest idea what they were likely to eat, but she knew nothing would be wasted as long as Ross was around.

The three Sinclairs appeared just after ten o'clock. Ally had set the table for three in front of the window, wondering as she did so if she should be setting up separate tables!

Randolph was first through the door, in designer jeans, a cashmere sweater and a cravat. 'Good morning,' he said, looking around. 'I hope we're not too late?' He went straight to the sideboard and poured himself a large fruit juice. He was followed by Giles.

'No, you're not,' Ally replied, 'but I would ask that you come down for breakfast at half past nine or ten at the very latest.' She cleared her throat. 'Did you sleep well?'

'It's a lot quieter here than down in that damned hotel,' he said by way of an answer as he carried his glass and heaped cereal bowl across to the table.

Giles followed behind him carrying an equally heaped cereal bowl. Just then Lavinia appeared, and Ally realised for the first time just how thin this woman was, scrawny in fact. She was fully made-up though, her long dark hair done up in a tidy chignon, bracelets jangling on her bony wrists. Ally could see that they all had the remains of suntans, which were unlikely to have been acquired around here.

'I can make porridge if you want,' Ally added. She thought she saw Lavinia shudder at the thought as she carefully helped herself to three prunes which she inserted into a cereal bowl.

There were no takers for porridge, so Ally said, 'Would you all like my standard cooked breakfast?' as she pointed out the printed menu on the table. Both Randolph and Giles indicated that they would have the cooked breakfast, and Lavinia, who was studying the menu with suspicion, shuddered.

'Is this organic?' she asked, pointing doubtfully at the muesli.

'No, I don't think it is,' Ally said, trying to remember what had been written on the packet, which she'd thrown out, because she kept her cereals in Tupperware boxes, and realising that she was probably about to fall at the first hurdle. 'But I can get some for you if that's what you'd like,' she added hastily. Was there the faintest chance that Queenie might just stock organic cereals?

'For God's sake, woman!' Randolph bellowed from the table, munching his cornflakes. 'Just bloody well eat what's *there!*'

Lavinia ignored him. 'I don't suppose you have oat milk?' she asked, suppressing a sigh.

'The thing is, Lavinia,' Ally said, 'I've had no indications beforehand of what your requirements were going to be. If I had, I'd have done my best to provide them.' Without much hope she asked, 'Will you be having a cooked breakfast?'

'That depends,' Lavinia replied. 'I'm vegetarian so I'll just have some scrambled eggs. Are your eggs free-range?'

'Yes, they are,' Ally replied, relieved at having something that might meet her approval.

That seemed to satisfy Lavinia for the moment as she sat down with her husband, son and the three prunes. Then she thought of something else. 'Could I have buckwheat toast?'

'Er, no, I'm afraid—'

'Sourdough then?' Lavinia interrupted.

'Yes, I do have sourdough,' Ally said, praying she still had a loaf in the freezer.

'In which case, I'll have two scrambled eggs on half a slice of sourdough toast,' she said, slicing a small piece of a prune with her spoon.

Both husband and wife wanted coffee; Giles wanted tea.

'You must have some Earl Grey,' Lavinia advised, patting her son's hand.

'Builders' tea,' confirmed Giles, 'nice and strong, please.'

When she got back into the kitchen, Morag was preparing to go upstairs to tackle the bedrooms.

'*Three* rooms!' she grumbled, pulling on her yellow Marigold gloves. 'It disnae say an awful lot for the marriage, does it?' With a lot of tut-tutting she disappeared upstairs.

Ally wondered if she should cook Lavinia's scrambled eggs ahead of the two large breakfasts, reckoning she'd get the remaining prunes eaten before the other two got on the outside of their mountains of cereal. She decided she would.

Ross came in with an armful of logs which he'd been chopping up for the wood burner. 'How's it going?' he asked.

'More or less as expected,' Ally replied. 'Randolph and Giles don't appear to be fussy, but Lavinia is vegetarian and obsessed with everything being organic and all that.' She grinned. 'I found a few slices of sourdough in the freezer, and I can only hope that Queenie might stock some oat milk.'

'Oat milk!' said Ross. 'Whatever next?'

Breakfast went well, and Lavinia seemed satisfied with her eggs. Ally did her best to keep the tea and coffee flowing, in an attempt to keep them in the dining room for as long as possible so that Morag could get on with their bedrooms.

When, finally, the family drifted upstairs, Morag reappeared, her eyes like saucers.

'Ye should see that woman's *wardrobe*! And did ye know that they make clothes in a size *six*?'

'I'd heard rumours,' Ally replied, laughing.

'When they go out,' Morag continued, 'ye should go upstairs and just have a look at their stuff! Ye wouldnae believe it! Ye're no' goin' to find a high street label up there! It's all French and Italian and that. Do ye know, I never thought I'd run my fingers over an Armani suit, but *he's* got one!'

'Apart from the wedding, I shouldn't think he'll have many occasions to wear an Armani suit up here,' Ross said as he prepared to leave. One of his five granddaughters had a birthday today, and although they'd kindly asked Ally to the birthday tea as well, she'd opted to stay at the malthouse on this occasion. She didn't really know his family very well yet, and she was also worried at leaving the Sinclairs there on their own on their first full day. And she had to admit that the prospect of a four-year-old's birthday party, with four sisters and goodness knows how many friends running around, wasn't exactly her idea of relaxation on a Sunday afternoon. It wasn't Ross's either, he admitted, but he had little choice.

'Fancy a cuppa before you go, Morag?' Ally asked as she cleared away the breakfast dishes.

'Aye, I will,' Morag replied as she helped to load the dishwasher.

When she sat down with a mug of tea, Morag continued, 'That woman is *that* untidy! Clothes all over the floor, make-up everywhere! Am I supposed to be a lady's maid, Ally?'

'No, no,' Ally soothed, terrified that Morag might change her mind about her two hours at the malthouse. Plainly she was never going to forgive Lavinia for being a size six. 'They've only just arrived, so let's give them a couple of days to settle in, and then, if Lavinia continues to scatter her stuff all around, I'll have a word with her and explain that it means the room can't be cleaned properly.'

'*Lavinia!*' scoffed Morag, taking another swig from her mug. 'What sort of a name is that?'

'Well, it appears to be the only one she's got!'

'Them toffs come up with some weird names,' Morag said, shaking her head as she finished the last of her tea and then deposited her mug in the sink.

After she'd gone, Ally sighed. During these past few weeks, minus guests, she'd got used to a more leisurely lifestyle, seeing Ross more often, having long walks with the dog. She had to get back into her stride now, take control and maintain standards.

And find some oat milk.

Randolph had gone out briefly after breakfast, presumably to get a selection of Sunday papers. They then spent most of the morning in the sitting room, reading them. Ally knew that allowing her guests to use the sitting room wasn't standard practice in B&Bs, which were, by definition, exactly that – bed and breakfast only. But, as Ally only used the kitchen, her little snug with its old squashy sofa and the television, plus her own sleeping quarters immediately overhead, she saw no reason why her guests shouldn't use the formal sitting room, which, along with the dining room, was at the front of the house. She'd put books, magazines and some board games in there, because she felt sorry for people trying to keep themselves occupied somewhere indoors in inclement weather. And there was usually a fair bit of inclement weather, it had to be said. They did, however, go out at lunchtime, and shortly afterwards, Hamish arrived.

'I see they've gone out,' he said, following her into the kitchen. 'I hope they're behaving themselves?'

'Yes,' Ally replied, 'but I have to tell you that they've taken all three of my rooms. You'll only pay for two, of course, because that's what you booked.'

'Nonsense!' Hamish exclaimed. 'I'm more than happy to pay for three rooms if it keeps them from complaining and upsetting everyone. And that is *so* typical of them! Of course Randolph and Lavinia haven't been getting on for years, so no surprise there. The only reason Lavinia is sticking around is because she's determined to become the Countess of Locharran! She's such a snob! I think Randolph would be glad to be rid of her, but she isn't going to move an inch as long as there's any chance of this inheritance. You can understand why I wanted an heir! Now. Your car should be ready very soon as I'm told that the work is nearly completed.'

'Thank you.' Ally studied him for a moment. 'How *are* you, Hamish?'

'Fine, fine, thank you,' he replied briskly.

'No, I mean, *really*. Are you getting over the shock of what's happened?'

Hamish paused for a moment. 'Well, everyone's been so supportive, you know. And, of course, it's not as if I'd really *known* Elena very well – or had a relationship with her for years or anything. So yes, the shock is wearing off a little now, but of course I'm very sad. She was so young and so beautiful, and if I hadn't brought her up here, she'd still be alive now. But Simon has been such a great help to both Magda and myself. We're both beginning to start to come to terms with things.'

'How is Magda?'

'She's quite an inspiration. Let's face it, she's lost her only sister and she's made the decision to stay in Locharran for now, but she's making a real effort to fit in. Simon's chatting to her right now, so I thought I'd leave them to it, escape for half an hour and find out how things were going down here.'

'So far, so good,' Ally replied, crossing her fingers.

He declined her offer of tea because he wanted to get back to the castle before Simon left. 'Don't put up with any nonsense from them!' were his parting words as he made his way towards the door.

After he'd gone, and as the Sinclairs had gone out too, Ally felt at a bit of a loose end. Ross was most probably up to his ears in birthday cake, and so what did she want to do now? She felt like some company, and Flora needed a walk, so Ally decided this might be an ideal time to pop in to see Linda.

'Believe it or not,' said Linda as she filled the kettle, 'I had four people for dinner last night! Four! They all had three courses, bottles of wine, coffee and liqueurs. It was good to be doing some proper cooking again after it being so quiet recently. So, how are things at the malthouse? I hear the Sinclairs have moved in?'

'They have indeed,' Ally said, rolling her eyes. '*She's* somewhat demanding, but I'm coping so far.'

'They're suspects though, aren't they?' Linda asked as she made a pot of tea.

'Yes, they are.'

'So you could be sleeping under the same roof as a killer, or a family of killers?' Linda remarked, looking wide-eyed at Ally.

'The thought has crossed my mind,' Ally agreed, 'but, as you know, my sleeping quarters are quite separate from theirs, and I have good locks on the door! Anyway, it's not as if I had much choice in the matter because there was nowhere else for them to go, and Hamish doesn't want them at the castle any more than they want to go there.'

Then she told Linda about her wrecked car.

'Oh, Ally, how terrifying! What have you done to upset anyone? Probably some maniac who doesn't like women drivers. What about the insurance?'

'Believe it or not, the earl insisted on having it fixed. He thinks it's something to do with Magda, but I'm well aware that it's me.'

Linda nodded. 'The only consolation I can offer you is a slice of my pineapple cake.'

'I'd die for a slice of your pineapple cake,' Ally said, laughing. She knew that denying herself this treat wasn't going to reduce her to a size six overnight. 'How're things with Callum?'

'Yeah, it's good.' Linda handed her a cup of tea and a

hefty slice of cake. 'Isn't it strange that we've lived virtually next door to each other for years, and it only really began when we bumped into each other that time in Glasgow of all places!'

'*Glasgow?*'

'Yeah, a few weeks ago. Didn't I tell you about that? I'm sure I did.'

'No, you *didn't*,' Ally said, her ears out on stalks.

'Well,' said Linda, 'what happened was that I went down on the train to Glasgow to visit a friend in hospital and decided I might as well have a meander round the shops while I was there. And' – here Linda giggled somewhat coquettishly – 'who should I bump into at lunchtime – none other than Callum Dalrymple!'

Ally almost choked on her tea. 'What was *he* doing in Glasgow?' As if she didn't know!

'He was on a hotel managers' course at the Osprey Hotel. Lovely place – do you know it?'

'No, I don't.' Ally shook her head and laid her cup down carefully.

'Oh, it's so luxurious! You and I must go on a shopping trip one of these days and have some lunch there!'

'So you met Callum?' Ally prompted.

'Yes, he had an hour off before he had to go back to the conference room where the course was taking place. So he insisted on taking me back to the hotel for some lunch at the bar and that's when we got chatting.'

'I thought you got chatting when you began making desserts for the Craigmonie?' Ally said.

'Oh no, it was because of our chat in the Osprey that he asked me if I'd be prepared to make the desserts as the previous supplier had pulled out.'

'You certainly didn't tell me any of this!' Ally exclaimed.

'I didn't think it was important,' Linda replied. 'It's not as if

I got to really know him that day or anything, although I must admit I thought he was rather nice.'

'So he was definitely on the course,' Ally said more to herself than to Linda.

'Yes, of course he was. At two o'clock he bade me farewell and joined a bunch of other grey-suited guys going into this conference room. He'd told me that there was to be an evening session as well, with lots of role playing, and he wouldn't be driving home until the next day, otherwise he'd have given me a lift.'

Ally took a deep breath. 'And you can remember when this was?'

Linda refilled their cups. 'Yes, because it was the day that poor woman's body was found in Loch Soular.'

Involuntarily, Ally let out a long sigh of relief.

'Why are you so interested?'

'I knew that Callum was supposed to be on a course, but...'

'You didn't honestly suspect him, did you?' Linda asked.

'I'm afraid I've been suspecting everyone,' Ally admitted, declining another piece of cake.

'Well, I can assure you that Callum was in Glasgow, and Ivan was apparently going crazy in his absence – rushing around like a madman, so I don't think he'd have had much time for killing either!'

'I'll just be so relieved to delete them both from my list of suspects,' Ally said with a sigh.

'You have a list?'

'In a manner of speaking,' Ally replied, thinking of her two dials and the motley collection of Post-its.

Linda grinned. 'I know you'll think I can see no wrong in Callum,' she said, 'because our relationship is so new, but, believe me, that man could no more kill anyone than I could fly to the moon!'

'You know something, Linda? I do believe you.'

'And you can forget all those rumours about Ivan changing his mind about getting married. One of the waitresses was telling me that, on the day Kristina should have got here, Ivan was so excited, even although he was manically busy. He kept rushing out to the bus stop to see if she'd arrived. We all know he drinks too much, but he would have had no wish – and certainly no opportunity – to kill poor Kristina.'

Ally nodded. She had no reason to doubt Linda and, when she got home, she would take great pleasure in removing two Post-its from her suspect board: Callum and Ivan.

TWENTY-TWO

Back home, Ally wasted no time in removing both Callum and Ivan from Kristina's dial. That only left Desdemona, who'd known for some weeks beforehand about Hamish's plans to marry. As did Randolph, Lavinia and Giles, of course. She doubted that any of them could have met her earlier though, but any of them could have mistaken Kristina for Elena, particularly as both women, who were of similar build, with blonde hair, had been due to arrive at the airport at about the same time on the same day. However, the Sinclairs had presumably been in London until just before the wedding.

As far as Ally could see now, it was obvious that Kristina's murder had been a case of mistaken identity. She removed the original two pieces of paper with the two clock faces drawn on them, took a fresh piece of A4 and fetched a plate from the dresser, round which she carefully drew one new clock face. She re-tacked the piece of paper to the back of the painting, picked up some fresh Post-its from the drawer and began to place her suspects round the dial.

There was no two ways about it: Desdemona had to be the prime suspect and so was placed firmly at twelve o'clock. Next came the Sinclairs. Should she post them on as one family or as individuals? After a moment's thought, she decided to post them as individuals, because Lavinia seemed – to her anyway – to have the greatest motive; she wanted to be a countess, and she wanted her son to be the earl. Besides which, Ally didn't like the woman and wouldn't put anything past her. Then there was Randolph – he was the one who would become the earl, with great status, the castle, the thousands of acres and a considerable fortune. Not that he wasn't rich enough already! She put Lavinia and Randolph either side of Desdemona at eleven and one. What about Giles? She knew little about him yet, but, of course, he would eventually become the heir. She had a feeling that he wasn't that bothered, but, nevertheless, he was a suspect with a motive, so he must go on the board. She put him at the bottom of the dial at six o'clock.

Who else? There was Mrs Fraser and Mrs Jamieson, of course. Ally still couldn't get Queenie's comment out of her mind that Mrs Fraser was glad that Elena had been got out of the way. But then it seemed that they didn't know about Elena's imminent arrival until the day before! So there was no way they could have mistaken Kristina for Elena. Nevertheless, there was still the very faint possibility that Kristina had tripped, fallen and bashed her head before she fell into the water, because according to Rigby, Kristina's post-mortem hadn't been a hundred per cent conclusive. And they were still suspects for Elena, so she positioned them at five o'clock and seven o'clock.

With the thought in mind that Kristina's death could have been accidental, it suddenly occurred to Ally that she had to consider the possibility that Magda could be a possible suspect – much as she hated the thought.

There was a lot she needed to discuss with Ross.

. . .

Morag arrived at nine o'clock the next morning, just before the Sinclairs sauntered into the dining room at half past. Ally had laid out all her usual supplies but had been unable to add anything extra because Queenie's shop did not open on Sundays between October and April.

Nevertheless, breakfast progressed smoothly, with Ally confirming that the milk had originated from a cow and not a goat. At which Lavinia had wrinkled her nose and asked, 'No chance of oat milk or almond milk in these backwoods, I suppose?'

'I'll check it out today,' Ally replied, watching Lavinia about to feast on her three prunes again. Fortunately, there were no complaints from husband and son, who seemed to have voracious appetites.

It was while she was delivering their two breakfasts that Lavinia, having almost finished her prunes, said, 'Have you ever considered an interior designer to jazz up this place a bit, Ally?'

While Ally was rendered momentarily speechless, Giles choked on his hash browns and said, 'You looking for a job then, Mother?' He and his father both sniggered.

'Of course not!' Lavinia snapped before turning back to Ally. 'I admit my charges are a little high,' she said, daintily removing a stone from the final prune and setting it neatly on the side of her bowl with her long, red fingernails, 'but I have transformed some of the most luxurious residences in the South-East, and I'd be happy to give you some free advice.'

'Well, thank you,' Ally said, 'but I prefer to keep my décor simple, using natural materials where possible. This is just a simple, country guest house, you see.'

'It's fine as it is,' Randolph muttered.

'Perhaps,' Lavinia continued doubtfully, 'but I feel the need for *colour* – some feature walls perhaps.'

'I'll keep your very generous offer in mind,' Ally said before escaping to the kitchen, hoping she didn't sound too sarcastic and trying not to feel too irritated by Lavinia's remarks. Ally liked the malthouse the way it was, with its golden oak beams and doors, flagstone floors downstairs and the chalky off-white paint.

No doubt about it, Lavinia was a bossy, self-opinionated woman, and if Ally had to choose which of the Sinclairs was a killer, Lavinia would definitely be her choice. Ally was now hoping she could take Desdemona out of the twelve o'clock spot and replace her with Lavinia.

A little later, when the Sinclairs had gone back up to their newly serviced rooms, and Morag had collapsed onto a kitchen chair, accepting a mug of tea, Ally asked casually, 'How are you getting on with cleaning their rooms?'

'Now, I'm glad ye brought that up because ye're goin' to have to tell that woman up there to stop leavin' her stuff all over the floor, Ally! I'm not a lady's maid! Ye can tell her that it's stoppin' yer cleaner from doin' her job properly, like ye said. And there's make-up on the pillowcases, so why does the silly cow not take off her make-up when she goes to bed? Tell me that?'

'That I don't know,' Ally replied with a sigh.

Later, when Morag had gone home and Ally had cleared up downstairs, she decided to take Flora for a walk. After they'd set off, Ally found herself automatically on the path which led to Loch Soular. She was determined not to let Kristina's death put her off one of her favourite walks to her favourite place. It was also a twenty-minute walk each way through the heather and, even today under cloudy skies and a brisk wind, there was something special about it. There was now a thick carpet of leaves around the whole area, which crunched underneath her feet. The purple of the heather was beginning to fade a little, and the surface of the loch was quite rough, so there were no reflections to be seen, but the setting was still magnificent.

She watched Flora digging happily in the sand, and as she watched a seagull landing on the roof of the little rustic boathouse, Ally remembered again why she had fallen in love with this little corner of the world.

She found her thoughts going back to that day when she first found Kristina's body floating on the loch. Ally was, by now, almost certain that Kristina's murder had to be down to a case of mistaken identity. And if that was the case, Desdemona had to be the main suspect for both murders. She wondered if Rigby had come to the same conclusion. Should she go and tell him about the monkshood in Desdemona's garden? She realised now that she should have told him this before. It could be a key piece of evidence.

'Oat milk?' Queenie exploded. She looked at Ally as if she'd gone completely bonkers. 'Oat milk? What's that?'

'It's a very healthy option to animal milk, I'm told,' Ally said, burrowing through the cereals to find one with the magic label 'organic'.

Queenie shook her head. 'There is nothin' unhealthy about cow's milk, or goat's milk,' she said, 'or sheep's milk, for that matter!'

'Yes, I know that,' Ally said, 'but I have this guest...'

'The one that was at the Craigmonie?' asked Queenie.

Ally sighed and nodded.

'Aye, well, they were always wantin' somethin' and makin' a fuss. I did warn ye.' Queenie shook her head in disbelief. 'Oat milk!'

'Yes, and I don't suppose you do almond milk either?'

'Almond milk!' Queenie looked above for guidance. 'Can I tell ye somethin', Mrs McKinley?'

'Oh, please do,' Ally said.

'I might've left school at fifteen, but do ye know what? Ye *canna* milk an oat or an almond!'

'That's true,' Ally agreed, 'but I just thought I'd ask.'

As she walked home, Ally tried to decide if she should order a supply of oat milk and some different organic cereals from Inverness or somewhere, or stick to what she could source locally. She wasn't due to do a big supermarket shop in Inverness until the next week, so she decided she'd see if Callum had oat milk in the kitchens at the Craigmonie that she could buy to placate Lavinia for now.

In fact, apart from Lavinia's requests, the family were – so far anyway – behaving perfectly reasonably. Of course, they weren't paying this time – Hamish was, unlike at the Craigmonie. And she only saw them at breakfast time, when she avoided conversation where possible, fearing that they could bring up the subject of Hamish and his bride again. Ally couldn't forget their harsh remarks at the wedding reception.

In the meantime, she had to find a polite way to ask Lavinia to remove the pile of clothes from the floor so that Morag could get the vacuum cleaner in.

Ross called in for a cup of tea before starting his evening shift at the surgery.

'How's it going with the Monsters?' he asked, referring to her guests.

'Better than I expected, although Lavinia wants to add walls of colour all over the malthouse.'

'*What?*'

'Apparently she's an interior designer, and colour would appear to be her forte.'

Ross shook his head. 'Don't you let her anywhere near your walls. This place is perfect just as it is.'

Pleased with the compliment, Ally then related her conversation with Linda and the subsequent removal of Callum and Ivan's Post-its from Kristina's dial, meaning that she could reduce her board to one dial instead of two.

'That sounds very sensible,' said Ross. 'And where have you put the Monsters?'

'Well, even though the Monsters were presumably in London until just before the wedding,' Ally said, 'I've put Lavinia at eleven o'clock, Randolph at one o'clock and Giles at six o'clock.'

'Very wise,' said Ross.

'And I'm bringing Mrs Fraser and Mrs Jamieson down to five o'clock and seven o'clock.'

'What about Magda?' Ross asked.

'Strange you should mention her,' Ally said. 'I've been thinking about Magda.'

'You can't rule her out as a suspect for Elena's murder.'

Ally nodded slowly. 'I've realised that.'

'I know you've become fond of her, and so it's difficult for you to see this dispassionately, but—'

'No buts,' Ally interrupted. 'She's on the clock face now because I realised she had to be a suspect, assuming Kristina's death could have been an accident.'

'I'm glad you agree. Let's face it, we don't know anything about them or about their life before we met them here. Maybe they've never got on. Perhaps Magda was jealous that Elena was prettier and more outgoing? Perhaps Elena had always stolen Magda's boyfriends? I mean, what do *we* know?'

'In that case, why would she accompany Elena to Scotland? Why not stay at home and be glad to see the back of her?' Ally asked, wanting to find a reason for Magda not to be a suspect.

'Perhaps Magda too wanted a new beginning, particularly after losing her parents and then having that difficult break-up with her boyfriend,' Ross suggested. 'She may have thought she'd have more luck finding love somewhere new. Then, when she arrives here, she sets eyes on the castle – and the earl – and decided that's what she'd like for herself. As a devoted sister, it would have been comparatively easy for her to pop something into Elena's drink or food before, or during, the reception.'

'That's possible,' Ally replied reluctantly.

'I'm glad you're beginning to see it from my point of view. If you hadn't become fond of Magda, you'd have had her high up on your clock face from the beginning.'

'No, I'm convinced it was one killer, and that Kristina's murder was a case of mistaken identity. Magda hadn't arrived in Scotland until after Kristina's death, but if Kristina's death was an accident, which seems unlikely, then Magda's not off the hook.'

Ross glanced at his watch, still looking somewhat unconvinced. 'I'd better go. I've only ten minutes to get down there. But how about I come up tomorrow evening and we have a takeaway pasta of some kind?'

'That would be lovely,' Ally agreed as they hugged.

'I'm sorry if I've offended you with what I said about Magda,' he said as he kissed her, 'but think it over.'

'I will,' Ally said and gave him a kiss.

After he'd gone, Ally did think that what Ross said was possible, even though she didn't like the idea. She knew that, but, after all, she had come to the same conclusion herself. And she couldn't forget the way Magda had looked so adoringly at Hamish whenever he appeared. She'd got herself a bedroom next door to his, and he was giving her a dog. And, not to make too fine a point of it, she had recovered remarkably quickly from the death of her only sister. Had Rigby noticed any of this? Did he suspect her?

Ally felt rather surprised to discover that she really needed to have a chat with Rigby before too long. Apart from anything else, she needed tell him about the monkshood in Desdemona's garden. Well, at least it would be an excuse to get to talk to him. After all, at the present moment, Desdemona really was the prime suspect, unless Ross's suspicions were right and the Sinclairs might have been in Scotland at the time of Kristina's death. How could she find out? Which of the family would be best to gently interrogate?

Ally looked down at the dog. 'I'm not much of a detective, am I, Flora?'

TWENTY-THREE

The following morning after an uneventful breakfast, Ally remembered that she was supposed to be doing something about Lavinia's clothes strewn across the floor. She also knew that Morag would be eavesdropping to make sure that she did. And so, as Lavinia made her way towards the staircase, Ally asked, 'Could I have a word, please?'

Lavinia turned, frowning. 'Yes?'

Ally cleared her throat. 'My cleaning lady is a little concerned about not being able to clean your room properly because of clothes lying on the floor, so I wonder if you'd be kind enough to remove them, please?'

'Is there some reason why *she* can't pick them up?' asked Lavinia. 'Is she disabled or something?'

Ally swallowed the fury she could feel rising in her stomach but knew she had to keep her cool. 'No, Lavinia, but she is *not* a lady's maid, and she should not have to tidy up after you in order to clean the room! She's an excellent cleaner, and I am not prepared to lose her services.'

Lavinia snorted. 'I should have known that coming to an inferior establishment such as this would present problems.'

Ally could control her anger no longer. 'Perhaps it's slipped your mind that the reason you're all here is because you are suspects in a murder case, and there was nowhere else for you to go! And may I remind you that your very generous cousin is footing the bill! So please remove your clothes from the floor. May I also ask you to remove your make-up before you go to bed because it's ruining my bed linen.'

Without waiting for a reply, Ally marched out of the hallway and into the kitchen, slamming the door behind her and almost colliding with Morag, who'd had her ear pressed close to the door.

'Och, ye did well, Ally!' Morag said, giving her ear a rub.

'Remains to be seen if it has any effect,' Ally said. 'But what a despicable woman she is!'

She heard the sound of a motor outside and, on looking out, Ally was delighted to see her silver Golf, good as new, sitting on the drive.

Randolph and Lavinia disappeared shortly afterwards. Ally had no idea where they went, but they always took their car, so it was unlikely to be anywhere nearby. In their absence, she vacu-umed the dining room and hallway, and then looked into the sitting room to ensure that it was tidy, where she was surprised to see Giles Sinclair sprawled on the sofa with his phone.

'Sorry, Giles, I didn't realise anyone was in here,' Ally said, switching off the vacuum cleaner.

'That's OK – go ahead,' Giles said, glancing up from his phone. 'I'm sorry, but I get fed up of being in my room.'

'Your parents have gone out somewhere then?'

'They're both golf mad,' Giles said. 'It's the only place where they get on. Thank God they found a golf course here, somewhere down near the coast.'

Ally felt a rush of sympathy for this rather lonely boy,

remembering how he'd loved playing with the dogs in the garden and how he wasn't allowed to have one himself. 'Well, if it's of any interest, there are some board games and jigsaw puzzles in the cupboard over there,' she said rather lamely.

'Not really my thing,' Giles said, wrinkling his nose, 'but it's OK because I've got my phone.'

Which is fine, Ally thought, as long as the Wi-Fi doesn't go on the blink. 'I should warn you, Giles, that we do sometimes get power cuts. It's to do with our position here in the mountains.' Seeing panic in his eyes, she added, 'But not very often.'

He nodded in a resigned way. 'How are the dogs?' he asked somewhat wistfully.

'Well, the larger one, Ebony, isn't here at the moment because that's my friend's dog, but Flora is in the kitchen. I try not to let her stray into the rest of the house.'

'Oh, OK,' he said.

Then a thought occurred to Ally. 'You're welcome to come into the kitchen to see her, if you'd like to.' Even as she spoke, she could see him brightening up.

'Could I?'

'Of course. Follow me.'

As they entered the kitchen, Flora leaped up, excited at the prospect of a visitor, tail wagging furiously.

'Do sit down,' Ally said, holding Flora back with her collar, 'but don't let her jump all over you because she's been out in the garden and has muddy paws,' She had visions of a confrontation with Lavinia on the subject.

While Giles was stroking the dog, he looked round the kitchen. 'This is nice,' he said. 'I like the stove.' He pointed at the wood burner.

'It's my favourite room,' Ally confessed.

'Wish we had a kitchen like this,' he said wistfully.

'I'm sure you have a very beautiful kitchen,' Ally said.

Giles snorted. 'You wouldn't want to sit in ours,' he said,

'even if you were allowed to! All streamlined, state-of-the-art, very shiny. Nothing on display. Sterile.'

Ally could well imagine the Sinclair kitchen. She resolved never to let Lavinia get her nose round the door of this one. 'And I bet you have an *island* in that kitchen of yours!' she exclaimed.

'A huge island,' Giles confirmed. 'And stools along one side which no one's ever sat on.'

For the life of her, Ally couldn't imagine Lavinia doing any cooking, so she wasn't surprised. 'Would you like a cup of tea or coffee?' she asked him.

He looked up from fondling Flora's ears. 'Could I have a hot chocolate?'

'Yes, of course you can. In fact, I quite fancy one myself,' Ally replied as she delved into the cupboard.

There was a comfortable silence while Ally made the hot chocolates and Giles continued petting the dog. Then, as she handed him his drink, she asked, 'Are you in college, or university or whatever?'

He pulled a face. 'I'm just about to move up from Westminster. Westminster School, that is.'

Yes, of course, Ally thought, if it wasn't Eton, it would be Westminster. 'So you'll be heading for university then?'

'There's a slight difference of opinion as to where I go next,' Giles replied. 'The parents want me to do law or financial studies.'

'And you don't?' Ally sat down opposite him.

'Not really my thing,' he replied, 'because what I'd really like to do is media studies, but they both go ballistic if I even mention it.'

'So what would be your ultimate aim?'

'Production, direction, in the film or TV business,' he said. 'Something like that.'

Ally proffered the box of shortbread, from which he carefully selected a large piece.

Flora was now on high alert. 'Don't give her any,' Ally said. 'Flora, like all Labs, is extremely greedy and liable to become overweight.' As she replaced the box, she pretended not to notice Giles breaking off a tiny piece and dropping it on the floor where Flora moved at the speed of light to gobble it up.

'The film world can be very precarious,' Ally said, chucking another log into the stove.

'I guess so,' he said, 'but it's what I really want to do. I guess there are loads of jobs in the industry that I haven't even heard of.'

'Before I came up here,' Ally said, 'I was a researcher for a TV company in Edinburgh. I know how many people it takes to put a TV programme on the screen, far less a movie. There are hundreds of jobs involved, Giles. You don't have to be a big-time producer or director, you know. As far as production is concerned, you'd spend all your time getting the finances to put the thing together, so you'd be better off with a maths degree than anything. And, for everything else, you could do what I did when I was starting out – make the tea and run errands.'

'A runner?'

'A runner,' Ally confirmed, laughing. 'I can't help feeling that a degree in English or politics could lead to an interesting position in the film business.'

Giles shrugged as he stared into the fire. 'They were making a film near Culloden Battlefield when we were in Inverness,' he said. 'I'd like to have been an extra, but neither Mum or Dad were prepared to run me out to the set each day.'

Ally was suddenly alert. 'When was that?'

'Shortly before we came here,' Giles replied, munching the last piece of his shortbread.

'So you didn't come directly up from London for the wedding?' Ally asked.

'Hell no! We've been up here for *weeks*! They found this golf course near Inverness, out near the airport somewhere, and they played there every damned day.'

'Did they now?' Ally asked.

Ally hadn't set eyes on Rigby for quite a while, and so decided it was time to visit the little police station which had been set up in the village 'temporarily' but, as yet, showed little sign of closing.

'The inspector is a busy man,' said the constable importantly when she rang up in the afternoon to make an appointment.

'I should hope he is,' Ally retorted, tempted to add 'with two murders to solve'. Instead she said, 'I was hoping he could spare me fifteen minutes or so as I have some information for him.'

She could hear a sigh at the other end of the phone. 'Well,' said the constable grudgingly, 'he could probably spare you a few minutes at quarter to five.'

'I'll be there,' she said. Of course he could spare her a few minutes because he hadn't made any arrests yet! *And he'll be sure to wonder if I know something that he doesn't.*

In fact, at a quarter to five, Rigby was quite amenable.

'I was thinking of coming up to see you,' he informed her after they'd exchanged pleasantries. 'I wondered how you were getting on with the Sinclairs? I'm sorry you got landed with them, but I didn't trust them to move out of the area.'

'Well, I'm aware that I've got three possible suspects under my roof, so thought it was time I updated you,' Ally said with an exaggerated smile.

'Are they behaving themselves then?'

'Randolph is OK, not particularly friendly but doesn't complain – so far at least,' Ally said. 'But Lavinia is a complainer, very untidy, wants food that's difficult to get round here, that sort of thing. I like the son though.'

'He always appears bored with the whole thing,' Rigby said. 'Did you know that they've actually joined the Faoileag Club?'

'What on earth is that?' Ally asked.

'It's a very exclusive golf club, the only one down here, down near the coast. Very few people get accepted, not even – I'm told – a certain American president with a Scottish mother! Don't know how true that is, of course. But when I interviewed the treasurer, he said that the only reason they were accepted was because they are reckoned to be the likely heirs to the Sinclair Estate and the golf course is, part of it at least, on the earl's estate.'

'Lavinia must be in her element!' Ally exclaimed.

'What it indicates to me,' said Rigby, 'is that they have every intention of inheriting now that Elena is out of the way.'

'I had wondered where they went every day,' Ally said, 'because, until this morning, I had no idea there was a golf course round here, until their son said they'd found a club in the area, but he didn't tell me it was such an exclusive one. What did you say it was called?'

'Gaelic pronunciation isn't my thing,' Rigby said, 'but it sounds like "feolag" although it's spelled FAOILEAG which, I'm assured, means "seagull".'

'Interesting name.' Ally paused. 'The boy, Giles, doesn't go with them. He stays in the malthouse, obviously bored and lonely.'

'A potential killer, would you say?'

'Very unlikely, Inspector. But he has given me some interesting information. Which is why I decided to talk to you today.'

'And what's that?' Rigby asked.

'The Sinclairs were in Scotland, in Inverness, for a couple of weeks before the earl's wedding,' Ally said.

'Yes, we knew that,' Rigby said, somewhat dismissively.

'Oh,' Ally said, taken a little aback. 'And you don't think that's strange?'

'No, not very,' Rigby said.

'Well, did you know that they chose to play their golf at a course close to the airport as opposed to the one in Inverness itself?'

Rigby shrugged. 'We didn't check out specific golf courses. Perhaps they just liked to be out in the countryside?'

'But the proximity to the airport could be important because Hamish's bride would have flown into Inverness.'

Rigby looked thoughtful. 'Did you manage to squeeze any more information out of the son?'

'Well, we did get quite chatty, and I've told him he can take my dog out for a walk any time he likes. He loves dogs but isn't allowed to have one. He's confided in me that he wants to work in films, but his parents want him to have a degree in finance or something.'

Rigby rolled his eyes. 'Do you think he might open up some more to you?'

'Possibly. I could do some gentle probing.'

'Do that, please,' said Rigby. 'They are suspects, of course, but I'm more interested in Desdemona Morton. She was in no hurry to inform me about picking up Kristina from the airport. And nobody saw her when she supposedly broke down at Cairn Cross, so we only have her word for that. No chance, I suppose, that you're on a chatty basis with her too?'

Ally realised that Rigby was, in his own way, asking for her help. 'I'm not exactly on a chatty basis with her, but I could try. In fact, I've just recently bought another of her paintings, which she hasn't delivered yet, so perhaps I should go to collect it?'

'Perhaps you should,' Rigby said with a slight smile.

'As a matter of interest, have they discovered yet what the poison was that killed Elena?'

'They've excluded a whole range of unpronounceable poisons, but they're no closer to coming up with a definite cause of death,' Rigby replied.

'I feel I should tell you that Desdemona grows monkshood in her garden,' Ally said.

Rigby frowned. 'Monkshood?'

'A very poisonous plant with purple flowers. It certainly looked like monkshood to me anyway when I saw it growing in her borders.'

Rigby studied her for a moment. 'And how come you know so much about this?'

'I used to be a researcher for a TV company and, while I was working on a crime drama, I had to research it because they wanted to use it as the method of killing. It was chosen because it's highly poisonous and very difficult to detect.'

'How very interesting!' Rigby looked thoughtful and began to scribble on his notepad. 'Perhaps it's time I visited Miss Morton again – and take Sergeant Shaw with me this time. He's a manic gardener, spends every free moment digging, cutting, pruning and all that.'

Ally nodded. 'Before you go, it might be an idea to have him google monkshood, so he knows what it looks like. I can't imagine he grows a row of it between his potatoes and his carrots!'

'Good point,' Rigby remarked, scribbling furiously. 'Thank you for that information – it's certainly not something I'd ever have picked up on.' He paused for a moment. 'No one else in this place has anything much to do with any of the suspects on a personal level, so if you do get chatting, perhaps you'd pass on anything relevant.'

This time Rigby was actually asking for help.

As Ally stood up to go, he said, 'I'm convinced we're looking for just one killer for both these murders.'

'I think so too,' Ally said.

'And, in my opinion, it must have been a case of mistaken identity as far as Kristina's death was concerned,' Rigby added.

'Most likely,' Ally confirmed.

'Keep in touch, Mrs McKinley,' he said.

TWENTY-FOUR

'You must meet my puppy!' Magda sounded positively childlike in her enthusiasm when she called Ally the following morning.

'Why don't you bring him down here?' Ally asked.

'But I'd rather not come to the malthouse, please. I don't want to see *them*... I still think they killed my sister.'

'That's not been proved yet, Magda,' Ally reminded her, 'but I can understand how you feel. So why don't we meet up at the little shelter? It's the little stone hut halfway down the path from the castle towards my house, with a wooden seat inside. Wait for me there, and we can walk across the moor together. I'll be finished by about midday, and the Sinclairs have already gone out.'

She then proceeded to have a look into Lavinia's bedroom. Morag had only said that 'things are a bit better', but due to the fact that she hadn't gone on and on about it, Ally guessed that things must have improved greatly.

It was fairly tidy, with only a damp towel on the bathroom floor. Ally could see that Morag had been polishing mirrors, and she took a moment to study the collection of very expensive cosmetics and perfumes on the dressing table. Then, on impulse, she had a quick look in the wardrobe and was appalled to find so many designer clothes hanging haphazardly, half on and half off hangers, and an equal amount lying on the floor below. What had the silly woman done – just kicked them from the bedroom floor into the wardrobe? Well, that was Lavinia's problem, and as long as it didn't affect Morag's cleaning, it wouldn't affect her either.

Shortly before noon, Ally and Flora set out to meet Magda and Benny. When they arrived at the little stone shelter, Magda was already there, sitting inside on the wooden bench, and throwing a ball for yet another black Labrador puppy. He was bigger than Ally had anticipated.

'Here's Benny!' Magda said proudly, pointing towards the dog. Benny was more interested in his ball and playing with Flora than he was in meeting Ally.

'He's a big boy,' Ally remarked.

'Yes, they didn't give him to me until he'd had all his jabs,' said Magda.

'He's lovely, Magda,' said Ally, watching Flora and Benny chase each other.

'I know – he's so sweet. He's still such a baby.' She sighed. 'It always make me sad that I never had a baby of my own...'

'There's still time, surely?' Ally asked. 'I had my children when I was about your age.'

Magda nodded sadly. 'I've been told by several doctors that it might not be possible to have children.'

Ally felt a wave of sadness at the tone of Magda's voice. She gave Magda a little hug. 'I'm so sorry,' she said.

They set off across the moor with the dogs cavorting together.

'How are *you*, Magda?' Ally asked, noting that Magda was still wearing make-up.

'I'm doing better, thank you, Ally,' Magda replied, her eyes sparkling. 'Hamish is so kind to me, and I finally feel safe.'

'I'm so glad,' Ally agreed with a smile. 'And is Simon still helping you?'

'Yes, he also is a very kind man. Sometimes I think it's like he sees inside my head.' Magda pointed at her forehead. 'Like he knows what I'm thinking. And the pills he's giving me are making me feel less mixed up.'

Ally frowned. 'Pills?'

'I can't remember what they're called, but he says they're for my anxiety,' Magda said, nodding, 'I haven't been taking them for long, but I think they're helping.'

In spite of being somewhat surprised that Magda needed medication, Ally supposed she couldn't really argue with that. 'Good. And... I hope Hamish is behaving himself?' Ally wondered if she should warn Magda of Hamish's reputation as a bit of a ladies' man.

Magda laughed. 'Oh no, Hamish is wonderful. He's been so kind to me, and I love living with him at the castle. He's a very good boy!' Here she dissolved into giggles.

Ally stole a sideways glance at her as they walked. Magda had appeared partial to Hamish from the beginning, but was it possible that she was falling for his undoubted charms? She glanced at her and was struck again by how happy she looked. She'd never seen Magda look anything other than a little sad and fearful, forever in the shadow of her pretty sister. But hopefully, she thought, this change of demeanour was due to the dog.

As they tramped through the heather, Ally remembered Ross's words. Not for a moment did she believe that Magda had killed her sister, and she most definitely had had nothing to do with Kristina's death as she hadn't even arrived in the country then. And Ally, like Rigby, was certain that there was only one killer for both women.

'I must be back for lunch at one o'clock,' Magda said, consulting her watch and turning around. 'I don't want to keep Hamish waiting.'

They began walking back towards the castle. 'Have they released Elena's body yet?' Ally asked quietly, knowing full well that this was highly unlikely.

Magda shook her head. 'Not yet. But when they do, Hamish says we'll bury her at the castle. Then I'll always be close to her.'

Magda was plainly not planning to move out any time soon. Ally couldn't decide if this was going to prove to be a blessing or a disaster. Perhaps it was time to say something.

'I know that Hamish is a kind man,' she said, 'but he's very fond of the ladies, you know.'

'Yes, yes, I know,' Magda replied brusquely. 'Angus said so too, while I was helping him with the dogs.'

'What did Angus say?'

'He said something about Hamish having trouble keeping it in his trousers. That he needs to grow up. Grow up?' Magda exploded with laughter at the idea. 'He's over seventy!'

Well, she's been warned, Ally thought as they parted company at the shelter shortly afterwards. *She has been warned.*

When she got home, she prepared a casserole for the evening. Ross was doing an afternoon shift at the surgery and was coming up later. As she sat down with a sandwich and a cup of coffee, Ally felt strangely restless, recalling her conversation with Rigby and her meeting with Magda. She could do little about Magda, who was a grown woman with a broken engagement in her past, and who should have some knowledge of men by now.

If she was falling in love with Hamish, there was little Ally could do about it. Although, if it weren't for the fact that Magda wasn't in Scotland when poor Kristina died, Ally would have had Magda firmly stuck to her clock face. Magda was obviously besotted with Hamish, and he certainly was a catch in spite of his age. Sisters had been murdered for less. But somehow, Ally was certain Magda wasn't responsible for *her* sister's death.

When it came to Desdemona, Ally wasn't so sure... Desdemona had a Land Rover, of course, but goodness only knew what colour it originally was, since it was permanently covered in a layer of mud. And Ally was pretty sure it hadn't been a woman who'd knocked her off the road.

Rumours were rife in the village that Desdemona had poisoned her own sister out of jealousy because Ophelia had stolen Hamish from her all those years ago. Desdemona was one of the few people Hamish had confided in about Elena, so would have been well aware that his new fiancée was coming to Scotland.

When she offered Kristina a lift, Desdemona could easily have mistaken Kristina for Hamish's wife-to-be, and might have wanted her out of the way. Perhaps she still hung on to dreams about becoming the Countess of Locharran – even after all these years? She had the means and the motive to kill Kristina, albeit through mistaken identity, and she also had the means and the motive to kill Elena. She'd been at the top of her suspect list for a while now, and the more Ally thought about it, the more credible it seemed that Desdemona really was the key suspect, but how could she prove it?

As she had promised Rigby, she would attempt to get some more information from Desdemona. As an excuse for a visit, she could collect her painting, since Desdemona had plainly forgotten about delivering it. It was a bit of a drive out to Desdemona's remote lochside residence, with no guarantee of her being there, and she didn't have the woman's mobile number, so there was no way of checking. Flora was fast asleep in her basket but, remembering the bunch of noisy, muddy dogs, perhaps it would be best to leave her there. Just as she was trying to make up her mind about this, there was a knock at the front door.

When she opened it, Ally couldn't believe her eyes. Because there stood Desdemona, as if Ally's thoughts had magically summoned her, complete with the bubble-wrapped painting. For a moment, she was completely dumbstruck.

'Sorry for the delay in delivering this,' Desdemona said. 'I forgot all about it.'

'We must be telepathic,' Ally said, 'because I was just, this very minute, planning to come up to you to see if the painting was ready. Do come in.' She stood aside to let Desdemona and the painting in, before leading the way into the kitchen.

'Whew! It's warm in here!' Desdemona exclaimed, casting off her fur-lined gilet.

'Well, the Aga's in here as well. It provides the central heating and does most of my cooking,' Ally said, pointing across the room. She'd never been inside Desdemona's residence – apart from her gallery – but didn't imagine there'd be a great deal of heating going on in there.

Desdemona handed Ally the painting.

'Oh, that's so beautiful!' Ally exclaimed as she removed the wrapping. 'Thank you so much!'

'Well, you paid for it,' Desdemona said, warming her hands in front of the wood burner.

'How about a cup of tea?' Ally asked, standing back to further admire the picture. *This woman really is a very talented artist*, she thought, wondering how much paintings such as these would cost from the gallery in London.

'Black, please,' said the artist, 'and two sugars.'

'I take mine black too,' Ally said.

Desdemona stood and looked around the kitchen and then her eyes alighted on the oranges, lemons and grapes on the wall. She walked straight across to it, her nose almost touching the canvas. 'This is very good,' she said. 'Who painted this?'

'I've no idea,' Ally replied. 'My grandmother brought it back from Italy.'

'The brushwork is quite superb,' Desdemona said. She stroked it gently. 'Is there a signature on the back?'

'No, no,' said Ally hastily. 'I've checked it very carefully!' How would Desdemona react if she saw the board on the back with the clock face and discovered that Ally had her down as the chief suspect for both Elena and Kristina's murders?

Ally made a mug of tea for them both and then sat down opposite, wondering how to broach the subject of the recent murders. After a minute, she said casually, 'I think Hamish is now beginning to get over the shock of Elena's death.'

Desdemona frowned. 'There wasn't much to get over, was there? He hardly knew her.' She took a noisy slurp of tea.

'Well no, but I think he really loved her. And it must have been an awful shock to have his bride die just hours after the wedding,' Ally said.

'I've no doubt he'll find solace elsewhere,' Desdemona said sharply. 'It didn't take him very long after my sister died.'

'That must have been awful. I believe she had an allergy, didn't she?'

She gave a deep sigh. 'Well, that's what they came up with in the end, but I never knew her to be allergic to anything. And I wasn't even able to be at her funeral because I'd had my appendix out the day before she died.'

Ally was taken aback for a moment; this wasn't at all what she'd been led to believe. Then she noticed Desdemona's eyes had filled with tears.

'She was my little sister and I loved her dearly,' she said. 'Do you have a sister?'

Ally shook her head. 'No, but I have a brother, and I'd be devastated if anything should happen to him.'

'Of course, everyone thought I wasn't at the funeral because I was jealous,' Desdemona went on. She looked hard at Ally as she spoke, as if challenging her to deny it. 'But nothing could be further from the truth.'

'I don't pay a great deal of attention to local gossip,' Ally said, placing the biscuit tin on the table. 'Would you like a biscuit?'

'No, thank you. I don't eat sweet stuff.'

Ally desperately wanted to keep the conversation going. As she tried to think how to coax more information out of her, Desdemona said, 'Hamish and I were lovers once, you know.' She gulped some more tea. 'For several years.'

'I had heard something to that effect,' Ally said cautiously.

'He wanted to marry me.' She gave a sigh. 'I've never wanted to be married. I like being on my own.'

Before Ally could decide what she should say next, Desdemona continued, 'Our relationship finished well before Ophelia came on the scene. I found something out about Hamish that ended things for me.'

Ally took a deep breath. 'Which was...?'

Desdemona shook her head. 'Ask him yourself since you're so friendly with him. Anyway, it finished our relationship as far as I was concerned. I told Ophelia because I felt she had a right to know, but it didn't bother her at all. Each to their own.' Desdemona sighed. 'Hamish and I have remained close friends since Ophelia died, but on a purely platonic basis. No one believes that, of course!'

'Whatever Hamish confided in you, it must have been something you felt very strongly about?' Ally asked hopefully, trying to tempt her into telling more.

'For me, yes. But as I say, not for my sister, and perhaps not for you.' She sniffed. 'You still like the picture?'

'I *love* the picture!' Ally said truthfully. 'I've hung your other paintings in the bedrooms but I'm going to keep this one downstairs.' She looked at the tiny Lowry-like figure near the loch – a feature in all of Desdemona's paintings.

Desdemona drained her tea and stood up. 'I hear you've got the dreaded Sinclair family here, so good luck with that.

Rather you than me having a family of killers under your roof.'

'You really think they're the killers?' Ally asked as they reached the front door.

Desdemona turned round and stared defiantly at Ally. 'Who else did you have in mind?'

Ally gulped. 'No idea really,' she said hastily.

'I'm not sure our Inspector Rigby has much idea either,' Desdemona said as she headed towards her muddy old Land Rover. 'Thanks for the tea.'

As Ally watched her climbing into the Land Rover she peered at the number plate. It was covered in mud, but she could clearly see an X, and what could well have been a nine.

'I've had quite a day,' Ally told Ross when he arrived in the evening. 'Desdemona delivered my painting, and I had a good look at her Land Rover. There was definitely an X in the registration, but I couldn't be sure about the nine. It could easily have been the one that pushed me off the road.'

Ross looked horrified. 'Have you told Rigby about this? After all, she was the chief suspect on your board, and now you're telling me she might have been the person to knock you off the road. Promise me you'll get in touch with Rigby tomorrow?'

Ally nodded. 'OK, I promise. How was your day?'

Ross shook his head sadly. 'Not the best. I've had to put down a lovely old Border collie that I've known since he was a pup. He's had a good innings though because he was nearly fourteen and still working. Even the farmer, normally a stalwart old fellow, had tears in his eyes.'

'Oh, that's the worst part of caring for animals,' Ally said, giving him a hug, remembering her own grief when they'd had to have their old Labrador put down years ago.

'So I need cheering up,' Ross added with a grin, 'and a gin and tonic would help!' With that, he produced a large bottle of Bombay Sapphire and several cans of tonic.

'You sure know how to win round a lady,' Ally joked.

'You ain't no lady – you're a one-off,' Ross quipped, taking two glasses down from the shelf.

'If you say so, sir,' Ally replied, getting ice from the fridge.

A few minutes later, as they sat down with their drinks, Ross said, 'Fire away. What's been happening up here?'

Ally recounted her conversation with Giles.

Ross was astounded. 'What? They actually *chose* to play their golf out near the airport? The golf course in Inverness is far better.'

'He didn't elaborate,' Ally said, 'but I'm hoping that, now we're on a friendly basis, he might tell me more. I've been to Rigby and told him.'

'Do you mean Rigby didn't *know*?'

'He knew they were in Inverness before Hamish's wedding, and he knew they were golfers, but he didn't think to ask them *where* they played,' Ally said.

'Very remiss of him,' Ross remarked.

'I thought so too,' Ally said before telling him of her walk across the moor with Magda and her puppy. 'I think Magda is really smitten with Hamish.'

Ross shrugged. 'Not much we can do about that.'

Then Ally told him about Desdemona's visit. 'That I found *very* interesting. After years of being lovers, she ended it suddenly when she found out something about Hamish. I tried to wheedle it out of her, but she wasn't having any of it.'

'As you've already found out for yourself,' Ross said, 'folk round here much prefer to believe the juiciest rumours.'

'She'd finished with Hamish well before her sister came on the scene,' Ally said, 'and the reason that she didn't attend Ophelia's funeral was because she was having her appendix removed at the time. But she and Ophelia had never fallen out over Hamish, and although Desdemona and Hamish are still great friends, it's purely platonic.'

'Well, you've certainly succeeded in getting her to divulge the information,' Ross said admiringly. 'She's normally very standoffish with everyone, so I'm very impressed. Now, you've got to get chatting to that Sinclair boy again, Ally, to see if he comes out with more information.'

'Shouldn't be too difficult,' Ally said, 'because he's hanging around the place most of the time, utterly bored, and he's very fond of Flora. I've just got to find the right opportunity.'

TWENTY-FIVE

The opportunity was handed to Ally on a plate the following morning at breakfast time, after her usual contretemps with Lavinia, who always managed to find something wrong. She was obviously still seething under the surface at being asked to tidy her room and, to show her disapproval, had reverted to calling Ally 'Mrs McKinley'. Today her soft-boiled egg wasn't soft enough. 'It was far too hard!' she snapped.

Ally apologised, explaining that it had been boiled for the same amount of time as usual, and that there was no way of seeing inside an egg. It was at this point that Randolph – who'd cleared his plate and was standing up preparing to leave – said, 'I wonder if you could do us a favour?'

Ally stiffened, wondering what was coming.

'Lavinia and I have become members of a most prestigious golf club,' he said importantly, brushing breadcrumbs from his paunch onto the floor, 'and tonight they are having a special centenary dinner to which we have been invited. Obviously, Giles will not be with us, and we wondered if perhaps you could provide a meal for him?'

This was plainly news to Lavinia. 'He's perfectly capable of going out, or sending out for a pizza or something,' she snapped. 'He's done it often enough before.'

Giles, in the meantime, was staring moodily out of the window.

'That's as maybe,' Randolph continued, 'but he's eating rubbish far too often, and I wonder if Ally might perhaps cook something for him, something nutritious with vegetables perhaps?' He turned back to Ally. 'You'll put it on the bill, of course.'

'That's not a problem,' Ally said, 'because I shall be cooking something for myself anyway and would be happy to cook a little extra.'

'And eat it here in the dining room, Giles,' ordered Lavinia, 'and not in your bedroom.'

Ally saw Giles turn round and roll his eyes. 'If he doesn't mind, he can eat with me in the kitchen,' she said.

'In your *kitchen*?' Lavinia appeared horror-struck. Nobody had obviously ever dared eat in hers. 'The kitchen is Mrs McKinley's domain,' she said, turning to Giles.

'He'd be very welcome if he doesn't mind,' Ally replied, seeing Giles nodding out of the corner of her eye. 'We can have something to eat and then perhaps watch a movie or something. I believe Giles is keen on films.'

'Perfect,' said Randolph gruffly, heading towards the door. 'Like I said, pop it on the bill.'

Ally noticed that Giles had brightened up considerably, but Lavinia was regarding her with pure hatred. *Perhaps I should be putting an extra lock on my door*, Ally thought.

Ross, being the gentleman he was, helped her clear away the dishes from the dining room because Morag was still working upstairs. A pattern had been established in that the minute the Sinclairs appeared for breakfast, Morag would shoot upstairs to clean and tidy the rooms. She did Lavinia's first because it was the messiest and took the longest, then Randolph's and finally Giles's, because Giles didn't care if Morag was still pottering about in his bathroom or somewhere when he got back.

Ross was about to leave because he and his son, Will, were going to a veterinary conference in Inverness at lunchtime. This event occurred once a year in various places and although Ross had officially retired, he still enjoyed meeting up with other so-called 'retired' vets, a couple of whom he'd actually trained with in university. 'Just need to check they're still alive,' he'd joked. This conference culminated in a dinner and an overnight stay in order to dilute the alcohol before heading home next day.

As Ross was leaving, he said, 'Remember, you've got to get in touch with Rigby.'

'I will,' Ally agreed.

Later, when Ally tried to get in touch with Rigby, she was informed that he was out all day. Ally was almost relieved. She still couldn't quite believe that it could have been Desdemona who'd tried to run her off the road. But she had to tell him somehow.

As Ally was standing in the kitchen trying to work out what to cook, there was a gentle tap on the door, and there stood Giles.

'Any chance of a curry tonight?' he asked.

'Most definitely,' Ally replied. 'I was just thinking of something like that. How about a vegetable one, to please your father?'

'Fine,' he said.

Ally had a good recipe from years back, which her children had loved, so hopefully Giles would too. Not only that, she was pretty sure she already had all the vegetables necessary.

Later, as she awaited his arrival, she prepared some side dishes and brought out the mango chutney. Then, just before seven, there came a timid knock on the door and in came Giles brandishing a bottle of Sauvignon Blanc.

'Don't know a lot about wine,' he said apologetically, 'but it was on display down in the shop.' Here, he raised his eyes to heaven. 'I had a right grilling from that old woman.'

'Queenie?' Ally asked, laughing, after she'd thanked him.

'Is that her name? She wanted to know why I was on my own, where were my parents? Was I old enough to purchase alcohol? Was I happy in The Auld Malthouse? On and on she went, the old bat.' Suddenly he put his hand over his mouth. 'Oh God, I hope she's not a friend of yours!'

'No, she's not,' Ally confirmed, 'but she's very nosy and the epicentre of village gossip.'

'Well, I guess we've all given her plenty to gossip about,' Giles said. He sniffed deeply. 'That smells good.' He laughed, fending off Flora, who was jumping up enthusiastically at the sight of her new friend.

'Now, would you like some wine, or would you prefer a beer?'

'Beer, please,' he replied.

Ally wasn't sure how old he was, but he only had to climb the stairs up to his room afterwards, so she poured him a lager and one for herself. '*Slàinte mhath!*' she said.

Giles nodded. 'Yes, cheers!' he said before taking a large gulp. 'This is very kind of you. I could easily have got a pizza or something delivered, but both Dad and Mother have got this bee in their bonnets about junk food, as they call it.' He sighed as he stroked Flora.

'You must be pretty bored being up here in Scotland for so long,' Ally remarked as she stirred the simmering curry and checked the rice.

'It's supposed to be my gap year, but they insisted I came up with them to decide what I was going to be studying. We were supposed to just be here for a couple of weeks and then going straight home after Hamish's wedding. But, of course, that didn't happen – and isn't going to happen until these murders are solved. So, yes, I'm bored and wasting time because I was supposed to be backpacking through Europe and Asia with my mate, but he's set off without me.'

'Oh, I'm so sorry about that, Giles. How disappointing. Still, if they let you go home within the next few weeks, would you still be able to join him somewhere?'

'I could probably fly out to wherever he's got to. He's in Croatia at the moment and says it's beautiful,' he said wistfully.

'I'm sure it is,' Ally said, feeling more and more sorry for this unfortunate young man. 'Well, the curry's ready, so, if you'd like to come to the table...'

When they were seated, she noticed that he'd drunk most of his lager and wondered if she should offer him another. Perhaps she was being too canny because, doubtless, boys of his age had been knocking back alcohol – and goodness knows what else – for years on the quiet. 'Shall I top up your drink?' she asked.

'Yes, please.' He was already tackling the food with gusto. 'Great curry,' he said.

Ally breathed a sigh of relief as she topped up his glass. They ate in silence for a few minutes before Giles asked, out of the blue, 'Do you miss your family?'

She was taken aback for a moment. 'Yes, I do, but they're all grown up now, with families of their own. And I've made some good friends up here. Mind you, both my son and daughter thought I'd gone bonkers when I told them I was heading to the wilds, at my age, to open a bed and breakfast!'

'But you came anyway?'

'I did,' Ally replied, 'and I'm glad I did. Sometimes you've just got to follow your gut feeling.'

Giles looked thoughtful for a moment. 'Mmm,' he said. 'I think you're right.'

Ally pointed at his rapidly emptying plate. 'Would you like some more?'

'Yes, please.' He took another large gulp of his beer as Ally filled up his plate again.

'You mentioned your parents are very keen golfers,' Ally said casually as they resumed eating.

'Bloody fanatics, more like,' Giles muttered.

'Well, I've heard this very prestigious golf club they've joined here is extremely selective, so the club they found in Inverness must have been outstanding if they were prepared to go out to the airport each day?' She paused. 'I'd always believed the golf club in Inverness itself was considered to be excellent.'

'Yeah, but they wanted to be close to the airport,' Giles replied, piling some chutney on the side of his plate.

'Why was that?'

'Because they were hoping to waylay Hamish's fiancée before she got any further,' Giles said in a matter-of-fact manner.

Ally almost choked. 'Why on earth would they want to do that?' she asked when she regained her composure. 'And didn't they think that Hamish would be at the airport to meet her?'

Giles shrugged. 'No idea. Anyway, they took turns at meeting every flight from London, holding up a board with "LOCHARRAN" written on it.'

'But *why*?'

'I believe they thought they could dissuade her from going any further. Talk her into going straight back home, stuff like that. They probably planned to offer her a load of money.'

'But they never saw her?'

'Oh yes, Mother *thought* she did, although now we know it wasn't her anyway! But that Morton woman had got in there first and was leading her into a muddy old Land Rover.' He carried on eating with enthusiasm.

'So, did your mother go back to her golf?' Ally asked, hardly able to believe what she'd just heard.

'No, she said she tried following the Land Rover, but she couldn't keep up with it. Apparently, the Morton woman is a fast driver, and Mother wasn't used to these Highland roads with all their passing places, so she lost track. I only know that later, when they arrived back in the hotel, she and Dad weren't talking to each other. Must have been a fun day.'

'Your parents feel *that* strongly about retaining their inheritance?' Ally asked.

Giles pulled a face. 'It's mad, isn't it? No offence or anything, but who would want to live in a freezing-cold old castle in the middle of nowhere? I'd much prefer to be in London, thank you very much.' He finished his second helping and laid down his fork. 'That was awesome,' he added, draining his lager.

'I can't claim to have made a dessert,' Ally said, 'but I have defrosted a chocolate gateau I had in the freezer, and there's cream too.'

'Yes, please,' said Giles.

Ally, her head in a whirl, was relieved that he managed two portions, leaving another two portions for herself and Ross later in the week. When she half-heartedly suggested watching a film afterwards, she was relieved when Giles asked if she'd mind if he went upstairs to play an online video game with his friend, Oliver.

'Not at all,' she said, desperate to sit down and sort out her chaotic thoughts.

After he'd thanked her profusely and gone upstairs, Ally sat down with a brandy. Was Lavinia the killer? Had she *really* given up tailing Desdemona's Land Rover? Surely she knew where Desdemona was going? Well, she'd have known the road as far as Locharran perhaps, but she'd never have made it up to Loch Trioch and the track to Desdemona's residence. And if she'd got as far as Cairn Cross, she would have presumably found the broken-down Land Rover, *if* the Land Rover had broken down.

The whole thing was beyond ridiculous. How possible would it have been – in the unlikely event of Lavinia coming face to face with the *real* Elena, *and* Magda, of course, with no sign of Hamish – that Elena would have been persuaded to return home? Ally had been convinced, in the short time she'd known Elena, of the strength of her feelings towards Hamish, and doubted very much that she would have come all this way to turn on her heel and go all the way back because some strange woman had offered her money at the airport! It only served to underline the depths of Lavinia's desperation.

Ally sat by the fire, stroking Flora's head. Most of the evidence still pointed to Desdemona. But what could have been Desdemona's motive if she was no longer interested in Hamish as a lover? If only Ross was here because she desperately needed to talk to someone sensible about what was going on.

Nothing made sense, and Ally knew she wasn't going to get much sleep.

In the morning, Lavinia arrived in the dining room ahead of the other two and greeted Ally with, 'I think your maid has stolen my pearl earrings!'

'*What?*' Ally asked, startled, as she set out the cereals on the sideboard.

'My pearl earrings have disappeared,' Lavinia continued, 'and I distinctly remember leaving them in that little ashtray thing on the dressing table a couple of days ago.'

Ally bristled. 'Morag would never steal anything, I can assure you,' she said firmly. *Little ashtray thing* indeed! That was a pretty little Spode dish that had belonged to her mother. And Morag *never* wore earrings.

'I think you should be more choosy about your staff,' snapped Lavinia, 'and, let me tell you, these are genuine pearls and extremely valuable.'

'Morag will *not* have taken them,' Ally repeated.

'How dare you doubt my word!' Lavinia shouted haughtily.

Ally had had enough. 'And how dare you accuse my cleaner! And, Lavinia, while we're talking about people being guilty, perhaps you can explain why you attempted to intercept the woman you *thought* was Hamish's fiancée at Inverness Airport?'

Lavinia stiffened. 'What are you talking about?'

Ally took a deep breath. 'I'm talking about *you*, at Inverness Airport, hoping to persuade the woman you thought was Elena to go back where she came from. But Desdemona Morton got there first, and so you followed them in your car.'

Lavinia had paled noticeably. 'What business is this of yours?' Her voice had faltered somewhat.

'You had every intention of stopping that marriage by any means you could,' Ally said, 'and I intend to inform Detective Inspector Rigby of this.'

'What the *hell's* going on?' Randolph asked loudly as he came in through the door.

As he spoke, Lavinia sat down and began to weep. 'I haven't hurt anyone,' she sobbed. 'Just because I wanted to waylay Elena...'

'For God's sake, shut up, woman!' Randolph bellowed at his wife.

'But she *knows*!' Lavinia wailed. 'She knows about me being at the airport—'

'That'll doubtless be thanks to Giles,' Randolph interrupted, glaring up at the ceiling, 'who's wisely keeping out of the way.'

'I didn't wish her harm,' Lavinia continued, wiping her eyes. 'I was only trying to retain my husband and son's rightful inheritance.' Her shoulders shuddered again. 'I thought maybe Hamish had sent that woman Morton to meet Elena, so I followed them. But she was driving like a maniac, and I had to keep pulling into these damned passing places to let things pass.' She wailed again. 'Don't tell Rigby, please!' She turned to her husband. 'Do you think they might cancel our membership of the Seagull Club because of this? Oh, I can't bear it!' More tears, more shuddering.

'I fully intend to go to see Rigby later,' Ally said as firmly as she could.

Randolph held up his hand. 'Fine, fine! You can tell the inspector that my wife will be happy to answer any questions just as soon as my lawyer gets here from London. And I'm calling him *right now!*' With that, he pulled his phone out of his pocket and walked back into the hall.

At that moment, Morag came rushing down the stairs and poked her head round the dining-room door. 'I've just found a pair of pearl earrings which had rolled under the bed, Mrs Sinclair, and they damn well nearly got swallowed up by the vacuum cleaner. Could ye please be more careful with yer jewellery?'

With that, Lavinia gave another wail.

'Breakfast looks like being a little late this morning,' Ally said to Morag.

TWENTY-SIX

Breakfast was, indeed, a little late and eaten in complete silence, Randolph wolfing down everything at speed and Lavinia picking listlessly at a boiled egg. There was no sign of Giles.

It wasn't until they'd both set off in their car, some half hour later, before Giles tapped on the kitchen door. Ally and Morag were halfway through their mugs of tea and analysis of this delicious new gossip.

'I'm sorry you missed breakfast,' Ally said, 'but I'm sure you could hear what was going on.'

Giles nodded in a resigned way. 'My fault, of course. Perhaps I shouldn't have told you what I did last night, but I'm so bloody tired of being told to not-say-this and not-say-that! And I don't want to be the damned earl one day anyway!'

Ally grinned at him. 'How about I make you a nice, big bacon sandwich?'

'Awesome,' he said, grinning back. 'I've left the TV on, so I'll go back upstairs for a minute.'

'It'll take me only a couple of minutes,' Ally said.

As he headed upstairs, Morag remarked, 'Nice boy.'

· · ·

Shortly after Ally had made and delivered the sandwich, Murdo arrived with the post.

'Ye'll never guess the latest!' he announced gleefully.

'Better come in then,' Ally said, wondering what the latest piece of gossip was that he was about to impart.

In the kitchen, he laid a couple of letters down on the table, blew a kiss to his wife and said, 'They've just arrested Desdemona Morton!'

'Are ye certain?' asked Morag.

'Oh, aye. Paul at the polis station told Freddy down at the garage, and he told me just half an hour ago when I dropped off his heart pills. He always gets them in the post, see.'

'Aye,' Morag agreed, draining her mug. 'If he didnae get them delivered by the post, he'd have to go all the way to Fort William.'

'Desdemona has been *arrested*?' Ally asked, still trying to get her head round the morning's events. 'You're sure?'

'Oh, definitely,' said Murdo, looking at the teapot. 'Any chance of a quick cuppa?'

'Aye, well, we always knew she wouldnae be happy with the earl marryin' someone else,' Morag said sadly. 'And she likely did away with her own sister. Jealousy's an awful thing.'

Ally didn't want to waste time arguing with them. These two, like most of the villagers, had long since decided who was guilty and why. She made a mug of tea for Murdo, then went to fetch her coat. 'Have you any idea where they've taken her?'

Both of them looked at her in astonishment as she put on her anorak.

Then Murdo shrugged. 'Well, they havenae any cells round here,' he said, 'so my guess would be Fort William.'

Ally, heading towards the door, said, 'Lock up and let yourself out when you're ready, Morag. I've something urgent to do.' Morag, like the guests, had her own key.

As she closed the door behind her, Ally could hear Morag mutter, 'Well, I never!'

As she made her way down the road, Ally realised she was probably being somewhat hasty. It was very unlikely Rigby would be there because he would most likely be in Fort William, or wherever they'd taken Desdemona. Her mind was in turmoil; had this arrest been made because she'd told Rigby about the monkshood? Perhaps they'd confirmed that it was the monkshood which had killed Elena? But why would Desdemona have wanted to kill Elena if she said she now had only a platonic relationship with Hamish? Had she been telling the truth?

And what about Lavinia?

Since Lavinia's breakdown this morning, Ally was more convinced than ever that Lavinia was guilty. Why else would the woman have lost control so completely when she was challenged?

And why was Randolph in such a hurry to summon his London lawyer?

Had Lavinia perhaps followed Desdemona all the way to Cairn Cross and then picked Kristina up when she started walking towards Locharran?

Ally could feel a headache coming on as she approached the little police station. She'd also convinced herself that Rigby wouldn't be here, and that she should have phoned first. And so she got quite a shock when the first person she saw, deep in conversation with the constable on the desk, was none other than Rigby himself.

At the sound of her footsteps, he turned round. 'Ah, Mrs McKinley,' he said.

'I've some information,' she said.

He gave her a glimmer of a smile. 'No doubt. Better come through to the office.'

She followed him along the corridor to his office, where they both sat down in their respective seats and faced each other.

'Let's hear it then,' said Rigby, stifling a yawn. 'I hope this is good because I was on duty very late last night and I'm not going to last much longer without a bit of kip.'

'I hear you've arrested Desdemona?'

'Blow me, that didn't take long to get round! It was late last night, so the Locharran bush telegraph has excelled itself.' He looked impressed.

'Did you arrest her because you found the monkshood in her garden?'

'Yes,' said Rigby. 'We've identified that Elena was poisoned with monkshood.'

'I'm shocked,' Ally admitted, 'but not entirely surprised. But surely it doesn't prove conclusively that it was Desdemona? I mean, anyone could have got it from her garden.'

Rigby frowned. 'So you're still not entirely convinced of her guilt?'

'Well, you asked me to get chatty with her, and with Giles Sinclair, and I've managed to do that,' Ally said. 'Desdemona actually delivered my painting and stayed for a cup of tea. And she told me that she'd finished her affair with the earl long before he married her sister. She'd discovered something about him that ended their relationship.'

'And that something was...?'

'She wouldn't tell me,' Ally admitted. 'But she had nothing to do with her sister's death because she was having her appendix removed at the time, which doubtless can be proved. And, since then, she and the earl have been purely friends.'

'Similar to what she told us, Mrs McKinley, but why should we believe her?'

'But surely it could have been proved that Desdemona was in hospital when her sister died?'

'There are always buts, I'm afraid,' Rigby interrupted. 'In here we only work on facts. Proven facts. Furthermore, I'm trying to solve two murders at the moment, and what you're now referring to must have happened about forty years ago and is, I hope, dead and dusted. I'm certainly not going to dig that all up again.'

'But if she was innocent of killing her sister, then surely she'd have no reason to want the earl's wife dead?'

'Possibly. But it's also possible she suspected the earl had a hand in killing her sister, and Desdemona Morton killed his new wife in revenge. Now, was there something else you wanted to tell me?'

'Yes, there is,' Ally said firmly. 'I gained the confidence of Giles Sinclair last night. He told me, without any persuasion, that his parents had chosen to play golf at a course near Inverness Airport so that they could meet the flights from London and check to see if Elena appeared on one of them. They even had a board with "LOCHARRAN" written on it, which they held up as the passengers came through. This was, of course, a week or so before Elena actually arrived, but nevertheless it appeared that both Desdemona and Lavinia thought Kristina was actually Elena.' Ally went on to relate how Lavinia had then tried to follow Desdemona's Land Rover. 'And she actually admitted at breakfast this morning that she was doing this purely to protect her husband and son's rightful inheritance.'

Rigby scratched his head. 'So where was Randolph Sinclair when all this airport meeting business was going on?'

'Presumably playing golf. Apparently, they took turns at meeting the flights, and it was Lavinia's turn when poor, innocent Kristina showed up, with no one to meet her, having missed the bus and then been offered the lift from Desdemona, which that poor woman must have considered to be a godsend.'

'Didn't either of these two stupid women not think that the earl was likely to be there to meet his fiancée?'

'Perhaps they assumed he'd been delayed or something,' Ally said lamely, although she'd been thinking much the same thing herself.

'So, we're to assume that Lavinia Sinclair gave up following the Land Rover at some point?' Rigby asked.

'That's what she said,' Ally confirmed.

'But she didn't say where exactly?'

'No.'

'Well, I'll ask her when I get to question her,' Rigby said.

'Randolph was phoning for his lawyer as I was leaving,' Ally told him.

'I bet he was,' Rigby said, unperturbed.

'So, where have you taken Desdemona?' Ally asked.

'For the moment, she's in Fort William,' Rigby replied. 'And later today, I shall be going there again to question her further.'

'Will I be able to visit her?' Ally asked, starting to feel guilty for the part she'd played in Desdemona's arrest.

'Not at the moment,' said Rigby. 'Possibly later.' He shook his head. 'Why ever did I think that policing up here was going to be a doddle? The occasional drunk at closing time, the occasional sheep rustler perhaps?'

'It's not quite worked out like that, has it?' Ally said with a smile.

When Ally got back to the malthouse, she found the place empty. Even Giles appeared to have gone out, and Flora was looking at her hopefully.

'I know, Flo,' she said, stroking the dog's head. 'You need a walk. Just let me have something to eat and then we'll go.'

Ally glanced at the clock to discover it was half past two. No wonder she was hungry! What a weird morning it had been.

She hadn't served breakfast until half past ten, and then she'd got to Rigby's office around midday.

As she made herself a sandwich, Ally's thoughts veered from Desdemona to Lavinia and back again. Either woman could have killed both Kristina and Elena; mistaken identity in the case of Kristina, absolute certainty when it came to Elena. Whoever had done the killings had been determined that Hamish must not marry. At least Lavinia had confessed to trying to preserve the earldom for her husband and son. Not that her son even wanted it! But what possible motive could Desdemona now have, if she was telling the truth? Could Rigby's suggestion be right? Did Desdemona blame Hamish for her sister's death?

Ally sat down with her sandwich and a coffee and decided that Flora's walk should be up to the castle, because it was high time she had a talk with Hamish.

Hamish was in his study when Ally and Flora arrived and were duly ushered in by Mrs Fraser.

'Good to see you, Alison. It's almost teatime, so let's join Magda and Simon in the sitting room,' he said enthusiastically.

'Before we do,' Ally said, 'I wondered if we might have a private word?'

'Yes, yes, of course.' He filed away some pieces of paper and gave Ally his full attention.

'I suppose you've heard that Desdemona has been arrested?'

'Yes, word has got around. Poor, poor Desdemona.' He looked gloomy.

'But what I don't understand, Hamish, is what Desdemona's motive could be because she told me that you stopped being lovers some time before you married Ophelia.'

Hamish looked surprised. 'You are very honoured,' he said, 'because Desdemona is not known to reveal her private life to anyone. But she was right, of course, because at one time we were indeed lovers.'

'I'm flattered then that she chose to confide in me,' Ally said truthfully, 'and I've actually become quite fond of her and would like to see her released as soon as possible. Thing is, everyone in the village seems to think she had something to do with Ophelia's death because of jealousy, and now they all think she's killed the two women who she thought to be your next bride. Those rumours could go against her.'

Hamish gave a long, exaggerated sigh. 'I really didn't think you listened to gossip like that.'

'You know what, Hamish? I think the fact that she was in hospital at the time of Ophelia's death should be publicised.'

'Yes, yes, it was proven she was in hospital at the time, but the locals all chose to ignore that. Somebody must have acted on her behalf, they said. It was all completely ridiculous!'

Ally took a deep breath. 'One of the things she told me was that your love life finished after you told her something which she found completely unacceptable.'

'Did she tell you that?' Hamish stared at Ally with a look of horror on his face.

'She did indeed,' Ally confirmed.

Hamish was silent for a moment, looking somewhat lost and confused. 'Did she tell you what it was?' he asked eventually.

Ally shook her head. 'No, she wouldn't tell me.'

'In that case, Alison,' he said, smiling, 'if she wouldn't tell you, then I won't divulge what it was either.'

'But it could be important—'

'In that case, we'll worry about it if and when the time comes. I'm quite sure they'll release Desdemona soon. Now, why don't you and Flora come through and join Magda, Simon and myself for a nice cup of tea? Simon has been absolutely magnificent; so extremely attentive. And, as you must have observed, Magda is a completely different person now!'

. . .

In the sitting room, there was a moment or two of chaos while Flora and Benny renewed their friendship and jumped around together, causing general mayhem. When they'd quietened down, Simon stood up from where he'd been sitting next to the fire and offered Ally his seat.

'Thank you, Simon, but I'm feeling quite hot from the walk up here. It's a bit of a climb, you know,' Ally said. 'So, if you don't mind, I'll sit over here.' She sat further back, facing the fire. Magda was sitting on the opposite side to Simon, and next to Hamish.

There was general chit-chat for a few minutes before Mrs Fraser trundled in with her tea trolley, laden with sandwiches, scones and cakes – an afternoon ritual which Ally had experienced more than once. She wondered how any of them managed to keep their figures.

Magda, now very much the lady of the house, took over, pouring tea for everyone and offering round sandwiches. Ally permitted herself a couple of dainty triangle-shaped sandwiches, at the same time noting how happy Magda seemed to be.

Simon appeared to have noticed too because, as he sipped his tea, he said to no one in particular, 'I'm so pleased with the progress I've made with Magda. She's regained her confidence and is a different person from just a few weeks ago.'

Magda, her eyes sparkling, said, 'And it's all because of you, Hamish.' She moved closer towards him and gave him a long, loving look, followed by a kiss on the cheek.

Ally noticed Simon also looking at Hamish and frowning for a moment, before looking tight-lipped and downright angry. He was plainly annoyed, as he probably had every right to be, as he'd spent so much time here talking to her. Ally wondered how much he normally charged for this kind of therapy and whether

Hamish was actually paying him. Whatever the arrangement, his personal pride must have been severely dented by Magda's thoughtless remark.

After all, it was thanks to him that Magda had been persuaded to leave the castle at all and, in such a short space of time, found it possible to be able to face the world again. He certainly deserved some credit.

As Magda handed Hamish his cup of tea, she said, 'I love it here with you, Hamish – you've changed my life!'

Hamish beamed. 'And you've changed mine too, Magda!'

Ally was surprised. She'd realised that Magda was infatuated with Hamish, but this was the first indication that he might be feeling the same way.

She glanced across at Simon, wondering if there was any indication of what he might think of their mutual admiration.

She was shocked. There was an expression of total loathing on his face as he looked at them both.

TWENTY-SEVEN

Ally felt a distinct sense of uneasiness as she and Flora made their way back down to the malthouse. She also had a definite sense of foreboding. Why had Simon given Magda and Hamish such a hateful look? Was it because Magda was crediting Hamish with her progress and not him? Surely it couldn't only be that his professional pride was sorely dented? It was much more likely that he'd begun to have feelings for Magda himself! Why hadn't she thought of that before?

Then there was Hamish. He was obviously no longer suffering from the shock and grief he'd exhibited after Elena's death. No matter how unlikely it seemed that Hamish could have been involved in his first wife's death, if Rigby's off-the-cuff remark was correct, it possibly indicated that Hamish was involved in Elena's death also. And it couldn't be denied that he'd recovered quickly considering his wife of only a few hours had been murdered.

He now seemed perfectly happy with the situation, including the fact that Magda obviously adored him. Had he come to adore her too, and if so, when? Could it possibly have been even before he married Elena? Were they sleeping together?

So many unanswered questions! Ally was beginning to wonder why she'd never considered giving Hamish a place on the clock face and, with that thought, she realised there was no way he could have been involved in Kristina's death, which brought her back to her senses a little – the whole idea was ridiculous. Wasn't it?

Ally's thoughts kept returning to Desdemona. At the moment, she was Rigby's prime suspect, partly thanks to Ally herself, but, of course, everyone thought it was high time Rigby arrested *somebody*. Ally was feeling more and more guilty about the matter of the monkshood. Had they tested the plants? Could it just have been something that appeared similar to monkshood? She was beginning to wonder if she should have mentioned it to Rigby at all.

Nevertheless, Ally had a gut feeling that the answer to the whole mystery must lie with Desdemona, whether she was guilty of the murder or not, and so she had to find a way to visit Desdemona in jail. She glanced at her watch and saw it was nearly five o'clock. There was little chance of Rigby working late, so she'd leave it until the morning.

Ross had arrived back from his vets' conference in Inverness mid-afternoon and, having reclaimed Ebony from his daughter-in-law, phoned shortly after Ally had got back to say he'd be over the following evening.

'I'm so glad because there is something I really need to discuss with you.'

'Oh, I'm intrigued! Can you tell me what it is now?'

'No, it's something I need to discuss with you face to face. I'll tell you tomorrow, and hopefully I'll have more proof by then.'

Ally reckoned that, if she could get the Sinclairs' breakfast things cleared away by half past ten the following morning, she could leave Morag to finish off the rooms. Then she could be at the police station by eleven or half past.

Breakfast presented no problems. Lavinia was silent, withdrawn and ate little. Randolph and Giles ate normally, but there was little conversation. And, as if on cue, they'd left the dining room by half past ten.

Ally got out her phone and hoped she sounded assertive. 'I need to see Detective Inspector Rigby today, please,' she said firmly to the policeman who answered.

'He's here until twelve,' the policeman replied, 'then he's off to see the chief constable in Inverness.'

'I'll be there in about twenty minutes,' Ally said.

Rigby looked exhausted, and Ally, for the first time, felt sorry for him.

'More news?' he asked hopefully.

'Not yet,' Ally said, hoping she sounded positive, 'but I do need to talk to Desdemona.'

'She's in jail,' said Rigby, stifling a yawn.

'I *know* that! And I'm quite happy to drive to Fort William to see her, if it can be arranged, *please*.'

Rigby regarded her quizzically. 'Why?'

'I think she has some relevant information, from years back, which could shine a light on this case.'

'I've no doubt she has,' said Rigby. 'A *confession* perhaps?'

'That's not what I meant, and you know it,' Ally retorted. 'I need to know why she and Hamish broke up all those years ago.'

'Oh, not *that* old chestnut again! I've told you before, I've got enough on my hands at the moment without having to dig up stuff from forty years ago.'

'You don't have to dig up anything, Inspector. Desdemona

has opened up to me over the past few weeks, so I'd like to strike while the iron is still partly hot, if you know what I mean? I think she can tell us something important.'

Rigby studied her for a moment, then sighed. 'I suppose you're only trying to help,' he said. 'I'll ring up and tell them that you'll be there about three o'clock?' He looked at her enquiringly.

'Perfect,' Ally confirmed.

'And I assume you have a driving licence or some means of identification?'

'Of course.' Ally grinned. 'Thank you so much!'

'You'll need directions,' he said, scribbling madly on a scrap of paper.

When Ally got back home, she found Giles in the hallway, looking thoroughly bored.

'Would you like a dog for the afternoon?' Ally asked, having been wondering what to do about Flora.

He brightened up immediately. 'Could I?'

'Well, I have an appointment in Fort William this afternoon, and I don't really want to take Flora with me,' Ally told him.

'I'd be happy to look after her,' he said enthusiastically.

'She's not allowed in the front part of the house or the bedrooms,' Ally said, 'although she has been known to escape now and then. But if you could perhaps take her for a walk and then shut her in the kitchen afterwards, that would be great.'

'But I mustn't take her into my bedroom?'

Ally smiled. 'Perhaps I shouldn't tell you this, but there's no way Flora would go into your bedroom anyway. She won't go anywhere near it. I inherited a ghost with this house, and apparently he's still in residence in your bathroom!'

'What? I've got a real ghost up there?' Giles looked delighted. 'No chance it's a gorgeous maiden, I suppose?'

'No chance at all! His name is Wailing Willie, who once drank himself to death in this very building and played his bagpipes, after a fashion, right up to his final breath. Legend is that you'll only hear the wail when someone's about to die though, so you've probably missed the last one by being in the Craigmonie!'

'Oh, wow!' said Giles.

The drive to Fort William was uneventful, apart from having to slow down to let a couple of wayward sheep cross the road. And it was raining, as usual, when she arrived in the town, the rain clouds obscuring any view of Ben Nevis. Even with Rigby's instructions, the police station took a bit of zigzagging around to locate.

When she got there, a young constable, who introduced himself as PC Malcolm, knew all about her impending visit. 'We don't often get to lock anyone up,' he said cheerfully, 'and she doesn't much look like a double murderer. Is she a friend of yours then?'

'An acquaintance,' Ally said as she followed him along a corridor to a sturdy door which he unlocked with great panache.

'Press the bell on the wall when you want to come out,' he instructed her, opening the door cautiously and peering in quickly.

'Thank you, I will,' Ally replied, walking into the small room where Desdemona was sitting on her bed, reading *The Scotsman*.

'I wasn't expecting a visitor,' she said, folding up the paper.

Ally looked around with interest. There was a toilet, a

washbasin, a small cupboard, one chair and a small table, as well as the bed and a couple of shelves.

'I brought you some fruit,' Ally said, offloading a selection of apples, pears and bananas.

'Thank you,' Desdemona said. 'It'll make a welcome change from the stodge they serve in here.' She pointed to the chair. 'Sit down. It's not the height of comfort but better than nothing.' She gave a half-smile. 'I suppose you've been sent to see if I'll confess?'

Ally nodded. 'That's certainly what they'd like, but I'm damn sure you're not about to confess to something you didn't do.'

'I'm glad you believe me, even if that Rigby doesn't.'

Ally had rehearsed what she was going to say to Desdemona all the way from Locharran, but now she couldn't remember any of it. Not a word. It was something to do with the way Desdemona was looking at her, in defiance almost. Here was a talented woman who'd chosen to stay single, who was very much a loner and who would not buckle under now.

'The thing is, Desdemona, I really do want to help you. But I'm going to need you to help me to see if I'm on the right track or not. Were you by chance driving from Inverness along the lochside just over a week ago?'

'You must be joking! I've told you about my problems with the tax and the MOT. I never take my old jalopy anywhere I might get pulled up by the police! Why do you ask?'

Ally told her about the attempt to push her and Magda off the road.

Desdemona shrugged. 'Every farmer and his wife, and his dog, has a Land Rover round here. And, come to think of it, every earl too.'

'The thing is, I really want to help you, but there's still a lot you can tell me, and I can't help you unless you help me.'

'I don't understand,' Desdemona said.

'You told me that you ended your relationship with Hamish years ago because of something you found out.'

'So what if I did?' Desdemona was beginning to look a little uncomfortable.

'I need to know what that was. It could, and I stress *could*, be very relevant to this case.'

'It's history now. Nothing to do with anything.' Desdemona glared angrily out of the tiny window high up in the wall. 'I'm worried about my dogs,' she said. 'If that boy from The Bothy forgets to feed them, I'm afraid the RSPCA will take them away.' When she looked back to Ally, there were tears in her eyes.

'Don't worry – I'll do whatever I can to help. And I'm sure Ross will help too, but as far as I'm concerned, you're innocent and you need to be released as soon as possible,' Ally said. 'I'm not a detective, but you need to tell me about what happened between you and Hamish all those years ago.'

Desdemona sat silently for a minute. 'I discovered he was having an affair with someone else at the same time as myself.' She hesitated.

'He confessed?' Ally asked.

'Yes, but only after I actually found them in flagrante! Can you imagine? I knew that he had a roving eye, was a bit of a flirt, but I didn't know he was the type to cheat. We had even discussed marriage at one point! That was before I decided to give up on men altogether. And I don't regret it.' She sighed, suddenly looking very tired and very small, despite her defiance.

Ally squeezed her hand. 'How awful for you. I'm going back to see Rigby and try to talk some sense into him.'

Desdemona looked up at her. 'Do you think they might release me then?'

Ally spontaneously leaned forward and gave her a hug. 'I'll do my best,' she said as she pressed the bell on the wall.

TWENTY-EIGHT

When she got home, Ally found Flora was fast asleep in her basket. The dog opened one eye, gave a feeble wag of her tail and crashed back to sleep again. Giles had obviously taken her for a good long walk.

Ross and Ebony arrived at about half past six. Ross told Ally he'd had a great time at the vets' conference: terrific speakers, a wonderful evening and a raging hangover next morning. Ross and Will hadn't set out on their return journey until nearly lunchtime. He was pleased to be home though. And what had she been doing? Anything exciting?

Ally filled him in on everything she'd learned that afternoon. 'With Desdemona off the hook as far as I'm concerned, I think maybe we need to look more closely at Lavinia and Randolph. There's something about the pair of them that makes me uneasy. But speaking of being uneasy,' she said, pouring them both large glasses of wine, 'I want you to tell me everything you know about Simon Hartley-Knott.'

Ross raised his eyebrows. 'What's he been up to then? He's not been trying it on with you, has he?' He laughed, shaking his head at the very thought.

'Why? Am I so undesirable?' Ally asked with a pretend pout.

'That's not what I meant!' Ross took a sip of his wine. 'I've always had him down as a bit of a ladies' man, but I thought age might have slowed him a bit. What do you want to know about him?'

'What you've told me is probably enough. Honestly, I think he might be in love with Magda!'

'Are you *serious*?' Ross asked, clearly surprised.

'I caught him looking at both Hamish and Magda – who were sitting closely together – with this terrible look on his face, and I can't really explain why, but I'm beginning to be a bit worried for Hamish.'

'Let me get this straight: you think that two old lotharios, in their seventies, are vying for the attention of a woman less than half their age?'

'It *could* be possible,' Ally said.

'Both in love with Magda? She seems like a lovely girl, but she doesn't exactly strike me as the type of girl who's used to a long train of suitors.'

Ally shrugged. 'She's attractive, she's a lovely person, she's caring and kind. I don't know, Ross, I just keep seeing the way that Simon looked at Hamish.'

Ross sighed. 'So, what are you going to do now?'

'I need to have a chat with Rigby,' said Ally. 'I'm hoping I'm wrong, but I have an awful feeling that Hamish might be in some sort of danger.'

'It won't be easy to convince him that Hamish is in danger,' Ross said, 'particularly as we have no proof one way or the other.'

'No,' said Ally, 'we haven't. But, nevertheless, I think we need to keep an eye on Hamish, just in case.'

. . .

After they'd eaten dinner, Ally felt an urge to phone Magda, to assure herself that all was well. And so it was with great relief that she heard Magda answer.

'Hi, Magda. Just thought I'd give you a quick call to make sure you're all OK up there?'

'Yes, of course, Ally – we're fine.' She sounded surprised.

'Is it just you two?'

'Yes. Simon was here yesterday, but it's just us today.'

'I just wondered how you and Hamish were. Ross is back now from his conference so we may take a walk up to the castle sometime tomorrow.' *After I've spoken to Rigby*, she thought.

'That's very kind of you, Ally,' said Magda. 'We're both fine, but it would be lovely to see you. Come whenever you like – you're always welcome.'

In spite of knowing that the earl was safe, for the moment anyway, Ally found it difficult to sleep. She kept seeing the look that Simon had given the two of them. This was a respectable, educated, clever man, who'd been married and had children. Surely he was past the age of lusting after younger women? Hamish wasn't, of course, she thought. Could Simon have been cut from the same cloth too? He was definitely a bit of a flirt...

Ally turned over slowly for the umpteenth time, hoping not to waken Ross. Then a thought occurred to her: what *was* it with these guys? Ken had been just the same. She'd be lying there worrying about everybody and everything, and he'd be snoring his head off. Did men have an 'off switch' which they pressed every night when they went to bed? To erase any worries and get a good night's sleep? Were women programmed to do all the worrying?

She sighed and began to count backward from one hundred, because she'd read somewhere that it helped to get to sleep, which it didn't. It was almost two o'clock before she finally drifted off.

Ross helped her with breakfast in the morning, although he kept a low profile in the kitchen. 'I really don't want to face that Sinclair family,' he said.

After the Sinclairs had gone their separate ways and Morag had had her cup of tea and departed, Ally telephoned Rigby. She was told that Rigby was in Fort William and, with some persuasion, was given his mobile number. That was a first, and the number could prove to be very useful.

'Yes?' Rigby sounded edgy.

'Good morning, DI Rigby. It's Ally McKinley.'

'What now, Mrs McKinley?'

'I assume you're not with Desdemona Morton at this exact moment?' Ally asked.

'Correct,' he said, 'I am not with Desdemona Morton at this exact moment. I am in the office.' He sounded quite ratty.

Ally wondered if this was a good time to inform him of her new theory. Probably not, but she'd tell him anyway. 'I think Simon Hartley-Knott might have fallen in love with Magda, Elena's sister.'

'Good for him. So what?'

Ally sighed. 'He's also been giving Magda therapy since her sister's death. It seems to me that it's suddenly dawned on him that Magda too has fallen for the earl's undoubted charms because I saw him giving Hamish a look of pure hatred.'

'So, are you saying that this other old guy is after that woman for himself?'

'I think it's a definite possibility,' Ally said, trying to ignore the disbelief in his voice.

'And what has that got to do with the murders of two women?' Rigby sounded impatient.

'I'm not sure,' Ally admitted. 'But something's not right. Would you do a bit of digging on him?'

Rigby sighed. 'I'll do my best, but I'm very busy today. If, in the meantime, you find out anything that might exonerate Desdemona Morton, I'd appreciate it if you let me know.' And he hung up.

'We need to have a chat with Hamish,' Ross said later, 'on his own. We need to talk to him about Desdemona and maybe ask him to speak with Rigby.'

'Do you think we should go up there right now?' Ally asked. 'And maybe while we're at it we can find out a bit more about Simon Hartley-Knott.'

'I think we should,' Ross said.

The weather had turned much colder now, but at least it was dry. Wrapped up in coats, scarves and gloves, Ally and Ross made their way up to the castle.

Ross tugged at the bell. 'We must insist on seeing Hamish alone.'

After a couple of minutes, Mrs Fraser duly arrived.

'We need to have a quick word with the earl,' Ross said, 'on his own.'

'He's in his study,' said Mrs Fraser, leading them into the Great Hall. 'I'll just check with him.' She set off along the corridor and left them alone under the sightless eyes of the countless stags' heads. When she returned, she said, 'He'll be pleased to see you,' and signalled them to proceed.

Hamish opened the door of his study where, thankfully, a fire was blazing in the hearth.

'Good to see you both. Come in, come in. What can I do for you?'

'The thing is, Hamish,' Ally began rather hesitantly, 'we need to ask you some rather personal questions.'

Hamish appeared mystified. 'My goodness, Alison, this all seems very intriguing.' He looked from one to the other.

'It concerns Desdemona,' Ally said. She looked towards Ross. 'We need to convince the police that your affair with her was over years ago, due to her finding out about you being unfaithful. At the moment, the police still think that she's jealous of any woman who comes near you.'

'Well, I can assure you there's no truth to that at all,' Hamish exclaimed. 'It's a ridiculous accusation.'

'But how are you so sure? We need to know the reason,' Ally said, 'in order to clear her name. It's very important.'

'Well, it's a very delicate matter,' Hamish said.

'That may well be, but I don't think you believe that Desdemona's guilty any more than I do. And there's another reason I'm here, Hamish; I'm worried about you.'

'Why on earth would you be worried about me, my dear Alison?'

'I saw Simon looking at you and Magda. And it was an awful look. It turned my blood cold the look he shot at you when Magda gave you a kiss. I think Simon might be in love with Magda.'

Hamish laughed. 'I can assure you there's no way Simon Hartley-Knott is in love with Magda!'

'Surely you must have considered it after all the time they've been spending together?'

'Alison, I can assure you there is no way Simon is attracted to Magda – believe me!'

'By the way,' interjected Ross, 'where *is* Magda?'

'She's taken her dog for a walk,' the earl replied.

'And where is Simon?' Ross asked, looking out of the window.

'He popped by earlier, but he's gone home,' Hamish said firmly. He glanced at his watch. 'He left about half an hour ago.'

'Is that not his Land Rover out there behind that tree?' Ross asked.

'No, no, it's probably mine,' Hamish said. 'Angus will have left it there.'

'I know your Land Rover,' Ross said doubtfully, 'and I don't think that's yours. It's hard to see from here; I'm going to go out to check.'

'I'm coming with you.' Ally felt suddenly afraid, though she wasn't sure why.

Hamish, watching her face, picked up on her change in mood because he grabbed his walking stick and got to his feet.

'I'll come too,' he said.

The three of them walked through the Great Hall and out of the front door.

'Oh yes, you're quite right, that *is* Simon's Land Rover!' said Hamish in surprise as they got closer. There, almost hidden underneath the branches of a tree, was a large, green, muddy Land Rover.

Ally gasped. There was an X and a nine in the registration.

TWENTY-NINE

'If Simon's supposedly gone home, then how come his vehicle is out here?' Ross asked, his voice suddenly tense.

'That's very strange,' Hamish admitted.

Ally felt a cold surge of fear. 'Hamish, I'm not sure what's going on, but I'm afraid Magda might be in danger.'

'Why on earth do you think that?' Hamish asked.

Ally gestured to the registration plate. 'I'm damned certain that's the vehicle that tried to push me into Loch Ness!' she said. 'And if that was Simon, there are only two people he can have been trying harm. Me or—'

'Magda!' Hamish stopped in his tracks. 'Oh God, there's no time to lose. She normally walks Benny down by Loch Soular,' he said, withdrawing his keys from his pocket. 'It'll only take me five minutes to drive over there.' And before they could stop him, he shot off towards the other side of the castle to where he normally parked his own vehicle and, a few minutes later, he could be heard revving the engine.

Ally was only aware of a sense of foreboding and rising panic. 'We should have gone with him...'

Ross looked around. 'But Simon could be around here somewhere.'

'No, I don't think he *is* around here. I think he's gone with Magda, meaning that Hamish and he could be fighting it out over there. Oh my God! Why didn't we drive up here this morning?'

'Don't worry.' Ross took her hand reassuringly. 'We can be there in less than twenty minutes.'

Half walking, half running, they set off.

'I don't think I can run all the way,' Ally gasped, stopping to get her breath back after a few minutes.

'Neither can I,' Ross agreed, slowing down, 'not any more! God, I hate being old!'

'Better than the alternative,' Ally reminded him as she resumed a steady trot.

'Possibly a wild goose chase anyway,' Ross said, having regained his breath. 'What's the betting that she's sitting happily by the loch, alone, with her dog?'

'So where's Simon gone then?' Ally asked.

'Something could be wrong with his car. Perhaps it wouldn't start? He's gone down to the garage?' Ross suggested between gasps.

'I don't think so,' Ally said.

'I don't think so either,' Ross agreed grimly.

They were within sight of the loch now, and the first thing they saw was Hamish's Land Rover but no sign of Hamish. And the boat had been removed from the boathouse and was half in and half out of the water. For a brief moment, Ally wondered if Hamish had guessed wrong, and Magda must have gone somewhere else, but just as she was trying to work out where else she might have gone, she saw, tied to a post, Magda's puppy, Benny. He'd seen them and began to bark excitedly.

'Is that Magda's dog?' Ross asked, stopping in his tracks.

'Yes, that's him,' Ally said, staring down towards the boathouse.

The door swung open, and a familiar male voice yelled, 'Shut up, you stupid dog!'

Ally looked round in panic, trying to see if there was anywhere to hide.

'Quick! Get down!' Ross said, grabbing her arm and pulling her down into a small hollow.

Ally peeped over a tuft of heather to see Simon Hartley-Knott stepping out from the boathouse, looking around. Ally pulled her head down again as far as she could.

'Can you see him?' she asked.

'Yes,' Ross said, hardly above a whisper, 'but I'm pretty sure he's not seen us.'

They lay there until he'd gone back inside, and then, warily, Ross got up and helped Ally to her feet.

They advanced slowly towards the boathouse, making as little noise as possible. Benny had stopped barking but was whimpering and wagging his tail. Ally, who had some dog treats in her pocket, withdrew several and scattered them on the ground, much to the dog's delight. He settled down to tackle a chew as Ross inched his way towards the door, holding out a restraining hand towards Ally.

'Let me deal with this...' he began, and then his voice faltered as they both saw Hamish's body lying sprawled inside the boat. Ally rushed to Hamish's side and could immediately see that he'd been knocked out by a blow to his head. There was a wide gash above his left eye, but at least he was breathing and moaning quietly. Ross checked his pulse and pulled up his eyelids to examine his eyes. 'Who did this to you, Hamish?'

'Simon,' Hamish murmured.

'Stay with him, Ally,' Ross said as he made his way towards the door.

'Stay awake, Hamish,' Ally urged. 'We'll get help soon, so just hold on there!'

Hamish was now beginning to sit up and agitatedly pointing towards the boathouse, before collapsing again.

'I'll be OK,' he muttered. 'Please help Magda.'

Trembling, Ally approached the building, her heart in her mouth. As she peered into the gloom, the first person she saw was Magda, crumpled in a heap with a syringe sticking out of her thigh, fighting for breath. As her eyes accustomed to the dark of the boathouse, she saw Ross furiously struggling with Simon.

'What the hell have you given her, you bastard?' Ross was shouting. Seeing Ally, he gestured at Magda. 'Ally, get that syringe out of her leg and call for help!'

'What do you think you're doing here? I'm only trying to help her,' Simon shouted back.

'Like hell you are!' Ross exploded, lunging at him and grabbing him by the throat.

Simon threw himself against Ross, and they both collapsed on the ground. Simon scrambled to his feet and made to run towards the door, before Ross grabbed his foot and sent him sprawling again.

Her heart racing and her fingers trembling, Ally dialled 999 and pulled the syringe out of Magda's thigh, studying what she could see of the contents. It appeared to be three-quarters full. She looked round for somewhere to put it safely, finally laying it on top of what looked like Magda's coat, crumpled up on the floor in the corner. Magda was drowsy but not quite unconscious, and Ally knew that somehow or other she should keep her awake. Goodness only knew what he'd injected her with!

'No, no, Magda, don't close your eyes!' Ally tried to get her into a sitting position, and at the same time trying to keep an eye on Ross and Simon, grappling a yard or so away from her on the floor of the launching platform.

It was at this point that Hamish, holding his head and looking very shaken, stumbled through the door. 'You bastard!' he shouted at Simon and rushed to Ross's aid. Between them, they dragged Simon towards the door. 'I should bloody well kill you!' Hamish added.

'You wouldn't,' Simon said clearly. But, suddenly, all the fight appeared to have gone out of him as he lay panting on the floor. In the meantime, Ross had staggered to his feet, nodded at Hamish and, together, they hauled Simon up against the wall into a semi-sitting position. He was still breathing heavily, his face badly swollen, and for the first time, Ally could see the real man, old and exhausted, far from the debonair image he presented to the world. She almost felt sorry for him.

'You jealous bastard!' Hamish repeated quietly, looking anxiously towards Magda. 'What have you given her?'

'It was for *you*,' Simon muttered. 'I did it for you!'

Ally, still supporting a sleepy Magda, exchanged glances with Ross.

Hamish shook his head slowly. 'No, Simon, this is all about *you*, isn't it?'

'No, my love, it's about us *both*!' Simon had a strange smile on his face. 'I don't expect you to understand just yet, but what I did, I did out of my love for *you*! My undying love, for nearly sixty years, ever since we arrived in Cambridge all those years ago! Such a magical summer, wasn't it?'

'That was a long, long time ago,' Hamish said sadly.

'It was a different time, and I couldn't even *contemplate* pursuing the love I yearned for. But oh, *how* I longed for you!'

Ally was saddened and shocked, but not altogether surprised.

There was no stopping Simon now. 'Ophelia wasn't right for you. I could see that straight away, and so it was necessary to eliminate someone who could only bring you years of misery.'

He gave a half-smile, as if pleased with what he'd done. Hamish was staring at him in complete shock and disbelief.

Simon continued. 'So long as you were single, I dared to hope that you might turn to me again. That's why I moved up here.' He frowned, as if remembering something. 'I had a happy enough life with Elizabeth, of course, and I thank God for our beautiful children.'

'Simon, for heaven's sake...' Hamish was now looking increasingly horrified.

Ally was holding her breath.

'You'd told me about Elena, when she was due to arrive at Inverness. I didn't know what I was planning to do, but I went to the airport that day, looking for her. And saw Desdemona Morton giving a lift to a woman who looked just as you'd described Elena. I followed them.' He gave a shrug. 'I couldn't for the life of me work out why you hadn't met her yourself but supposed that Desdemona had offered. I must admit I was at a loss to work out why she didn't seem to understand what I was saying. I didn't particularly enjoy disposing of her, Hamish, and of course later it turned out that I needn't have done.' He sighed. 'I must admit I do quite regret that.'

There was a stunned silence as they all stared at Simon.

'And then, at the wedding reception, Elena conveniently laid her plate down on the table for several minutes while she spoke with the minister, so that one was easy. I knew that Desdemona grew monkshood in her garden; I thought that it would point the finger at her if anyone discovered what had killed Elena. Neither she nor Magda would ever have brought you the happiness that I could, Hamish. It's sad that you never realised the joy that we might have had together.'

Hamish had limped across the floor to where Magda was now sitting bolt upright and put his arms round her. 'Magda,' he managed before he gave in to tears himself. 'What has he done to you, my darling?'

After what seemed like an eternity, Ally heard a strange droning sound somewhere outside.

'What's that noise?' she asked Ross.

Ross was smiling as he looked up at the sky. 'Have a guess!'

The air ambulance and the police helicopter containing Rigby and several of his constables landed within minutes of each other, both hovering to find a flat piece of ground before landing. The ambulance landed first, with two paramedics racing out.

'You leave her with us,' the younger of the two paramedics said reassuringly as they lifted Magda gently from the floor. 'I think she's going to be fine.' Hamish accompanied them, keeping a tight hold on her hand.

Ross was keeping an eye on Simon, who was still sprawled against the wall, and it wasn't until two uniformed policemen hauled him upright and dragged him to the helicopter that Ross crossed over to Ally and took her in his arms, holding her tight. 'Don't cry,' he murmured softly into her hair. 'We arrived in time, thank God!'

Ally nodded mutely. Rigby had found the syringe and was placing it in a plastic bag. 'Is that her coat?' he asked.

Ally nodded.

'We better take it with us then.' He looked at Ally and Ross. 'I'm going to need a detailed statement from you two,' he said with a hint of a smile. 'But I'll let you recover first. After you called, Mrs McKinley, we did a little digging on Simon Hartley-Knott. Turns out he wasn't in Zurich at the time of Kristina's murder as he claimed. I was about to call you when you called us!'

'We'd better walk back,' Ally said, 'because we have Magda's dog.'

She realised that this was the first time she'd ever seen

Rigby smile properly. 'There's room for you *and* the dog,' he said, beaming, and pointing at the helicopter. 'Ever ridden in one of these before?'

THIRTY

Ally hadn't seen Hamish and Magda for some weeks over Christmas because Hamish had whisked Magda off to the French Alps to 'get away from it all'. Apparently Magda liked to ski, but Hamish didn't, so he just concentrated on the apres-ski, he said when he phoned up to issue the invitation to dinner.

'Do you think I should wear the dress I wore on Christmas Day?' Ally asked anxiously. She and Ross had spent a quiet Christmas together, some of it at the malthouse, and some at Ross's place, still a little shaken by their experience at the loch.

Ross shrugged. 'I don't see why not,' he said, then added, 'but why on earth have we been asked up to the castle anyway?'

'Hamish said he had some very important news for us,' Ally replied, lifting a dark blue midi-dress out of the wardrobe and holding it up against her. 'What do you think?'

'I think he'll tell us when we get there,' said Ross.

'What I mean is, do you think I should wear this dress?'

'It looks very nice,' Ross replied. 'If it's a dress-up affair, am I going to be OK in a roll-neck sweater?'

'Oh yes, he said it was informal. Just the four of us. Probably just wants to say "thank you" to us for rescuing him and Magda.'

'So you don't think I need to rush home to get a suit?' Ross asked.

'Of course not! But I must find some warm underwear because you know how cold that castle is,' Ally said with a laugh.

There was, for once, much needed warmth, and a feminine touch, to the dining room in Locharran Castle. There was a roaring fire, and an electric heater plugged in at the far end of the room, along with some beautiful flower arrangements and candles everywhere, on every surface, and all along the length of the dining table.

'I'm trying not to think of the fire insurance!' Hamish quipped.

The meal had been sumptuous. Magda and Mrs Jamieson – who were now firm friends – had been toiling for hours in the kitchen apparently, on an absolutely delicious three-course meal that everyone agreed was the best they'd had in years.

Leaning back and patting his tummy, Ross said, 'I shall *never* need to eat again.'

'Neither will I,' Ally agreed, sitting back to let Mrs Fraser clear away the dirty plates while Hamish produced an array of liqueur bottles. After Mrs Fraser returned with the coffee, she asked, 'Will that be all, sir?' to which he replied that it certainly would be all.

Hamish waited until Mrs Fraser left the room, then cleared his throat and said, 'I hope you don't think too badly of me after Simon's revelations?'

'Why would we think badly of you?' Ally asked.

Hamish looked embarrassed. 'We had one summer together when we met at Cambridge, and looking back, I realise now that it meant far more to him than it had to me. And then there was another time, some years later, when I was with Desdemona. He'd visited for the summer, and one evening when I'd had too much to drink, we... spent another night together. Unfortunately, that was the evening Desdemona decided to drop by unexpectedly.' He sighed deeply. 'I know I have a reputation as a flirt, but until that moment, Alison, I had never been unfaithful.'

So that was the night that had ended Desdemona and Hamish's relationship. Ally had suspected something of the sort, but it all made sense now.

'And,' Hamish continued, his voice breaking, 'to discover that he's the one that killed not only Elena but my poor Ophelia too, and that poor woman in the loch...' He shook his head mutely. 'How can one man cause so much evil? How was it that I never once suspected him?'

'Because he was cunning and clever. There was no way you could have known,' Ross said.

'I knew how he felt about me when we were young men,' said Hamish sadly. 'But I thought that when he married Elizabeth, he had put all that behind him. But I see now that he only married for respectability because his father was a bishop and it would have – at that time – been such an almighty scandal, and because he wanted children to carry on his family name. I don't think Elizabeth ever knew.'

'You've got to put all this behind you,' Ally said, 'and look to the future now.'

'I intend to,' Hamish said, 'but it isn't easy.' He looked fondly at Magda. 'I can only thank you both from the bottom of my heart for saving Magda from a similar fate.'

'He was going to drown me,' Magda said. 'He got the boat out and told me that he wanted to take me for a nice row around the loch. I told him that I was a bit afraid of water and would prefer not to go, but then he pushed me into the boathouse and took that syringe out of his pocket and...' She shuddered. 'He said, "I had to hurt that other woman, but this will be much gentler." I was so afraid.' She curled closer to Hamish, who put his arm around her.

Ally was rendered speechless. She looked at Ross and saw that he, too, was taking time to digest all this horrendous information.

When he eventually found his voice, Ross said, 'That monster killed three innocent women and tried to kill a fourth. Not to mention you too, Ally!'

'Thank God you two came along when you did,' Hamish said. 'He hit me with an oar, you know. I wouldn't have come round in time to save Magda.'

'I hardly know what to say.' Ross shook his head slowly.

'Well,' said Hamish, 'you could always say "congratulations!"' He was smiling now.

'Congratulations?'

'Magda and I are getting married, in Inverness, next Saturday, very quietly, and we would be honoured if you two would accompany us, and be our witnesses,' Hamish said.

'*What*!' they echoed.

'Yes,' Magda said. 'We want to have you there. Just you two.'

Ally looked at Ross and shook her head in disbelief.

Ross had now regained his composure. 'Then we must raise our glasses and toast you both. Oh, this is *marvellous*! That some good should come out of all this.'

'That's not all,' Hamish said, exchanging looks with Magda.

Magda smiled, her hand straying to her stomach. 'We're having a baby,' she said. 'So you really saved *two* lives when you both saved me!'

'You're having a *baby*?' Ally exclaimed, wondering how many more shocks she could absorb.

'Next summer,' Hamish said proudly.

'Oh, that's just *wonderful.*' Ally was trying hard not to cry. '*Wonderful.*'

'We weren't planning on doing anything much next Saturday, were we?' Ross said, grinning from ear to ear, as he looked at Ally.

'Nothing at all,' Ally confirmed as they laughed and raised their glasses. 'Why don't we go to a wedding?'

A LETTER FROM DEE

Dear Reader,

I hope you've enjoyed the second Ally McKinley story, set in my native Scotland, and that I kept you guessing until the end! And there are more Ally McKinley stories in the pipeline, which I hope you will enjoy. If you'd like to read my women's fiction novels or my Kate Palmer series of crime novels, set in Cornwall, then please just sign up with the link below.

Your email address will never be shared and you can unsubscribe at any time.

www.bookouture.com/dee-macdonald

If you feel like writing a review, I'd be very grateful, as I like to know what readers think, and it keeps me on the right track! And you can get in touch with me at any time on social media.

Thank you for reading my book!

Good wishes,

Dee

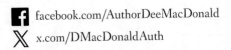
facebook.com/AuthorDeeMacDonald
x.com/DMacDonaldAuth

ACKNOWLEDGEMENTS

My very sincere thanks to my lovely, helpful editor at Bookouture, Lizzie Brien. Without her expertise and help, this book would not have taken shape. And thanks, Lizzie, for your enthusiasm and faith in me.

Thanks, too, to Natasha Harding at Bookouture, and to my agent, Amanda Preston at LBA, for her input and ideas, as well as looking after my interests.

A huge thanks, again, to Rosemary Brown, who helps me plot and plan my stories, and who reads over what I've written with an eagle eye. She is a true 'writing buddy' and every author should have one!

Thanks to my husband, Stan, of course, for leaving me in peace to write and offering refreshments from time to time! And to my son and grandsons for being much more computer savvy than me and sorting out my technical problems.

There is a huge team at Bookouture who help to produce the books, including Ruth Tross, Alba Proko, Melissa Tran, Peta Nightingale, Mandy Kullar, Stephanie Straub, Occy Carr, Jane Eastgate, Laura Kincaid and Lisa Brewster.

Not only are they all helpful and talented, but they are the friendliest publishers on earth! And I must add a special thanks to Kim Nash and Noelle Holten for the amazing promotional work they do on behalf of all our writers.

Last, but certainly not least, thank you to you, the reader! Thank you for buying my books and for some of the lovely messages I receive. I am so grateful to you all.

PUBLISHING TEAM

Turning a manuscript into a book requires the efforts of many people. The publishing team at Bookouture would like to acknowledge everyone who contributed to this publication.

Audio
Alba Proko
Melissa Tran
Sinead O'Connor

Commercial
Lauren Morrissette
Hannah Richmond
Imogen Allport

Cover design
The Brewster Project

Data and analysis
Mark Alder
Mohamed Bussuri

Editorial
Lizzie Brien

Copyeditor
Jane Eastgate

Proofreader
Laura Kincaid

Marketing
Alex Crow
Melanie Price
Occy Carr
Cíara Rosney
Martyna Młynarska

Operations and distribution
Marina Valles
Stephanie Straub
Joe Morris

Production
Hannah Snetsinger
Mandy Kullar
Jen Shannon
Ria Clare

Publicity
Kim Nash
Noelle Holten
Jess Readett
Sarah Hardy

Rights and contracts
Peta Nightingale
Richard King
Saidah Graham

Made in the USA
Middletown, DE
04 March 2025

72233079R00146